M Y
INESCAPABLE
VOW

A Stella Kirk Mystery #7

L. P. Suzanne Atkinson

lpsabooks
http://lpsabooks.wix.com/lpsabooks#

Cover Design by Majeau Designs
Editing by Tim Covell

ISBN
978-1-7776005-9-4 (Paperback)
978-1-0689911-0-3 (eBook)

1. Fiction, Mystery/Detective-Cozy/General
2. Fiction, Mystery/Detective-Amateur Sleuth
3. Fiction, Mystery/Detective-Female Sleuths

Distributed to the trade by the Ingram Book Company

Table of Contents

Perhaps our only sickness is to desire a truth which
we cannot bear rather than to rest content with the fictions
we manufacture out of each other.
—Lawrence Durrell, Clea (1960)

It's one thing to show your love for someone when everything is
going fine and life is smooth. But when the 'in sickness and in
health' part kicks in and sickness does enter your lives, you're tested.
Your resilience is tested.
—Patti Davis

Other works by L. P. Suzanne Atkinson

~Creative Non-Fiction~
Emily's Will Be Done

~Fiction~
Ties That Bind
Station Secrets: Regarding Hayworth Book I
Hexagon Dilemma: Regarding Hayworth Book II
Segue House Connection: Regarding Hayworth Book III
Diner Revelations: Regarding Hayworth Book IV

No Visible Means: A Stella Kirk Mystery #1
Didn't Stand a Chance: A Stella Kirk Mystery #2
Sand In My Suitcase: A Stella Kirk Mystery #3
Fictional Truth: A Stella Kirk Mystery #4
Mallory Gorman Won't Be Buried Today: A Stella Kirk Mystery #5
Fate Deals The Cards: A Stella Kirk Mystery #6

~E-Book Bundles~
Station Secrets / Hexagon Dilemma: Books I & II
Segue House Connection / Diner Revelations: Books III & IV
No Visible Means / Didn't Stand A Chance: Books 1 & 2
Sand In My Suitcase / Fictional Truth: Books 3 & 4

For David, always

Thank you to Marguerite, Harriet, Barb, and Beverley
for your feedback, and a special thanks to my editor Tim Covell for his
patience and support.

Much appreciation to Donamae Kutska, and Tyna Derhay, who each won a
Cozy Mystery Party contest, and permitted their name to be assigned to a
character in this book.

Finally, this book is dedicated to my friend and cousin,
Karen Fresque (1954–2024). I miss her terribly. She asked that I name a
character "Hermione" and despite the fact she won't see the results,
I honoured her request. Rest in peace.

Recurring Characters:

Stella Kirk............................Partner in Shale Cliffs RV Park; amateur sleuth

Aiden North ....RCMP Detective

Sergeant Moyer.. RCMP Sergeant

Rosemary North....................Aiden's wife (Mary Jo and Toni are her sisters)

Nick Cochran .... Partner in Shale Cliffs RV Park; Stella's love interest

Paul Morgan...Park Employee

Eve Trembly ....Park Employee (Del. Trembly's granddaughter)

Duke (John) Powell................. Park Security (Cloris Kincaid—love interest)

Kiki .... Duke's Pomeranian, adopted by Nick and Stella

Merrilee Wild..........Replaces Alice Morgan as Admin. Assistant at the park

Trixie Kirk ....Stella's younger sister (Val Reguly—love interest)

Brigitte & Mia Kirk.............................. Trixie's daughter and granddaughter
(Runs Yellow House, Carter Stephens—love interest)

Norbert Kirk .... Stella & Trixie's father

RV Park Residents .... Mildred Fox, Buddy McGarvey,
Curtis Walsh & Elroy Brown,
Sally & Rob Black, Ted Metcalfe

Jewel & Ken Winslow ....Caretakers at Painter Farm

Cavelle Painter........................... Real Estate Agent, friend to Trixie & Stella

Hester Painter...................Friend to Stella (Angus Raspberry—love interest)

Jacob Painter .... Brother to Cavelle & Hester

Chapter 1

Silence Mysterious

Rough and calloused square hands, farmer's hands, clasped between denim knees. Red beard resting on plaid flannel chest. Angus Raspberry never imagined his fate when he called the police last night. To find a man dead on your barn floor, the body still warm but the light gone from his eyes, resulted in a series of events for which he was unprepared. Angus found himself alone and afraid for the first time since his parents died, ten years ago.

Police, unfamiliar men and women, asked him questions, over and over— different questions, trick questions, troubling questions. Did he know the man? Why was he in the barn? Did he work with the man? Where did he spend his evening? Did the man own the truck parked in the yard? His mind muddled. He was confused, and his head ached. He requested permission to call Hester. He was polite. He didn't lose his temper. He didn't let himself become frustrated. No. They told him he would be held overnight. What about his dog? What about Orion? He needed to call Hester to go take care of Orion. Sleep never came.

A few minutes ago, Briggs Moyer brought him a tray with toast and coffee. They were in school together. Two big guys who weren't bullied because of their size, although neither fit in. He thanked Sergeant Moyer and felt bad he didn't have an appetite. The coffee wasn't as good as Jewel made at Painter Farm.

The door unlocked for the second time in ten minutes, and Moyer stepped inside again. "I've done you a favour, man, but you can't let on to anyone else," he said, in a tone so low Angus could hardly hear. "I called Hester Painter. She's a good person. I told her to come to the station as soon as possible."

A warm wash of relief spread through his stiff and aching joints. He couldn't find proper words of thanks and settled for a nod.

"I don't know if the detective will let her see you, but I thought she should know what's happened. She's worked with Detective North and said she'd come right away."

****

Hester Painter isn't given to overt displays of emotion. Their earlier telephone call proved a clear exception. Despite necessary attempts at a calm analysis of the current state of affairs, Stella's brain flips forward and explores the potential consequences. By the time she pulls her dilapidated Jeep, the vehicle used by her father when she first assumed operations at Shale Cliffs RV Park in late 1978, into a parking spot at the front of Painter Farm, her mind has conjured theories of increasingly chaotic magnitude. She stops beside Cavelle's electric blue sedan. Jacob's truck sits nearby.

The shadow of Hester hovers behind the screen door. Dressed in a green wool coat which probably belonged to her dead mother, she sports a cloche pulled tight over her ears. Her long and stringy hair sticks to the sides of her face. Even though she's overdressed for a balmy May 8, 1982, Stella notes Hester carries her forty-one years well.

Shale Cliffs RV Park opens to the public in thirteen days. The staff start their work on Friday. Stella planned direct avoidance of any investigations, at least for the summer. With the new septic system in place, sites added for seasonals, and the updated water and electrical systems, they expect a banner year. She hopes Aiden will sort through the assumed legal misunderstandings with Angus Raspberry today, and refuses to be absorbed into Hester's vortex of unease—yet.

When Stella received the call from her friend earlier, near nine-thirty, she learned how the police arrested Angus, Hester's boyfriend. He contacted the RCMP following dinner at the Painter farm and his return to his home, located around the point, last night. From what Stella understands, he found a familiar truck in his driveway and a dead man on the floor of his barn. Kind Sergeant Moyer called Hester at the start of his shift. Angus resembles Hester, in that he has limitations and withdraws when under pressure. Moyer acted out of concern, with good reason.

One might describe Hester's personality as unique. Others often view her as aloof and odd. Her parents never sent her to school. Her primary interests were plants, the garden, and higher education through self-teaching. She designed her room as a library. Her book knowledge encompasses her beloved topics, but reaches much farther. Social cues are a mystery to her, although since resolving their major family problem, Hester has emerged from her shell. Opal Painter, the oldest of the four Painter siblings, killed both their parents. The birth of Jacob, the youngest, precipitated their mother's murder. Opal wanted the baby for herself because of a twisted interpretation of her parents' inability to care for another child. The death of their father happened after he entertained the idea Hester should receive a public education. Hester gathered and hid proof of Opal's involvement but volunteered nothing. With the sudden demise of Lucy, Jacob's bride, Aiden enlisted Stella and Hester responded.

Although Stella is older than Hester, the two women have maintained a friendship since the Lucy Painter investigation. When they were young, and Stella's sister Trixie chummed with Hester's sister Cavelle, Stella paid attention to Hester, even when others avoided her. She established a trust which continues into the present. When law enforcement investigated Hester's family, Hester didn't volunteer information which might incriminate a sibling, but answered questions if posed specifically. In the long run, the police, with Hester and Stella's help, exposed the murders and Opal Painter as the guilty party. With Hester no longer influenced by Opal, she began tentative interaction with others—Stella in particular. Over the last few investigations, Hester has been pivotal in the conduction of formal searches, which unearthed necessary evidence, and resulted in justice for victims. Her current relationship with Angus suggests progress.

Aiden North did not contact Stella after Angus' arrest. She finds his silence mysterious. The usual chain of events involves the discovery of a body, Aiden's call for her to meet him at the scene, and a case where they both take on roles which play to their strengths. Perhaps his old partner, Essie Matkowski, has resumed work after her mother's illness. Stella admits, although in silence, that she and Aiden haven't been on the best of terms over the last while.

Separated from his wife, Rosemary, who suffers ongoing mental health challenges, Cavelle Painter has moved in with Aiden. Rosemary North threatened Stella, and Stella fears for Cavelle, now vulnerable to a woman who has a history of violence. She considers information shared with her by

Aiden's sister-in-law, Mary Jo Frost. Aiden isn't the man Stella presumed she understood. Despite having known him most of her life, and despite his role as her first lover when they were in high school, she missed his weakest link. She gathers the threads of her consciousness and focuses on the task at hand.

****

Jewel Winslow, the Painters' housekeeper and Hester's companion, wiggles her way toward the screen and pushes the door open. "Good morning, Stella. We're happy you're here." She leans closer. "Hester is in a state."

"Hi, everyone." Stella's eyes adjust to the gloom of the entry. Cavelle and Jacob linger in the passageway, which leads into the kitchen of the American Foursquare farmhouse built by their father, before his marriage in 1933.

Cavelle steps forward and places one unappreciated hand on her sister's shoulder. Hester's barely discernable shrink away from such a touch doesn't go unnoticed. "She insisted you drive her into the Shale Harbour RCMP Detachment, Stella." She waves a manicured finger around the tight space. "Any of us would oblige, but," she glances toward Hester, "she requested you."

As a local realtor, Cavelle Painter works alongside the business broker and owner, Farley Tompkins, at Grey Cottage Realty in town. "You rushed right over, Cavelle."

"Jewel called me." She nods, a silent acknowledgement of Stella's reference to her new living arrangement. "Aiden knows Hester's upset. I told him already." She turns her attention back toward her sister. "Aiden says he anticipates his case against Angus will be open and shut, Hester. Angus killed the victim after he returned from supper here. Time at our house earlier in the evening isn't an alibi."

Hester stares at her Oxfords. "Angus is gentle and unable to hurt anyone. Stella, please deliver me to the station. We must talk with Detective North and persuade him to let Angus go home. He has a dog."

"I'll run over and feed the dog, Hester. Where does Angus keep a spare key?"

"He never locks his house. Thank you. I'll share with Angus the kind act performed for him, Jacob. He will be grateful."

"Is the victim identified?" Stella's eyes scan the room.

"Cavelle knows but isn't at liberty to say." Hester sounds exasperated, as if Stella should understand every unexplained nuance.

"Don't forget, the one person who provided me with details is you, Hester. I agree, though. It's important we meet with Aiden as soon as possible."

"You'll hear no information from me," Cavelle flutters. "I'll telephone and ask if now's a good time, Stella." She turns toward the kitchen in the back.

Her command of their predicament shows how Hester's older sister relishes the indirect power gained from her relationship with the lead detective. Stella eavesdrops.

"No, they're ready to come in now. Hester wants time with Angus, and Stella wants a word with you."

"Understood. I'll explain the process. Afterward, I'm off into the office."

With everyone still muddled near the front door, Cavelle sidles her way back. "Jewel, why don't you and Kenny go into the kitchen and make a pot of coffee? Your cranberry muffins might be nice, too."

Jewel, her little boy wedged on her hip, follows instructions.

"Although she makes excellent coffee, we should leave now, Stella."

"What did Aiden say, Cavelle?" Stella's eyes fix on Hester while she asks the question.

"He says he needs an hour. They must interview Angus before laying formal charges. A legal aid lawyer will be engaged. Frankly, Aiden's frustrated, Stella. He never contacted you because the case against Angus is solid and your help isn't necessary." She turns toward Hester. "Angus has asked for you, and Aiden says you can visit after his interview. Take off your coat and hat. We'll pause for tea or coffee and a muffin."

With great, albeit silent, reluctance, Hester peels off her outer garments. She places them on the oak newel post, although she carries her bag into the kitchen.

The smell of Jewel's special brew wafts toward the doorway. Although Hester often sings the praises of their housekeeper's skills, she drinks tea. Jewel has the table arranged for four.

"None for me right now," says Jacob. "Save me some. I'll drive over to Angus' place and feed the dog. What's his name, Hester?"

"Orion. He's a big fellow and skittish, but he won't hurt you. Angus keeps his food on the back porch. Feed him two cups. He will stay in the yard." Even as she answers, her eyes remain downcast while she strokes Angel, the black cocker spaniel Jacob gave her after their sister went to jail. "Call him by name. He'll be fine and appreciate the sound of your voice. Angus talks to him." After a pause, she specifies, "in full sentences."

Jacob salutes and a moment later, the roar of his pickup reverberates through the house as the truck jumps to life.

"Where's Ken?" Stella pours cream into her coffee and addresses Jewel, still at the counter.

"Out on the disc harrow. Jacob wanted to stay inside until you arrived. Ken said he'd start. Lots of work to prepare for planting."

Stella first met Ken and Jewel Winslow when they were employed at the fish plant. They rented Lorraine Young's apartment the summer of her death. Although suspects for a short time, Stella never expected a circumstance where killing their landlord, to remain in their sub-let, seemed logical. After the incarceration of Opal, Ken and Jewel accepted positions as farm hand and housekeeper at the Painter farm. They live next door in the bungalow Jacob built for his bride. Lucy never crossed the threshold before she died from poison concocted by her sister-in-law. The arrangement with the Winslow couple has served both families well. Jacob needs help on the land, and Hester needs support.

"Great muffins. Will you share the recipe? Nick and I make different snacks for the staff."

"Thanks. I'll write the ingredients out for you. Cranberry and lemon are a yummy combination. One of Hester's favourites, although obviously not today." Jewel stares at Hester's plate where her muffin sits crumbled into pieces, untouched.

Hester looks at the clock on the kitchen wall. "Can we go soon, Stella?" Her red-rimmed eyes match her flushed face. She taps her foot and clutches her bag to her chest with desperate intensity.

After taking a last gulp, Stella stands. "Thanks, Jewel, especially for the recipe." She folds the lined yellow paper and stuffs it into a pocket of her trousers. "We'll be early." She speaks to Hester's back as she walks toward the front door.

No response.

"Aiden insisted he needed an hour, Stella."

The concept of Cavelle, now in the role of gatekeeper for Aiden, feels weird, if not troublesome. "The good detective's assessment of the case should prove interesting. Hester will settle once we're at the detachment, even if we must wait. I'll drive her home after our meetings with Aiden and Angus."

"Please call and tell me what happened." Jewel remains near the sink, with her little boy's hand in hers, but her eyes meet Stella's.

"Hester or I will phone you from town and then you contact Cavelle at work. Okay?" She looks at Cavelle.

"Fine with me, although I'll talk to Aiden directly after my property showing at eleven. Jewel, leave me a message regardless." She fusses with her purse. "Farley hired a new office administrator. Heaven." She rolls her eyes.

When Stella reaches the front door, she cannot find Hester. She peers through the screen and sees her positioned in the passenger seat of the Jeep, erect and expressionless, coat buttoned to her throat, hat pulled tight around her ears, and her canvas bag clenched in her fists.

She can't let her mind drift toward the worst case. Hester has improved in ways beyond calculation. This current circumstance might knock her progress back two years, to before Opal went to jail and before Hester learned to interact with others the way she does now. Stella closes her eyes for a moment before she hauls open the driver's door and climbs inside. If Angus Raspberry proves to be a murderer, Hester will never be the same.

****

She rocks from side to side, as much as her seatbelt allows, and stares straight ahead.

"We'll arrive in twenty minutes, Hester. Don't worry."

"No one ever stopped worrying because someone suggested the idea." She twists a ring on her left hand—a ring Stella hasn't noticed in the past.

"Nice."

"A present from Angus. The intent is friendship, but his gift symbolizes depth." She continues to twist. "Can you drive any faster?"

Since she's reached the speed limit, Stella ignores her friend's request and asks, "What did Moyer tell you again?" She remembers most of Hester's call, but hopes the woman's angst might ease if she focuses on the circumstances. "Let's do what we always do and review the facts."

"Kind Sergeant Moyer took a risk when he called. He said the RCMP arrested Angus last evening after he telephoned and reported he discovered a dead man in his barn. A patrol car and ambulance drove out to Raspberry Farm. They summoned Detective North, and he arrived thirty minutes later.

The person—the sergeant never revealed the victim's actual identity—lay deceased on the floor. After the forensics team assumed the scene, the police brought Angus into the detachment. They abandoned poor Orion at the farm."

"Jacob is tending to Orion. Angus will be relieved when he learns you managed his dog's care for him. Any reason for someone to be in Angus' barn when he's not home, Hester?"

"He rents the old building, identified as a barn, although the word might be an exaggeration if one considers its decrepit condition. A man stores a small motorboat there. He arrives on the property at all hours to launch the craft at high tide. The sergeant suggested the victim was the renter, but he never provided a name."

"Who rents from Angus?"

"Angus mentioned Vic Staples, but I'm not sure, because I don't live at Raspberry Farm."

"True. True." With difficulty, she masks her shock when she hears the name, but continues. "Angus ate supper at your place, right?"

"Yes. We enjoyed roast pork. I prepared the vegetables. Jewel and Ken joined us. Jacob and Maeve were there, too." Her cloche-covered head turns toward Stella. "I act the bigger person, as you've suggested in past exchanges, and ignore her boisterousness with my silence. Jacob laughs at everything she says, but she's too loud for me."

"Maeve Cavannah has a big personality, for sure." Stella smothers her amusement and prevents a potential snort from escaping her lips. The first time Stella realized Jacob was dating an old colleague of Lucy's was at Easter brunch last month.

Hester's eyes dart from side to side, as if in search of animals which might jump from the ditches into their path. One foot has tapped on the worn floor mat since they left the farm.

"Be prepared. They may not allow you to meet Angus. They'll find him a lawyer and do interviews—lots of interviews. And let me remind you, Aiden didn't call my house. I assume he doesn't want me involved. Maybe Essie Matkowski came back to work, or his superiors assigned him a new partner."

Her eyes squint into the windshield. "Detective North has decided Angus murdered the man he discovered. Angus reported the body was still warm when he called the RCMP and described the scene." She turns toward Stella. Tears well. "The detective is convinced Angus killed whomever. Now he sees no need for an investigation and no need for your help."

Wondering the same, she keeps her thoughts to herself. Hester is more emotional than Stella has ever seen. "I'll offer my services, for your sake. You've assisted in past cases. Aiden owes you, and I will be obvious that he should bear your contributions in mind."

Hester's chest heaves while she focuses on her lap. "You are a good friend, Stella. I acted wisely when I called you."

"Why not your sister? Cavelle lives with Aiden now. She's able to pull strings and convince Aiden to let you speak with Angus."

With her bag clutched ever closer, she blurts, "Cavelle is possessive of Aiden. I wanted to contact him earlier, after she arrived at the farm. She refused permission. She said he's busy and takes personal calls from her alone. I told her my call wasn't personal, but she stood her ground. She's become his social secretary." Hester's hands double into fists. "You were there and watched when she grabbed the phone, called, and made the arrangements. Cavelle has adopted a new role as Detective North's gatekeeper." She wrinkles her nose.

"I wonder what will happen the day Rosemary materializes on their doorstep." Stella knows her concerns regarding Aiden North's wife and her mental health challenges aren't the focus today.

"Stella, not to criticize, but Aiden's love life has little relevance to my distress for Angus and his predicament. I share your worries related to Cavelle and her arrangements with a married man and his unstable wife. I agree she's at risk, but she says she lives with a police officer, and he will protect her. Who are we to judge or interfere?"

They enter the crowded parking lot at the station. Stella silences further comments and wiggles the Jeep into a spot at the far end. The Shale Harbour RCMP Detachment sits on a side street off Main, housed in a structure which resembles a cinder block warehouse. With windows on one side and in the back, it doesn't welcome, by any estimation.

Hester lags, following Stella up the concrete steps with the metal pipe rails. "I'm nervous, Stella. What if he sends me away? What shall I do?"

"Let me talk to Aiden first." She glances toward the desk when she manoeuvres her way inside. "Thankfully, Moyer's on duty. I'll tell him I need a moment with the detective. Relax."

She graces Stella with a furrowed brow. Moyer lifts his hand in a wave but doesn't produce his familiar smile.

Chapter 2

Your Help And Support

"Sit down and wait for me," she instructs. Hester drops on the wooden bench with a thud, capturing the sergeant's attention. "Hester, stop tapping your foot. Moyer's still on the phone." With alarming abruptness, her friend has morphed into an incorrigible child.

"Right. Okay. Call me with any changes and I'll forward the message along." With the receiver in the cradle, he turns toward Stella. "North says he's busy. No telling how long he'll be. Will you bide your time in an empty office? I can deliver coffee."

Stella's nervousness fades. "Thanks, Moyer. Good idea. We'll remove Hester from the action. She's upset and afraid for Angus. I'll fetch us a hot drink, though, since you're on the desk."

Moyer and Stella met during her first murder investigation, where she consulted with Aiden. He was tentative in the beginning, but when she figured out who murdered Lorraine Young, and Aiden was still in Port Ephron and not available, he caught up to her at the bank and followed her instructions, albeit with hesitation. He trusts her now. During their last inquiry, he accompanied her on interviews while Aiden took part in hospital discharge meetings with his wife, sisters-in-law, and various psychiatrists, so the family could create a plan. She knows Moyer respects her work and her methods. An undefined ease surrounds her when he's nearby.

"Time for my break. You two make yourselves comfy in the second office on the right. Tea for Hester?"

"Yes. With whitener."

"Coffee for you. I remember." His face lights. After a constable covers the front, he lumbers off to the lunchroom.

"Come on, Hester. We are to wait for Aiden down the hall. Moyer's grabbing you a cuppa and joining us for a few minutes."

"When can I visit Angus, Stella? I need to check on him and not waste valuable time with Sergeant Moyer."

The word petulant springs to mind, but Stella perseveres. She expects a long morning ahead.

Damp and uninviting, with a government issue desk bereft of accessories save a multiple line phone where the buttons blink constantly, describes the unassigned office. She sees two chairs in front and one behind the workspace. An unused bookcase leans at an angle against the largest open wall. The trash can sits empty.

When the sergeant arrives, he has stacked Styrofoam cups with lids in one hand and a handled pottery mug in the other. "Sorry. No more mugs," he blusters. "They were all dirty. Tea for you, Hester." He hands Stella her coffee while he focuses on Hester.

Hester wrinkles her nose in silent protest. Insulting enough, that she's forced to drink tea with powdered whitener, but the ultimate insult is the Styrofoam cup. Stella understands her emotions but, mercifully, Hester keeps her opinions to herself.

Moyer positions one plump buttock on the corner of the desk and leans toward them. "Listen. Can you avoid tellin' the boss I called you, Hester? I've known Angus a long time and someone should watch out for him, but the detective will be mad as hell if he finds out I broke protocol."

"Shall I lie, Sergeant?"

"Gosh, Hester, we don't want to turn my call into a conspiracy. Avoid mentioning me, okay?"

Hester studies his face. "I will suggest, by omission, that Angus alerted me after he called the police. I assumed he was at the station because he wasn't at home today. Does my explanation work?"

Shocked at the ease with which Hester concocts a story at a moment's notice, Stella remains silent. The last time she was a witness to such evasion of the truth from someone happened when the financial clerk at Harbour Manor dug for information on her behalf.

"Besides, Detective North appreciates how smart I am and won't consider the possibility personnel at the station provided me with the facts. When I talk to Angus, I'll make sure he understands."

"The arresting officer didn't allow Angus a phone call?"

"Correct, Stella, and the reason I called Hester. I felt sorry for the guy." He shifts his backside on the edge of the desk in obvious discomfort but chooses the pain rather than the seat of authority behind him. "I ran into North when I fetched the drinks. He said he'd be another thirty minutes and you can wait here."

Her foot taps resume.

"He appreciates your concern, Hester, but Angus can't meet with anyone besides the legal aid lawyer, until he's finished his statement. I imagine they won't be long now."

"I don't understand, Stella." Hester's pale face pinches around her eyes. "I expected you and Detective North to interview Angus."

Despite potential rejection, Stella pats her friend on the knee. Hester doesn't pull away. "The first action the police complete, with a person under suspicion or a witness, is taking their formal statement. Once signed off, we can begin. I hope Aiden will let me sit in on his initial conversation with Angus."

"You mean I've waited, with patience, and I won't see him?" Her pale face flushes.

"Once we talk with Aiden, I'll make sure you visit Angus, even if we wait all day."

Moyer glances at his watch. "I'm due back on the desk. Thanks for helpin' a fella out, Hester." He heaves his body into a vertical position and closes the door with a soft click as he leaves.

For the third time in less than an hour, Hester's foot taps a steady rhythm on the tiled floor. She squeezes her eyes shut and bows her head.

"Are you okay?"

"Stella, Angus resembles me in temperament, but more extreme. I've improved, but Angus still has many challenges. I'm concerned the police will railroad him. Did I use the correct term?" She answers her own question before Stella replies. "Yes, railroad. With no other suspects, they might easily convince him of his own guilt." She sits straighter and clasps her hands in her lap. "We can't let law enforcement bully Angus, no matter what happens!"

"Okay, I guess." In the first place, he may well be their culprit, but Stella avoids the mention of an alternate possibility.

"You realize, Stella, I expect your help and support." Hester's eyes flash her demand.

****

Silence smothers her. The government issue clock, fixed to the wall, ticks louder than any clock Stella has ever heard. The cord plugs into an outlet near the baseboard. She watches the second hand and focuses on a topic unrelated to passing the time. Eleven-thirty.

"Hester."

"Yes." She studies her fingers and taps her foot in rhythm.

"While we wait for Aiden, describe Angus."

"Specific topics?"

"Whatever you can. The police focus on the here-and-now. I'm interested in his history, his background."

"If you insist." Hester adjusts her position on the wooden chair, straightens her posture, and wets her lips. "Angus Raspberry is thirty-five years old. He was born in 1947 in Ontario, where his parents immigrated after the war. They moved to Shale Harbour and bought Raspberry Farm when he was twelve."

"Does he have siblings?"

"No. An only child."

"Did they build the house and barns? They appear older."

"The Raspberry family purchased the farm from German immigrants who came here in 1940. He told me they are both dead and his parents are as well. The woman who lives up the road, Donamae—her father was a cousin to the original builder."

"They moved from Ontario to buy the property?"

"I assume, although he never said. Donamae keeps goats and delivers milk to Raspberry Farm every week." She curls her lip. "I often wonder how he drinks the stuff because of the gross smell."

Stella shrugs. "Maybe he pours it out once she's gone home. He's not the first person too kind to refuse a gift they don't want."

The slightest twitch of her lips betrays her thoughts. "I hope, Stella."

"What happened to his parents? Any idea?"

"Oh yes. His mother never enjoyed good health. She became bedridden and his father cared for her. He dropped dead of a heart attack and the ambulance took Mrs. Raspberry to the hospital. They said they'd find a nursing home for her, but she passed away before her move to Harbour Manor. Angus says circumstances broke her heart, but I'm not given to such fanciful thinking."

She provides Stella with a knowing look. "His parents both died, plain and simple."

"Do his neighbours help him?"

"I don't imagine, except for the odd meal and the milk. He doesn't speak about any kind of formal, or even casual, assistance." She stops and frowns. "Angus can be a troublesome man to understand. He's not fond of people. Even after all this time on his own, he still should have guidance every day to be independent."

"He's lucky he has you."

"True. We are two-peas-in-a-pod, as they say." She glances at the clock. "Will Detective North be here soon?"

The incessant ticking invades her consciousness once more. "I'll go out front and ask."

Alarm crosses her friend's face. "Try to be quick, Stella."

"Understood," she replies. "Remember, you have been a great help to Aiden over the past two years. I must admit, I'm surprised you're not comfortable around law enforcement."

"Let me remind you, I don't work inside the police station when Detective North requests my services. I attend a crime scene after the forensics team departs. We dig in the drawers of the deceased, Stella. I have never spent a morning sitting in an empty detachment office."

"Point taken." She foregoes her trip to the front desk for the moment.

"You and Angus are close. Tell me more."

"By the way, I appreciate your attempt at distraction from the incessant tick of the horrible clock on the wall, so I will satisfy your curiosity." She unbuttons the top two buttons of her coat. "Angus farms potatoes. He's talented. We study varieties as a team now and plan to experiment with three new types this year. He wants to grow his crops commercially but without pesticides." She studies Stella's face again. "Farming is hard when your goal is to be both competitive and responsible."

"I can't imagine."

"We want to start our life together as a couple after the harvest. You promised to come over when we tell Cavelle and Jacob."

Stella senses a slightly accusatory overtone. "I made you a promise and I will be there. Let's fix this mess Angus has gotten himself into first. Then, we'll both enjoy a great summer, after which you and Angus can start your life together." Her attempts to soothe float around the room unheeded.

"Neither Cavelle nor Jacob care now. They're busy with their own lives, but Jewel might miss me."

"Oh, Hester, don't fret. You'll be in and out of the farm every day throughout the season, managing your gardens. Jewel can teach you the skills you need so you can run your own house. Raspberry Farm has a prosperous future."

Hester snorts. "Not if he's in jail, Stella. I'm positive about one change, if we identify the actual murderer and Angus returns home. I inherited a small sum of money, and he will never have to rent his old outbuildings again to pay the bills." She stamps her foot and pats her satchel. "Now, I am prepared to sit here alone if you search for Detective North. Lunchtime is approaching and I expect poor Angus needs a break from lawyers and police officers."

Stella rises. "I'll root out more information, but don't feel disappointed if the wait isn't over. We can eat lunch at the café." She opens the door. "I won't be long."

Once in the hall, Stella reflects on her talk with Hester. She senses a change, an identified purpose. Hester sees herself as part of a couple. Her plans are inclusive and no longer self-involved. There were times she sat and read when Stella visited the farm, and her justification for not joining them at the table was that her book was more important than visitors. Those days appear to be on the wane.

Moyer remains at his post. "No sign of the boss, Stella. He told me he'd find you once Angus made his statement, but the legal aid lawyer took forever to drive here. Stephens and Stephens opted to refuse this case—too busy, I guess—and a legal-beagle from Port Ephron drove to Shale Harbour." He grabs the ringing phone and points his index finger into the air. "Detective North."

"Yes. Okay. She's here at the desk. Miss Painter's in the spare office."

"I'll tell her."

"Detective North says he'll be out in five minutes."

"Thanks, Sergeant." Stella returns and finds Hester with her eyes closed and her foot continuing to tap.

"Are you asleep?"

"No. I must focus on my breathing. I find anxiety creeps through my body if left unchecked."

"Aiden will be here in a minute."

Words leave her mouth just as an unkempt and puffing Aiden rushes through the half-open door.

****

The detective glances from one woman to the other, as if in search of mood indicators. "Good morning, Stella." A shock of white hair has fallen over his eye. "Hester."

"The hour approaches afternoon, Detective." Hester's focus remains trained on her lap.

"What's the story, Aiden? Can Hester visit with Angus now, or are you releasing him right away?"

His mouth drops open. He gapes at Stella. "No. A lawyer from Port Ephron arrived ten minutes ago. There's the formal statement, followed by an initial interview." He turns his attention toward Hester. "You may meet with him afterward but prepare for a wait. Get lunch at the café. Use the phone here and telephone an update to your family. Now, Stella. Come to my office."

"Sure." Concerned because of Aiden's abruptness, she asks, "Hester, are you okay for a moment or two?"

"Yes, Stella." Her voice betrays her impatience. "I'm a grown woman. I shall inform Jewel. After you speak with the detective, we'll go for lunch. Then I'll visit with Angus as promised." She punctuates her response with her jutted chin. "We finally have a plan of action."

In Aiden's office with the door closed, he removes his wrinkled jacket, throws the garment on his chair, loosens his tie, and waves his fists in Stella's general direction.

She does not waver.

"Honest to God, Stella. Why didn't you persuade her to stay home? You dragged her to the detachment and spent the morning locked away in an empty office."

Admonished but without remorse, she replies, "Hester Painter, Aiden. Remember her?" She points her finger. "You are aware you can't break her hold when she clutches an idea. Besides," her manner softens, "she's in love with the guy and will move mountains for him."

Aiden closes his eyes before he answers her with a question. "Do you want to sit in on his interview with me?"

"You never called." Her tone is accusatory, although her intention was to convey fact without emotion.

"He's guilty of the murder of Vic Staples, as far as the evidence points, but another opinion is never out of order, I guess." He frowns.

"Why are you so sure, Aiden? Hester said he arrived home after supper at the Painter's, and he found a dead guy. Vic Staples?"

"Yes. He rents the barn from Angus and keeps a boat stored out of the weather. The truck parked in the yard belongs to Vic, too." He stares at her. "How did Hester realize what happened?"

"Motive?" She avoids his question with one of her own.

"We're not sure, but I assume a drug-trafficking arrangement went wrong. Vic and Angus used the skiff to move contraband from the cove on to land and off for distribution."

"Proof?"

"Forensics found evidence of marijuana on the building floor. We'll confirm in a day or two. They'll assess the boat back in Port Ephron."

"What did Angus say?"

"He claims he does not know of any drugs. Big surprise. Vic often arrived and took his skiff out at high tide because he launched right from the rear door." He pauses and sips what Stella assumes is ice-cold coffee. "The barn sits so near the water, I'm surprised it hasn't tumbled into the cove during a storm." Before Stella voices a response, he continues. "I asked him about the status of the relic when I attended the scene. He said the dilapidated structure is in no condition to be moved and the ocean will win, eventually. When his parents bought the land, the high-water mark sat fifty feet away. He owns a second outbuilding further from the sea."

"Hester told me the cove is dangerous. She and Angus promised each other to never take a shortcut and walk around on the rocks, either from her place to his or the other way round, because misjudging the tide times means there's a good chance of becoming stranded. Once you travel away from Raspberry Farm, the beach turns into cliffs, the same as at the park. We installed stairs, but without them, or if you can't reach them, the circumstances become deadly in no time."

"True, and part of the problem, Stella."

"How?"

"If Angus didn't commit the murder, and we assume a third person in the picture, where did they go? The tide was high, and Angus claimed no one else was on the property or the road when he drove home." When the phone rings, Aiden grabs the receiver. "Okay. Tell him we'll be available in five minutes." He hangs up and returns his attention to Stella. "That was Moyer. Let's tell Hester to find lunch. You and I can sit in with the arresting officer while he takes Angus' formal statement before we conduct our interview."

"Okay. I'll call Nick."

Back in the spare office, they discover Hester and Moyer muttering together. She tells Hester she won't eat with her, so she can observe as the police take Angus' statement.

"I'm happy to join you at the café, Hester. A guy needs a break."

"Good idea, Moyer." Aiden interrupts. "You and Hester go. Stella and I will finish the interview. Hester, you can meet with Angus when we're done."

"I want Angus home, Detective." Stella hears a distinct tremor in her friend's voice.

"Sure you do, but the process requires patience. Did you contact the farm?"

"Yes. Jewel expected me, but she's preserved the salad for supper. Stella, shall I purchase you a sandwich at the café?"

"Thank you, Hester. How thoughtful. I'll telephone Nick and let him know I won't be back to the park right away. Aiden?"

Aiden pulls a money clip out of his pants pocket and offers Moyer a pair of twenties. "Buy lunch for you and Hester and sandwiches, to go, for Stella and me. Tell the front desk you'll be ninety minutes. We'll need at least an hour and a half." He slaps the bills into Moyer's outstretched palm. "I'll inform Angus' lawyer we're on our way, Stella. You make your call."

Once everyone leaves the office, Stella sits behind the fake oak desk.

"Shale Cliffs…." Nick answered.

"Hi." She's surprised to hear his voice. "Are you in the kitchen?"

"Hi. Yes. I gather you won't be home for lunch. Are you okay?"

"Fine, but the case isn't good for poor Angus. Aiden thinks he has the proof before the interviews. They found the guy a lawyer, who came from Port Ephron—the reason for the delay. We'll listen while Angus gives his statement before we complete our first interview."

"Where's Hester?"

"At lunch with Moyer at Cocoa and Café. They'll deliver sandwiches for Aiden and me later."

"You sound upset."

"Aiden says he's confident Angus killed Vic Staples, the victim, in a drug deal gone bad. Nick." She inhales. The words catch in her throat. "Angus is in trouble."

Chapter 3

A Thought

"Are lawyers younger these days?" Aiden mutters as they stand at the hallway window. Angus and his legal aid lawyer sit on the far side of the table. Roland Fulbright, with his chair pulled away and his elbows on his knees, attempts interaction with a reluctant Angus, who twists his fingers, head bowed.

"I'm not unfamiliar with baby-faced lawyers because of Brigitte's Carter Stephens. I must admit, I still consider them children. Where's the officer involved in the arrest?"

"Sergeant Herman Rose, at your service, ma'am." He stops short, papers askew under one arm.

Stella worries he might salute.

"Okay. Showtime. Stella and I won't interrupt unless the discussion veers off track, but I'll make introductions." Aiden pulls the door open. Stella enters first, takes her preferred seat at the corner of the oval table, while the two men settle across from Angus and his lawyer.

"Good morning, again. Please meet Stella Kirk, a consultant for the department. Stella, Roland Fulbright. Mr. Fulbright, let me introduce the officer on the scene, Sergeant Herman Rose. Ms. Kirk and I want to complete a more in-depth interview after Sergeant Rose finishes."

Roland nods to both Stella and Herman. "I've instructed my client regarding the statement. He has agreed to be interviewed, and then we request Mr. Raspberry's release."

Aiden coughs. "Don't jump ahead, Sir. With serious concerns regarding your client's involvement, we can hold him for twenty-four hours without charge."

"Ten o'clock tonight." Roland leans toward Angus. "You will sleep in your own bed. No need to worry."

The young lawyer's attitude impresses Stella, along with his long black hair slicked high above his brows—a style designed, she suspects, specifically for height and presence.

Sergeant Rose shuffles through his papers and grabs a notebook. "Shall we begin? Mr. Raspberry, you called 911 at eight-oh-five last night, Friday, May 7?"

"Correct." Angus does not lift his gaze when he answers the sergeant.

"Please describe, in your own words, the reason for your call."

Silence surrounds them. Angus bends forward. His scraggly beard trembles over his chest, and he pauses before he mumbles his response. "Went to Hester's for supper." He lifts his face and meets Stella's eyes. "Is she alright?"

Stella nods.

"Came home around eight. The sky was almost dark. Vic had parked his truck in the yard. I walked into the barn to say hello if he wasn't on the water. The tide was high. He could have been out, but I found him on the floor."

"Go on, Mr. Raspberry." Sergeant Rose writes with ferocity, despite the recorder.

"I saw his skull bashed in and my crowbar was layin' beside him." He looks at his lawyer. "I never touched nuthin'. I ran inside the house and called 911."

"What happened afterward?"

"Waited with my dog on the back porch."

"Did you know he was dead?"

"Sort of, but I told the operator to send an ambulance. You arrived soon after."

"Mr. Raspberry, please clarify, for the record, why the victim enjoyed access to your outbuilding."

"I rented the shed—Hester says the old place doesn't deserve to be called a barn—to Vic Staples for fifty dollars a month. He stores his little aluminum skiff inside and takes the boat out at high tide—two or three times a month."

"How did your arrangement with Mr. Staples begin?"

"Oh, easy." The muscles in his forehead lose a measure of tension. "Luther Greene, from the funeral home, asked Donamae, my neighbour from up the road, if I might be interested in rentin' the place. She told me. Vic and me, we discussed a charge. The money he pays covers my property taxes."

He turns his attention in Stella's general direction. His eyes glow. "Once Hester helps me, no more finance problems. She's a whiz." He heaves a sigh and settles.

"Mr. Raspberry, please describe the scene when you entered the barn."

"Like I already said, Vic Staples on the floor with my crowbar beside him. The boat was out of the water and pulled partway inside—the bow still hangin' out the door. There was seaweed tangled in the propeller. He'd been out. He always cleaned the propeller when he came back."

"Did you check on him whenever he used his equipment?"

Angus frowns. "No. Sometimes he left in the middle of the night when I was asleep, but if I saw his truck in the yard, I wandered over to the barn."

Sergeant Rose turns toward Aiden. "Questions, Sir?"

Aiden meets Stella's gaze and widens his eyes.

"One more detail, Angus."

The big man nods.

"Was Luther Greene ever with Vic?"

"Not so far as I know."

"Anyone else?"

Angus leans forward. "Another fella came out with him once, but I never met him."

"Can you describe the person?"

"He wasn't friendly. I hollered hello, but he never turned to face me. I didn't interfere. He was tall and kinda hunched."

Aiden jumps in. "Was he around last night, Mr. Raspberry?"

"No, Sir. I drove home at dusk. There was nobody on the road and no other vehicles."

The detective stands. "Thanks for permission to sit in, Sergeant Rose. Get Mr. Raspberry's statement typed as soon as possible. Stella and I will be back, Mr. Fulbright."

"When can Hester come see me, Stella?"

Stella glances at Aiden before she replies. "She'll visit you right after our interview." She watches the muscles in his face sag. "Not long now."

****

"I've advised my client he need not speak with you. Once he's signed his witness document, and if you do not charge him, we will request his release."

Aiden has not taken a seat. With his hands on his hips, he stares at Roland Fulbright while he asks, "Mr. Raspberry, are you willing to answer a few questions for us before we decide if we should lay charges?"

Angus glances toward Stella. Although wiser to follow his lawyer's advice, she is sure his help in their investigation will be advantageous. Information as to his arrangements with Vic Staples is critical. She's certain Angus notices her slight nod.

"Answerin' your questions ain't no problem. Please don't be mad, Mr. Fulbright. I want to be a responsible citizen, the same as Hester."

"Thank you." Aiden sits.

"You know, Detective, Hester told me how once you thought she was a suspect in the murder of her sister-in-law, Lucy, but in the end, and with her special information, you identified the real culprit." His face lights. "She harbours no grudges, and I won't either."

"Okay." Aiden's shoulders heave.

Stella can tell he has, in this exact moment, realized communication with Angus must resemble discussions with Hester—direct, and without the complications of compound questions.

"Please tell us, in as much detail as possible, about your interactions with Vic Staples."

"He knocked on the back door each month, near the first, and gave me fifty dollars in cash."

"Was there ever unusual behaviour when he came by?"

"No, except for his money. A brand new fifty-dollar bill—crisp—every time. You know, right from the bank."

"What did you do with the money after Vic paid his rent?" Stella hopes the bills weren't counterfeit, and he hasn't kept them under his mattress.

"I go into the Shale Harbour Savings and Loan once a month, after he pays me, and I make a deposit. I don't lock my house, so I don't keep money inside. Anybody could walk past Orion. He minds good, but he's no guard." Angus chuckles into his beard. "Hester's Angel makes a better watchdog."

Relieved, Stella glances at Aiden before she asks another question. "Did Vic visit the house at other times besides rent day?"

"Once, to use the phone. He called someone in town and told them not to drive to the farm."

"Do you know the identity of the person on the other end of the line?"

"Sorry, no."

"How long since you made your arrangement with the victim, Mr. Raspberry?"

"Comin' a year. He brought the boat out last summer—June." His eyes widen and dart from one to the other. "My bank book will show the first deposit, right?"

"Thanks. An excellent idea."

Angus sits straighter in his chair. "See. I can be a help instead of a suspect, same as Hester."

"Correct." Stella avoids any emotion, but she knows he isn't their murderer and consciously steers the interview in a direction where he might prove more useful in the investigation. "The tide was high when you found Vic."

"Off by thirty minutes—goin' out by the time I arrived home."

"Describe Vic's habits with his boat."

"Two or three times a month, he drove out and launched at full tide, be gone an hour or less, and return. He loaded the skiff right into the barn at the back, where the ramp sits."

"Anyone work with him?" Aiden questions.

"The man I mentioned, but I don't know if he worked for Vic. There could be others when I wasn't around or was busy. A potato farm is demandin'." His face assumes a surprised expression, and he rubs his beard. "I didn't spy on him, and you shouldn't be thinkin' I did. Vic rented the place and could come and go as he pleased."

"Is there any possibility another man was with Vic and left via the beach? You said before you saw no one on your drive home." Aiden pushes.

"A person couldn't walk the beach after dark at high tide, sir. The cove dips and the cliffs rise. You'd find yourself with no way up. I suppose somebody could've hidden nearby."

"Who lives on your stretch of road, Angus? You mentioned your neighbour, who connected you and Vic. There are two other properties besides hers, before you reach Raspberry Farm. Correct?"

"Yes. Dad said we were at the end of the line. Donamae Kutska lives across from us but further toward town. The place closest belongs to River and Saffron. The road follows the cliff and curves, running through the middle of their property, with the house on the left and other buildings on the right. I'm sure those aren't their real names. They dress like hippies and say they operate a hobby farm. Nice enough people—lotsa livestock. The pair collect critters for no good reason. Who needs one of every farm animal?"

"What do they do for income?" Now Aiden appears interested.

"Hester wonders if they inherited money and don't care, but they sell eggs on the side of the road, and Saffron makes bracelets out of beads. She peddles them in the craft stores in town, and Tiffany lets her ply her wares in front of Cocoa and Café."

"And the second place, Angus?"

"Jesse and Hermione Wigglesworth live before River and Saffron, on the left. They've been in their homestead since before we moved here in 1959. They're old. Hester and I take them bread or a casserole she and Jewel made."

"Describe Donamae Kutska."

"She keeps goats. Younger than my folks. Nice, but she meddles. She gives me goat's milk and cheese sometimes. They smell bad."

Aiden stands. "We've heard enough for the moment, Mr. Fulbright. We'll release your client before day's end, once the forensics team finishes on his property. I need time to complete the paperwork, too."

Angus' face flushes. He rubs his beard and fidgets in his chair. "Can I talk to Hester? Please? I'll tell her I was helpful and have permission to go home."

"Let me find Hester for you, Angus." Stella turns toward Aiden. "Shall we meet in your office while Hester and Angus visit, before I take her back to her place?"

He nods.

****

She finds Hester seated in the empty space where they waited earlier. Two brown paper bags rest on the corner of the desk. "Hi. How did you manage at lunch?"

"Sergeant Moyer isn't a great talker. We discussed food. I brought you a sliced vegetable sandwich on wholewheat bread." She taps the side of one parcel. "You've gained weight and should watch your diet. Nick is an excellent cook, but his culinary skills may well be a liability for a woman of your vintage." She stands and hands over two paper bags. "How's Angus?"

"Fine. Once the police are through at the farm, they'll release him and give him a drive home."

Her face beams, identifiable to anyone else who's hopelessly in love. "I want to hug him. You can take me back to collect Angel and supplies before I go to his place and wait for his arrival."

"Okay. I'll ask Aiden to call you when he's released. Workable?" *Hester wants to hug Angus.*

"Yes. Yes. May I see him now? Where is he?"

"Come along. He'll be in the conference room."

With eyes wide, her voice shakes when she asks, "Will the attorney stay with us?" Her face crumples. "Not acceptable, Stella."

"No. His name is Roland Fulbright, by the way. Mr. Fulbright is young, and I expect not very experienced. Be nice. He won't linger."

"I'll hire a better lawyer if necessary. Right now, I must speak with Angus and make sure he's okay."

Stella sneaks a glance at her friend, who is playing the unfamiliar role of caregiver. As they approach the room where Angus waits, Hester increases her pace.

She peeks in through the hall window. "There he is," she exclaims, as she pushes open the door. Stella follows her. The lawyer stands and extends his hand, but she ignores him while she rushes toward Angus, who struggles to his feet. She propels herself into his chest and he wraps both arms around her shoulders and rests his bearded face against her felt cloche.

"Mr. Fulbright, meet Hester Painter, Angus' close friend. Hester." She hopes Hester engages. "Say hello to Angus' lawyer, who kindly drove in from Port Ephron to help."

Hester stirs while she remains in Angus's arms. "Thank you, although we waited a long time for your arrival."

"My apologies, Ms. Painter. I expect the authorities to release Mr. Raspberry once the team finishes on his property, and after Detective North completes his paperwork. I am at your service and will remain in the break room until the statement requires review."

When she nods, Angus mumbles his thanks.

"I'll leave you two alone for now. There's a constable outside the door. When you're ready to go, Hester, ask him to fetch me." Stella waits for a reply.

"Are you okay? Did you eat?" Hester searches his face.

Dismissal occurs. She's suddenly invisible.

Back in the hall, she trots toward Aiden's office, but meets him halfway and waves the bags. "Sandwiches. Shall we debrief now?"

"Yeah. Moyer brought me my change but no food. I'm famished. Two-thirty is late for lunch."

Once they're alone, she hands him the bag marked with a V and opens the other one. Egg salad on multi-grain. Yum. Without further discussion, she munches and notes how his nose wrinkles when he pulls the slices of bread apart and discovers cucumber, tomato, and lettuce.

"Do I smell egg salad on your side of the desk?"

"Yup." She takes another bite while she crumples the corner of the brown paper with the E. "Lucky, I guess. Now, I told Hester you would call her place once you cleared Angus. She wants to meet him at Raspberry Farm."

"Tell Moyer on your way out."

"It's better Angus doesn't stay."

"At the moment, we haven't enough concrete evidence for a charge against him, but after the forensics team finishes with their fine-tooth-comb business, circumstances may change."

"I have a thought."

"Life never works out well for me when you ruminate, Stella." His expression remains blank.

She assumes the remark is a failed attempt to tease her. "We could visit the three farms on the road, and interview Luther Greene, too. He might know Vic's other contacts. Oh!" She gulps a mouthful of sandwich. "And the town office. We should talk with his co-workers."

Aiden's chest heaves. "Right now, there's no evidence of anyone else at the farm, Stella. Angus even admits he didn't come across a soul on the road when he drove home. The tide was too high for an escape along the shoreline."

"The person who murdered Vic might have hidden in a ditch or driven away in their own car. He said the time was dusk. The route goes right through River and Saffron's property. Let's ask the hippies if they noticed anyone around eight o'clock. A person could have walked the stretch once Angus drove past—a random guy out for a stroll."

"Fair enough. Lots of times, people don't understand or appreciate what they've seen. You take Hester home. Once Angus signs his statement, we'll call Hester before we deliver him to Raspberry Farm. I'll contact you once we receive a report from the crowd in the basement." He stuffs the remains of his lunch back in the wrapper and tosses the ball into his trash can. "How's Nick?"

Startled at the change in subject, she finishes her last bite before she answers.

"He's busy. The staff begin work next Friday. Duke is on board already. He and Cloris will connect their rigs into services right away. Nick's busy," she restates.

"Rosemary hasn't given Cavelle and me any trouble. I thought you'd appreciate knowing."

"Good." She covers her surprise and repeats her concern. "I worry about Cavelle. Rosemary is often unpredictable, Aiden. You and I both know she has a dangerous side."

"I can protect Cavelle."

"Right." She struggles but curbs any further comments. "I must go find Hester." She reaches for her handbag and turns toward the door.

"Do I sense a hint of jealousy in your tone?" He stares at the ceiling, a smirk on his face.

Caught off-guard again, she spins on her heel. "Not for a single second, Aiden." Her heart races, and her face feels hot. *How dare he?* "Number one: Nick and I are solid. Number two: current circumstances have you wedged between a woman who is smitten with you, and your wife, whose personality comes with challenges. I hope Cavelle doesn't get hurt, either physically or emotionally."

He remains seated, doesn't react, and changes focus again. "I didn't call you today because Cavelle and I discussed the case before we left the house, and she agrees Angus killed Vic in a fit of rage over a drug deal. She wants Hester out of their dalliance as soon as possible. Now she's found a practical excuse."

Stella stands with her fingers on the cool doorknob but remains turned away. "Hester's friendship with Angus has no bearing on whether he becomes a suspect, Aiden. You understand the principle of the evidence trail. Cavelle's feedback is based on her underlying motive—worry because her sister, long cloistered at home, has developed a life." There's a nick in the paint on the door. "Do you want my assistance, or need I run around unsupervised and interview witnesses and contacts on my own?"

"My apologies. Certainly, your help is invaluable, as you know, but Angus is our guy, even if you don't agree right now."

"Oh. One other piece of advice." She turns and observes his frown. "Sorry. Might you be wise to assign officers to walk the shore near Raspberry Farm? The person who murdered Vic Staples perhaps didn't understand the concept of high tides and the cliffs."

Chapter 4

Become Embroiled

Hester's tension fills the front seat.

"Did Angus describe his interview and statement?"

"No. He said he'd save the details for later. We discussed other stuff."

Stella and Hester, in the Jeep and settled, prepare for the return drive.

"You're upset." Sometimes the wiser option is to state the obvious.

"Although primarily good at his job, I don't understand why Detective North remains convinced Angus killed Victor Staples." She turns her pinched face toward Stella. "The man couldn't hurt a bug, let alone a person. You agree, right?"

"If I'm honest, Hester, I met Angus for the first time when you two attended Easter Brunch at the Shale Harbour Hotel. I don't know him."

Her eyes widen.

"I appreciate your confidence in Angus. You care a great deal for him." She hesitates and doesn't use the word love, which is presumptuous, at least now. "Aiden has a point. If no one saw a person or a car on the road and they found no one nearby, and the tide was high, where did the perpetrator go?"

"Here's my theory. The killer drove to the farm with Vic. They went out in the boat and fought after they returned. Did Angus tell you Vic's truck was cold, but the body was warm?"

"What? No. He never mentioned the vehicle, and neither Aiden nor I asked."

"Well, whoever killed Vic Staples remained on the property when Angus came home. The person, or persons, hid somewhere." She nods as she agrees with her own theory. "We need a more thorough search than Detective North's forensics team is likely to complete. We'll uncover a clue, I'm sure." She glares at Stella. "They bungled the Deena Finch investigation. Remember?"

"We can peruse the buildings once the police release the scene. Right now, the barn remains out of bounds. I expect they'll station a constable in a car nearby for a few more days." She drops the Jeep into reverse and navigates the vehicle out of the RCMP lot into the street. "We'll snoop around once we're given clearance. I promise. You and Angus talked for half an hour."

"Angus and I discussed our immediate plans," she replies, in a soft voice. "I will pack up a few personal items, Angel and her food, and the casserole Jewel stashed in the freezer two days ago. I told him I could catch a ride over and wait for him with the dogs."

"Do you need me to drive you?" Stella glances at her watch—six o'clock by the time she delivers Hester home. She can call Nick. He'll keep a plate warm for her.

"Unnecessary. Jacob and Ken are both at the farm. I already alerted Jewel."

"And you plan to stay at Raspberry Farm?"

"Yes. I realize I said the fall after the harvest is the better choice for us to begin our life as a couple." Her eyes widen. "Despite the circumstances, we decided, in consideration of the events we've experienced, we want to be together." She clutches her cloth bag against her chest and stares out the front window.

"Will your family approve?" In her mind, Stella has substituted Cavelle for family. She expects Jacob's support for the couple's decision.

As if she's read Stella's thoughts, Hester answers, "Cavelle's objections are anticipated. She doesn't want me 'tangled'—the word she used—with a younger person."

Stella can see Hester's smirk out of the corner of her eye.

"Cavelle is involved—and lives—with a married man whose wife has constant mental health issues," Hester continues. "She cannot say my decisions aren't wise. Angus and I are a good fit. She knows I'm right and hates the idea of my courtship with Angus; one which has a future." She pauses. "I predict a doomed affair between Cavelle and Detective North."

Avoiding disagreement, Stella asks, "Why are you convinced Cavelle and Aiden have no future, Hester?"

"To be frank, and you're aware I am a frank person," her lips twitch before she continues. "Cavelle acts needy. Her decision to move in with the detective was far too quick. She judges me but won't analyze her own problems."

"Do you still want my support when you and Angus break the news to your family, as you asked earlier?"

"I expect to need your endorsement soon. They will view today as an emergency with the sole purpose of assisting Angus. I'll travel back and forth but make my home at Raspberry Farm." She pulls her hat tighter around her ears. "Now," she adopts a professorial expression, "what details from his statement, his interview, and your discussion with Detective North are worthy of follow up by you and me?"

"As for you and Angus, you know I'll help in any way I can. I'm certain every word the man said was true. There's no direct evidence he wielded a crowbar at Vic Staples. Did you suspect Vic was involved in drugs?"

"No. Angus being dragged into a drug venture is preposterous, by the way."

"The police found traces of drugs at the murder site. Now, I must warn you that Angus's prints will be on the murder weapon because the crowbar belongs to him. Evidence particular to the weapon is circumstantial. Without a more defined story, there will be difficulty pressing charges."

"What else?"

"Aiden and I will interview residents of the three farms on the road which leads to Angus' place. In addition, I suggested he assign staff to walk the shore at low tide and that we could visit the town office and speak with employees."

"You and I can poke around in the barn once they release the scene, and we can search the house anytime. Good idea?"

"Yes. We need to conduct another examination with Aiden present, though, to avoid talk of planted evidence. Here we are." She pulls the Jeep into the gravelled lot in front of Hester's home. "I'll telephone Nick from here once we're sure you have a ride, okay?"

"Jacob or Ken can take me. Don't worry. Call Nick."

Jewel greets them at the door. She's aware of the plan from Hester's earlier contact. "Ken will drive Hester." Stress lines frame her eyes. "I set a frozen chicken and rice casserole on the counter, and filled a box with vegetables and bread, too." Stella isn't sure whom she's telling. Hester rushes toward the stairs and her room, while Angel trots behind.

"May I use the phone to tell Nick I'm on my way?"

The young woman points in the general direction of the telephone and saunters back to the sink. "Help yourself, Stella. In here if you need me."

****

She counts six risers before she reaches the deck of their veranda. Exhaustion overwhelms each step. He stands behind the screen, Kiki under his arm. "Hi. Sorry I'm late. A lawyer from Port Ephron took his own sweet time." He holds the door while she steps inside.

The grand old living room is awash in flickers of light from the fire. The wine glasses on the coffee table twinkle. She stretches on her tiptoes and plants a serious kiss on his lips. "Hello, again."

"You're beat. Let me take your coat. Sit. I'll pour you a drink and we'll visit." He stops and peers at her. "Tell me whatever you want. I can always entertain you with Kiki and Duke stories. Your choice." He plops the squirming dog on a couch and hangs her coat in the closet.

Stella absorbs the peace, Kiki, the warmth of the space, and this man who is the love of her life. She acknowledges the gift of Nick Cochran every day. He arrived on her doorstep in the spring of 1979, after she advertised for help; determined to open for the summer. The park had become rundown while her father drifted further along the road to dementia. Her sister, Trixie, refused involvement. Nick rescued both her and Shale Cliffs. As she slumps onto the leather sofa cushions beside Kiki, who wiggles for attention, she realizes he rescues her regularly.

"Bottle of wine on the way!" He shouts from the kitchen. "I'm afraid supper is sausage penné with a few mushrooms." He peeks around the corner. "Since Ms. Kirk promised to chef our meal tonight and," he pauses for effect, "didn't."

"For the love of God," she sputters, as she twists on the couch to better see him. "When Hester called, my plan flew out the window. My promise never crossed my mind." Her hand cups her mouth. "Nick, I'm sorry."

He rushes back with the wine. "Stop, Stella. I don't care. Duke showed his face after you left, but I ticked chores off my list, regardless. I raked the flower beds by the front door. Eve can get a jump start. I'll pick up our order of annuals on Monday." He wraps an arm around her shoulder while he fills her glass. "I was teasing. Making a meal is no problem."

"Dinner by me tomorrow."

"Maybe yes. Maybe no. A lot will depend on this case." He studies her expression. "I assume you've become embroiled."

"No doubt. Angus Raspberry found Vic Staples' warm body on the floor of an old garage, or barn, or whatever, when he arrived home after supper at Hester's last night. Before you ask, Vic rented the structure nearest the water so he could launch his motorboat two or three times a month." She inhales the fruity aroma. "Angus ignored Vic's behaviour, because Vic paid him with a crisp fifty-dollar bill as regular as clockwork. Aiden says they discovered indications of drugs on the property, and he suspects Vic collected the product offshore. We won't be certain until the forensics report comes in tomorrow."

"Did they hold poor Angus in cells? The guy didn't strike me as the adaptive type."

"Police held him overnight, but they'll release him within twenty-four hours." She glances at her watch. "Now Hester's on her way to his farm to be there when he returns. She packed Angel's supplies, a suitcase, and food. I expect she'll stay. As for Angus, once Aiden granted permission for him to see Hester, he relaxed and provided any information requested of him."

Nick sips his wine, open to listen but asking no questions.

"He didn't kill Vic Staples. He doesn't possess the intestinal fortitude necessary to slug a man with a crowbar."

"Ouch."

"Not pretty, from what I gather." She pats the dog. The muscles in her neck relax. "My biggest concern remains Cavelle."

"I bet she's interfered because she has Aiden's ear."

"What a very insightful guy you are." She leans against him. "Cavelle convinced Aiden, although he needed little convincing, that Angus was the perpetrator. The problem arises because Cavelle doesn't approve of Hester's liaison with Angus and wants the affair to break off. Hester has her sister figured out. I see no chance she'll leave Angus, no matter how difficult the circumstances might become."

"Want supper? Come out here while I cook the penné."

She reaches for the wine glasses. Kiki jumps to the floor and they both trot into the kitchen. "I'm hungry."

"You ate lunch, I assume?" He studies her face.

"Yes, Hester brought Aiden and me sandwiches from the café." She doesn't describe her sandwich switch. "Long time ago."

Nick turns on the stove to boil water for the pasta.

"By the way, Aiden bragged Rosemary has been among the missing and hasn't contacted either him or Cavelle. I sensed not-so-subtle admonishment because I'm now proved wrong in my concerns." She crosses her arms.

"Your response?"

"I expressed my support for them as a couple." She's never revealed her discussion with Mary Jo Frost, Aiden's sister-in-law, to anyone. Not even Nick. Mary Jo described Aiden as a philanderer for most of his married life. Whenever Rosemary went through a bad patch, he would find someone new, but they never lasted past Rosemary's return to a version of normal. Mary Jo expects, despite Cavelle's commitment to the detective, he'll repeat the pattern. At a point when the time is right, she'll tell Nick. Not now.

A tasty supper didn't cure her exhaustion. They drank maple liqueur in front of the fire before bed, talk of tomorrow's plans put on hold.

****

Side-by-side at the kitchen window, their warm bodies touch. He's in cotton pyjama bottoms and she wears an over-sized T-shirt. Last night, they revelled in the comfort of each other's company. This morning proved indulgent in other ways.

"We should discuss staff and schedule tasks, Stella. I expect you won't be home much until the police straighten out the current issue with Angus and Hester."

Loud thumps on the back screen door interfere with her answer. "Good grief." She glances at the wall clock. "Not even eight."

"Duke and Cloris are due around coffee time." He surveys her long legs. "You need pants."

"Right. And a sweatshirt."

Stella hears Duke's voice while she races for their suite upstairs. "Cloris will be here later, but I decided I'd drive out to the park and enjoy breakfast with you folks." After a pause where he must be assessing Nick's attire, he queries, "Did I catch you in the middle of somethin'?"

"Come on in, Duke. There's no rush today. Take a seat. Pat your dog. We'll be a few minutes. Have a cup of coffee."

"Honest to God, Nick." She huffs while she drags on her Acadia University sweatshirt as he appears at the door.

Nick grimaces. "Cloris objects when he mooches breakfast off us, although I imagine Duke misses his favourite time of day. Don't worry. Make him toast. You can keep him company while I wash. Afterward, we'll hook him into services. His trailer will need a serious clean. He'll soon be out of our hair."

His tone calms her. "Okay." She drags on yesterday's jeans. "I'll take a quick shower before Cloris turns up next."

Back in the kitchen, she plants her best indulgent boss expression on her face as she reaches for the near-empty coffeepot. Duke's butt swings in the air while his hands tap the floor in a game of don't-bite-me with Kiki. "Morning, Duke. You're here at the crack of dawn—on a Sunday."

"Eight isn't early in my world, Stella. Nice seein' you, too." He turns toward the dog. "Who's a good girl?"

She's now forced to converse with his rear end. "You managed coffee," she states, noticing one of her favourite cups perched on the edge of the table. She runs water for another pot.

"Wanted to be here pronto because I promised old Mildred I'd hook in her unit today and do her housework in the Cardinal as well. Between hers and mine, I'll be workin' until the sun sets. Cloris said she'd manage her own and didn't need my help. Okay, by me. My scourin' skills don't suit her."

Does she sense frustration? "Trouble in paradise?"

He clambers onto his feet and snuggles the dog under his arm. "Oh, we're fine," he grunts. "She likes stuff her way, and you understand my problem." He flashes yellowed teeth. "I sometimes ignore the rules."

"Toast? Nice of you to help Mildred."

"She's hittin' ninety soon. The old bat still has more life left in her, though. Cloris will tote her gear out in the pickup next weekend."

"Ninety? Are you sure? I assumed eighty. What a gal." Mildred Fox owns a minuscule Cardinal trailer, parked at Shale Cliffs RV Park for years now. They built her a new deck after hers rotted off the side of her rig and became dangerous. Paul helps her when he has spare time away from Nick. She lives in a senior's apartment in the winter but remains at the park for the summer. A young girl from town does her errands. She sits outside, under her flapping and torn awning, while she sips what she describes loosely as lemonade.

Stella plops two thick slices of brown bread toast on a plate and places them on the table near Duke. She contributes Hester's strawberry jam from the fridge and points her finger at her security guard. "Don't feed Kiki. We've broken her of the habit. Put her on the floor and I'll give you a kibble for her."

Duke pouts but listens.

Nick rumbles down the stairs as the coffee pot gurgles to completion. "Done." He reaches for his cup. "I can finish here, if you like." His breath touches the tiny hairs on her neck. She flushes.

"Okay, you two. We're at the breakfast table."

Despite his narcissism, Duke doesn't miss much.

By the time Cloris' enormous pickup pulls into the yard, Stella has readied herself for her day and the sink's full of dirty dishes. She watches from the kitchen window as the former transport and bus driver attaches her fifth wheel, parked behind the house, with no help from anyone. Once she's satisfied, she climbs the back stairs and knocks on the veranda screen door.

"Good morning, Cloris. Fancy job when you backed up the truck."

"The reason God invented mirrors, Stella. You don't need interference." She notes Kiki with a glance but doesn't pat her. "Nick around? Duke said I could move and hook into services."

"Ready when you are. They're at Duke's for now. We can walk over to his rig. Hold on." She grabs her coat and the dog's leash.

Duke's trailer sits at the far end of the park. They saunter along the road as Kiki skips ahead, the exact distance her tether allows.

"I hear Angus Raspberry killed Vic Staples."

"News travels fast. Vic Staples is dead, but police haven't charged Angus."

"Right. You're tight with his girlfriend, Hester Painter." She stops and faces Stella. "My sister says they ran drugs out of the Raspberry property. She told me everybody knows—Angus Raspberry's sunk up to his eyeballs in the drug trade. I hope your friend isn't involved."

Stella covers her shock with a change in subject. "You and Ruth are no longer on the outs because she dated Duke before you?"

"We're sisters, Stella. You understand. Besides, she dumped Duke. Anyway, Port Ephron folks say the case will be open and shut. Weird Angus killed Vic."

CHAPTER 5

Explain Your Theory

"Merrilee will have her work cut out for her if you're still involved in Vic Staples' murder investigation, Stella."

Leaving Cloris with Duke for the moment, Nick wraps an arm around her shoulder. They wander toward the house while Kiki trots ahead. The weight of him comforts her. Merrilee Wild, her new hire, took Alice's place in reception as her general assistant. Merrilee understood such a set of circumstances as the most recent murder could indeed happen. "You're right. I've allowed lots of time for her on Friday. Are you off to Cloris'?"

"Yeah. Duke is busy with his housework. He suggested we hook Mildred's Cardinal after lunch, so I'll help Cloris once she tears herself away from telling Duke how to clean. And you?"

"Off to Raspberry Farm to see how Hester and Angus are managing. Once the forensics report comes back, we'll assess our next moves."

As they reach the veranda stairs, he removes his arm. The chill of spring touches the warm spots left behind. "I don't imagine Cloris will need much help, but I can use the truck and keep Kiki with me. You'll want the Jeep."

She watches the two of them sputter off toward Cloris' assigned site at the opposite end of the park. He'll check the area over while he waits for her. She requested as great a distance from Duke's trailer as possible, suggesting she preferred not to run into him every day, especially in the event their affair fizzled. Cloris also doesn't want Duke on her doorstep for coffee and expectations she'll scoot around on the golf cart with him at a moment's notice. Stella shrugs. She might realize her concerns, regardless. They lived together for the off-season. She smiles as she enters her office and notices the blinking light on the answering machine. Cloris may prefer a single summer and a couple winter, but Duke has other ideas.

"Hi, Stella. I expect the forensics report in the morning, for sure. I called and asked. The overtime is going to kill me. Why do people commit murder on the weekend? Meet me for coffee at the café around ten tomorrow, and we can review the findings. I imagine a rearrest of Angus, but I'll reserve judgment for now. Call the detachment if you can't come. Otherwise, see you tomorrow." The machine clicks.

Before she presses the erase button, she sits. Aiden reserving judgment—encouraging. She hopes he's well-prepared to consider the involvement of someone else. Now, to find a way of balancing an investigation with her park responsibilities.

Nick's impatience always surfaces as they brace for staff and the commencement of a new season. He gets twitchy and dithers with the details. She jots notes and focuses on the business for a moment.

Paul Morgan, Alice's brother, has become Nick's right-hand man throughout the summer. The young fellow is sociable and helpful if someone needs a water filter in a hurry, or they experience a levelling issue with their rig. Paul listens well and can fix most problems. He loves machinery and has told Stella, in the past, he would work for them year-round, if he could.

Eve Trembly's an accountancy major at university, but her life's joy is the gardens and the lawn mower. She never seeks shortcuts, despite the daily grind, and cleans the public bathrooms and showers without complaint. She'll paint, plant annuals, weed, mow the lawns, and whipper-snip—whatever's needed. On a rainy day, Eve works inside the house and covers the front office if required. Stella appreciates their good fortune.

Once the three staff arrive on Friday, preparations for their first open weekend begin. Paul and Nick will tidy up the sites. Along with Duke, they'll deliver picnic tables and fire pit rings. Once they finish those jobs, Nick decides if they need more tables and Paul can build those. Eve spring cleans the bathrooms and laundry room. She runs each machine, checks every tap, and flushes each toilet. She'll plant annuals in the flower beds nearest the house. Registration cards and maps will be ready from Gorman Printing later in the week. Merrilee must become familiar with the seasonals as arrivals begin on Friday, May 21. She expects the weekend will be busy and hopes to work at her new assistant's side.

Satisfied with the list, she writes a note which says she'll be back for lunch and grabs the phone.

"Raspberry Farm."

"Hello, Angus. Stella here. I hoped to drive over for a quick visit. Are you and Hester around for the rest of the morning?"

"You should talk with Hester." The receiver clunks on the counter and she can hear muffled words—audible enough that she deciphers a measure of wariness on Angus' part.

"Stella."

"I want to visit with you. Okay?"

"Our coffee isn't as good as Jewel's, but you are welcome, nonetheless."

"Coffee isn't necessary. I need to see the scene with my own eyes."

"In the past, you have mentioned how imagination or descriptions cannot take the place of personal observations. You are most welcome, although we must suffer with a police car in the yard. They will stop you when you arrive on the property."

"Okay, Hester. I understand I can't go into any of the outbuildings, but I still want to lay my eyes on the farm. Angus sounds worried."

"He won't mind if I tell you, Stella. His time at the detachment upset him a great deal. He hasn't slept since the police brought him home. He's shaky and convinced Detective North plans to put him back in jail."

"Did he kill Vic?"

"How can you suggest such nonsense?" In a wobbly voice, she whispered, "We need you on our side."

"Give me twenty minutes."

****

Raspberry Farm nestles into the category of rundown—without exaggeration. The end of the road, which leads into the overgrown yard, is grassy and rutted. Any suggestion of gravel has long since disappeared. As Stella eases the Jeep to a halt, a young female constable approaches. Stella rolls her window open. "Good morning. Stella Kirk for Angus and Hester. They expect me."

She writes in her notebook and nods. "Thank you. Go ahead."

Stella can see a farm truck of nondescript origins parked inside the cordoned off area. Poor Angus. He can't touch his vehicle until Aiden clears the property.

The house, built around 1940 from what information she has already gathered, is a simple rectangular box with a closed-in veranda on the front and a four-paned dormer window in the centre above the porch. The siding colour suggests an apple green, now faded to a dirty shade of putty.

With no obvious pathway, she steps across the brown grass and makes her way toward the entrance. As she reaches her fist in the air to knock, the door squeaks ajar and Hester materializes, filling the opening.

"I heard the vehicle and came to check and see if you were here. Come inside."

Stella enters the cool and damp interior. The sun porch doesn't benefit from heat. The afternoon warmth of a fine weather day might enable the space to reach a temperature comfortable enough that guests could linger, but the northern exposure suggests the chances are rare. She notices the piles of discarded newspapers and boxes of random and broken tools, electrical appliances, and old clothes. The area has become another shed and trashcan, by the character of the contents. She swallows any mention of her observations.

"You said no coffee. For the best, I expect." She gives Stella a rare grin. "I made tea, and you may partake if you choose." She leads the way behind the central staircase into a kitchen at the back. They pass a living room on the left and a bedroom on the right.

One might assume the original owner didn't understand the art of construction, and crudely built the house from leftover materials and cast-off supplies. She can sense puffs of damp and cool air, from the hand dug basement, waft between the planks while she walks across the roughhewn wooden floor. The kitchen comprises a wall of open shelves, upper and lower. The counters are boards screwed into the vertical supports for the base shelves.

"We will renovate once our current issue," she pauses, and casts her eyes toward the water-stained ceiling, "gets sorted."

Angus, who has remained seated at the chipped orange Formica and chrome kitchen table, stands. Both dogs—Hester's cocker spaniel, Angel, and Angus' Labrador retriever cross named Orion—crawl out from underneath, seek pats, and withdraw to the porch.

"Sit, Stella. The tea is ready." She sets a floral pot with matching cups and saucers out before opening the refrigerator, circa 1960, and removing a small jug of milk. Hester reaches for the sugar bowl on a shelf near the sink.

"What a sweet antique tea set." Stella looks directly at Angus. "Was the china your mother's?"

"No. I don't remember ever seeing it. Hester found the pieces upstairs when she cleaned. I never used those rooms."

"I should show you, Stella. There are two alcoves under the eaves. The room on the front, with the dormer windows, is bright. The back space was sealed shut. I moved one plank before Angus helped me to tear down the false wall. I found the dishes and blankets." She wrinkles her nose. "The latter were moth eaten, and I put them in a box earmarked for the dump—once we can use the truck."

"Did someone sleep in there?" Stella's imagination bubbles as she envisions a person imprisoned in a secret hiding place with no windows.

Angus leans forward. "Not while we lived here. I slept in the front room upstairs and my folks were down here. I never noticed the other space until Hester asked for my help. The guy who built the house musta needed a spot no one could find." His enormous fists clutch the fragile cup. He sips his tea.

"Stella, the china is Bavarian." Hester returns the discussion to the china. "My research suggests the pieces date from before 1921 and were most likely brought here from Germany by the people who built the house. Angus' father purchased the property from them in 1959. Right?" She pats Angus on the hand.

He nods. "My folks came here and bought the place. They couldn't afford land in Ontario, but Dad wanted to farm. The German couple moved back to the old country. Donamae says they're both dead now."

"How is Donamae, your neighbour, connected again?"

"Easy. Donamae's father was a first cousin to the man who built our house. Even though we're no relation, she acts as if she's related because she feels attached to my place. I guess she spent lots of time here on the farm as a kid."

Hester has remained quiet throughout their exchange. "What's on your mind, my friend?"

"Cavelle came by earlier today. I spoke with the police because they didn't realize she's my sister, and they refused to allow her on the property. I recognized her car."

"And?"

"She expected me to go home with her." Hester scoffs. "As if I'm a troublesome child requiring removal." She returns to the counter and plugs in the kettle for more hot water. "I am forty-one years old, Stella. Despite my social challenges, Cavelle can't just cart me away." She settles into her chair once more and reaches for Angus' hand. "You and I, Stella, will solve Vic Staples' murder so Angus and I can make a life."

"Cavelle was angry."

"Infuriated. She was condescending, hurtful, and disrespectful to Angus, suggesting I'm cohabitating with a murderer." Her voice shakes. "I don't appreciate Cavelle right now. Her arrangements with Detective North have not enhanced her personality."

With his face bowed and his attention focused on the table, Angus whispers, "Stella, I hope someone finds out who killed Vic. Lots of trouble for me."

"Understood, Angus. I will do whatever's possible to get to the truth. Tomorrow, I will meet with Aiden after he receives the forensics report. Once he clears the outbuildings, we'll arrange for his visit out here and complete our own search. Right now, I must go."

Hester walks her to the door. "In the meantime, I continue to clean." Hester meets Stella's eyes. "There's lots of work. His parents died ten years ago, and he has done no maintenance besides the potato planting and harvest since."

"After we solve the murder, we'll organize a big party out here, Hester. We can paint, find new floor coverings, even snag a few doors for those open cupboards." She nudges her friend. "You wait and see what happens when we pull together."

****

She didn't want to abandon Nick again today. He supports her without complaint, and she often takes advantage. "Thanks, Tiffany." She accepts a cup of hazelnut brew from the café owner. Channelling Hester for a moment, she taps her foot with impatience on the pine floorboards, marking the seconds while she waits for Aiden. Cocoa and Café became a fixture in Shale Harbour once Tiffany and Andrew Blair purchased the business. Andrew provides chef services while Tiffany runs the restaurant. They hire one or two students in the summer because she excels on local tourism committees and their success means more help is required during the height of tourist season. The Blairs are another couple, like Nick and Stella, who work together—not an arrangement suitable for everyone.

Dust motes float in the quiet air. An older couple, seated at the sunny bistro table in the bay window, enjoy cinnamon buns and a pot of tea. The tinkle of the bells above the front door interrupts her indecision, related to whether a cinnamon bun will absorb a place in her own future. Aiden's blustery entrance contrasts with the warmth she has enjoyed at the back of the space until now.

He nods in Tiffany's direction and pretends to hold a cup, indicating coffee when she's able. Stella spies the manila file folder wedged in his armpit.

"Sorry I'm late. Been here long?"

"Not really. Wait until Tiffany delivers your brew, and we can talk."

Aiden slides the report across the tiny table. She makes room and opens the summary. Vic Staples owned a 1971 fourteen-foot aluminum utility boat with a fifteen horsepower Johnson outboard motor. They found a plastic box on the bottom of the skiff. Forensics detected cannabis inside, on the bottom of the boat, and on the floor of the barn. Aiden's gaze weighs heavily on her while she reads. "The victim's cause of death was, as we suspected, a blow to the skull with the crowbar located at the scene. The report suggests no evidence of another person besides Angus Raspberry nearby."

She closes the folder and slides the documents back. "We can assume the rumours are true and Vic Staples used his boat to collect drugs and deliver them to shore for distribution."

"Agreed. And Angus was his partner."

"No." She waves toward Tiffany, who bustles over, coffeepot in hand. "Thanks, my dear. I wonder if I need something stronger." Her smart remark elicits a titter from the owner before she turns her attention to the older couple at the front. "Vic partnered with someone, but not Angus." The scent of hazelnuts wafts around her face. "He doesn't possess the wherewithal, Aiden. His challenges are significant if his caregiver has become Hester Painter."

"Explain your theory, Stella."

Her shoulders heave with the burden of trust assigned by Hester and Angus. "Vic had company at the farm on at least one occasion, as Angus stated. Angus was oblivious to their actions. He wanted the fifty dollars. Honestly, Aiden. You should see the house where he, and now Hester, live. She tries her best, but the place is a dump. If he earned drug money, he didn't invest in creature comforts, for sure."

"True. Cavelle demands Hester be removed from the property." He snorts. "Cavelle assumes I possess superman credentials and because I'm a cop, I can make people do what I want, or in the case of her sister, what she wants."

"Cavelle—using your position as a police officer? I can't believe such a thing." Her eyes twinkle. "Her concerns don't surprise me after my visit yesterday."

"She's afraid Hester plans to sink her inheritance trust money into Angus' dilapidated farmhouse and will end up penniless."

"My personal bet? Cavelle should wrap her brain around the idea that Hester and Angus want a life together. Hester's a grown woman. She can do whatever she likes. As for the case, we need interviews with the neighbours and Vic's friends and co-workers. Who worked with Vic? Who chummed with him? Who might have been in cahoots with him?"

"Listen, I'll contact the folks who live on the road and make appointments for Wednesday. Let's search the farm ourselves before I sign off, okay?"

"Yes. I told Hester we could complete one of our famous searches, but with you present, to ensure no suggestion of impropriety. And Angus will remain away from the scene. We can snoop around tomorrow. I'll call her."

"We have a plan, but no Hester until we finish."

"Our staff start work on Friday, and my business doesn't run without my help," she reminds him. "As surprising as that may seem," she adds, with a smirk. "We need to discover the identity of Vic's partner and what happened after Vic's death, Aiden."

"Has Angus covered for the killer? Misguided third party loyalty? He wouldn't be the first."

"For what purpose?"

"Maybe he's afraid, or maybe the partner bribed him for his silence. He cared most about the fifty bucks each month. The killer could have made his silent support a lucrative option. Gotta go. Tell Hester I'll be at the farm by ten tomorrow."

She sits alone as the sounds of the bells over the door fade. Did the murderer bribe Angus? She closes her eyes and allows her mind to wander through all the possibilities. She's been wrong before. At least Aiden has no immediate plans to rearrest the poor guy. If he's accepted money from a drug smuggler, finding out shouldn't be a problem.

Chapter 6

More Worthless Details

The building sits close to the water's edge, sideways to the property, with two sliding doors, one facing the ocean side and one toward the yard. The young constable on duty mentioned he helped Aiden with the doors, both askew on rusted hardware. They forced the mechanisms to move despite the protests of metal on metal.

Aiden arrived at Raspberry Farm before Stella. She found Hester and Angus perched together on the back step, the dogs for bookends. "Detective North told us you do not need my help." Hester frowned and studied her shoes.

"He'll release the scene and we can snoop around afterward." Stella turned toward the barn. A tangle of thicket composed of brambles, prickles, and wild rose bushes smother one side. The place sits parallel to the sea. "Are there rooms inside?" She waited for Angus' stuttered reply.

"Nope. Open." Nodding when he answered, his beard scraped the front of his denim shirt. "The previous owner built the old machine shed when he moved here. I think they lived there until he finished the house. I asked Donamae, but she was little and doesn't remember."

"Are you with me, or did you come for a visit?" Aiden's voice, and attitude, spin across the yard on breezes from the water.

"On my way," she shouts. "I'll share anything we find out, you two," she mentions, before she leaves them.

"Good morning, Aiden. Trouble at home? You don't sound happy."

"I'm fine," he replies, although his tone is gruff. "Tell me your observations, because I can't, for the life of me, figure out how anybody else was inside the barn with Vic Staples."

With the back open as well, there's a spectacular view of the water, framed like a painting on the wall. "I hope the original family didn't spend a winter in this place." Light pours through. Yes, the structure could be a garage. Rocks and planks form a platform from the water's edge to the ocean side door, which makes sense for pulling a boat inside and undercover. The floor seems solid enough, with wide boards and a stone foundation around the perimeter. They constructed the building with more consideration and care than the house. A granite slab step provides easy access via the land side.

She stands still to absorb the space. One of her methods involves casting her eyes over objects. Stella prefers to note each item and assess their location. Here, she sees used tires stacked in a corner, dried potato vines scattered on the floor, and various small tools dropped in random spots—a screwdriver, a lug wrench, a level, and a tire iron. The murder weapon probably came from this varied assortment—a weapon of opportunity.

The roof must leak. Light tumbles through the ceiling slats. She suspects the structure won't stand against the weather and the sea for much longer. A healthy wind could mark the end. High tides and a severe storm will eventually wash away all evidence of its existence.

"Your assessment?"

"Both the forensics team's suggestions and our assumptions are true. Vic Staples used his boat and collected some product or other, offshore. He delivered the goods back here for distribution. They searched his truck, I assume. Did they find proof of drugs?"

Aiden nods. "He ran drugs, for sure. They scoured the house and Angus' truck before we released him but found no clues to his involvement. Odd." He wanders toward the rear door and stares at the water. "I thought they might discover traces on his clothes, or blood in a sink or the washer, but no."

"Aiden, Angus isn't our killer. Was someone else here in another vehicle? There was a three-hour window between when Angus left for the Painter farm and when he arrived home. Let's take a walk along the shore. The tide has turned, but there's still time."

He glances at his shoes. "You wore sneakers. Loafers weren't the best choice. Let me go put on my rubber boots first."

While he's gone, she studies the space once more. Light penetrates the roof boards, and various openings in three of the walls. Thicket must protect one side from the elements. She stares into the corners and imagines a family

50

living here for the spring and summer. The idea spurns a shiver, and she longs for the comfort of her leather couches in front of the fire.

Once Aiden returns, Stella leads the way over the makeshift ramp and onto the rock-covered shoreline. The mossy stones are slippery. She focuses on the packed flat sand spaces at odd intervals as she matches her steps so she can land on a stable surface as often as possible. Aiden bends and clutches larger rocks for balance.

"No one could walk out here, in the dark, at high tide, Stella. For God's sake, I can't stay upright in broad daylight at low tide. Besides, they'd have to swim once the water rises and the beach disappears, further along the shore."

"Agreed. I wonder. Did the killer arrive in their own car, or did they hide when Angus came home and left when the tide went out? Ample opportunity to leave something behind by mistake."

"Forensics combed the shore and came up empty. No one could have hidden out here when our members responded. They positioned floodlights, and the place crawled with police and crime scene folks." He stops and squints at the horizon. "No sign of a soul besides Angus."

"Okay," she sputters, avoiding an argument. "Too many loose ends and you haven't found enough concrete evidence for a charge yet," she reminds him. "Unless he confesses, we need information from more people. Did you make appointments for us with the neighbours?" She scrambles up the ramp once more, thankful for the separation from further prospects of a sprained ankle or broken wrist if she had lost her balance.

"Yes." He digs into his pocket for his notebook. "I confirmed Jesse and Hermione Wigglesworth for tomorrow morning at ten. I scheduled River and Saffron—the younger couple with the collection of animals—for eleven. We can go back into town for lunch."

"Break at the park, instead? My employees don't start until Friday. I'll tell Nick we'll be home at noon. Did you schedule Donamae?"

"I called her, and she'll meet us around two." He studies her face. "I understand we're short on time. No work for you after tomorrow, and I expect the next week to be quiet as well. Angus Raspberry won't run away."

As she squints over at the couple who remain seated on the step, she asks, "Will you release the scene? At least Angus can use his truck again."

"Yeah, but I don't want them in the barn where he found the body. Not yet. We'll explain before we leave."

****

Letting go is a challenge for many people. Mr. and Mrs. Wigglesworth live in a pert and modern bungalow with a ramp which leads to the front door. Behind the blue and white house an abandoned homestead languishes, rotting in the spring sun. Folks often build new, but never tear down the old.

The Jeep bounces to a halt after a successful navigation of the pot-holed driveway. A man in a wheelchair sits on the deck which faces the road. A woman, off to the left of the house, flaps both arms as she shouts instructions at the operator of a rusted and noisy rototiller. The brisk breeze carries her words away from Stella and into the garden. The worker cups his ear and frowns. Aiden pulls in behind her.

Hermione Wigglesworth pushes a strand of hair off her brow and marches toward the pair. "Good morning. Right on time. You said on the phone you wanted to discuss the night Vic Staples died." She slams her hands into her full-front apron pockets. "We're in bed before ten o'clock. I don't think we can help."

"Let's go inside, Mrs. Wigglesworth. You or your husband may have information you aren't even aware you possess." Aiden faces the house while he speaks.

"Jesse doesn't much notice the world except for mealtimes. I run the place now. Follow me." She turns on her heel, waves at the fellow in the garden, and trots along the wheelchair access, equipped with roof shingles as skid protection. "Say hello, Jesse. They're with the police and want a chinwag—the murder at Raspberry Farm." She flutters her hand in the air. "You don't remember I told you." She grabs the handles of his chair, spins him around, and frowns in Aiden's direction. He jumps forward and opens the door.

When she enters an unfamiliar residence, Stella always takes stock of the furniture, the condition of the floors, the colour of the walls—the normal accoutrements of life. In this incidence, she finds herself unable to tear her eyes away from the three rifles mounted on the primary wall of the living room, behind and above the couch—the spot one might expect to see a painting of a landscape or ocean waves. She turns and checks. Aiden has noticed as well.

"Never mind my collection. They're not loaded, and I own an FAC. I did your stupid paperwork." Her tone accuses. She settles her husband in a corner and stands by a side table as if prepared to give a lecture. "Two are antiques and came from my father. He taught me to shoot. I used to enter competitions. Those days are over. I target practise, albeit rarely, with the .22 Savage I've owned since I was a child. Sit. Sit." She flutters her arms again. "Can I make you a cup of coffee?"

Stella refuses. Aiden follows her lead. Once unceremoniously redirected from any talk of guns and their storage, Aiden starts with an explanation of their visit in more detail. "Our team determined Vic Staples' murder occurred on Sunday evening. You live on the one road which leads to the property, and the tide was high. We wonder if you glimpsed anyone walking or driving past around eight o'clock or sometime afterward."

"Not a soul, except for the cop cars cruising back and forth during the last couple of days, and dear Evan, who helps me with the garden."

"And you, Mr. Wigglesworth?"

"Don't mind him, Detective. My husband doesn't function in the here-and-now most of the time. He notices little."

"Sir?" Stella ignores Hermione's comments and focuses on Mr. Wigglesworth.

"Bedroom at the rear. I retire early."

"Enough, Jesse." She turns her attention back toward Stella and Aiden, both stunned into silence. "No one walked or drove by our place. I watch TV, but I notice what happens on the road." She stands. "Are we done here? Evan won't prepare the garden the way I want, without my supervision. Given the opportunity, he takes shortcuts."

"Evan who?" Stella's curiosity piques. She knows of an Evan, Evan Fleguel, and he's the town engineer for both Port Ephron and Shale Harbour.

"The town engineer, Evan Fleguel. He's our nephew and a big help. Took the day off to till my garden." She pats her husband's knee. "We're both proud of him."

****

"Now, are we off to visit River and Saffron's place?" Stella asks as they return to their vehicles.

"Their real names are Jonathan and Gail Carstairs and from my research, he comes from money and," he lifts both hands in the air, "they live their lives the way they want with a myriad of animals. They bought vacant land, built a small house and a barn, after which they accumulated the livestock."

"Should be fascinating." She climbs into her Jeep. "I'll follow you."

If anyone wanted a cute hobby farm on an acreage with a view of the water, the Carstairs property fits the bill. She pulls in behind Aiden's RCMP-issue sedan. There's a freshly gravelled driveway, a newly mowed lawn, and an enormous garden on the south side. A small and fenced field houses a llama, four goats, three pigs, and a cow. A coop for chickens sits near the barn. Both River and Saffron sway on a porch swing, hands wrapped around pottery mugs.

"Right on time, officers. Coffee?" River stands and leans on the rail.

Stella and Aiden refuse in unison. If one researched hippy couple in the encyclopedia, a picture of River and Saffron might adequately illustrate the culture. Both are tall and lean. River has the longest legs Stella has ever seen. Beads, frayed jeans, peasant tops, and an overabundance of thick, long curls create the image. As she climbs the veranda steps, she senses the faint odour of marijuana.

"Thanks, but no," Aiden says. "We won't trouble you for more than a few minutes. Meet my colleague and community consultant, Stella Kirk. We're investigating Vic Staples' murder, which occurred around eight o'clock on Sunday evening at Raspberry Farm. Did you folks notice anyone travelling along the road or the beach afterward?"

The couple shake curls and sip coffee in unison. "No one," River contributes. "We sat out here on the front porch until dark. It was quiet except for the time when Angus Raspberry rumbled past. We were relaxed." He glances toward Saffron and giggles.

"Who do you buy your weed from, River?" Stella tries the direct approach, although she expects she won't hear a straight answer.

Saffron takes the lead. "Why, Ms. Kirk, River and I appreciate a glass of port before bed." She pats her companion's hand. "Don't we, dear?"

He nods and giggles again.

"Were you acquainted with Vic Staples?" Aiden refocuses the pair back to the topic.

"We were friends of a sort, Detective."

"Are you aware of why he stored his boat at Raspberry Farm?"

"Because he didn't live near the water?" River's blank stare punctuates his response.

"Thanks for your time. We may return later if necessary." Aiden pivots and Stella follows.

"I told Nick we'd be back around noon. He's been hooking trailers into services—busy, busy."

"They smoke weed they bought from Vic Staples," he mumbles.

"Ya think?" Stella chortles.

****

She assured Nick she'd take care of the lunch details. She scrounged muffins from the freezer, sliced cheese, boiled the kettle for tea, and pulled a tray of vegetables out of the fridge. Aiden sat at the kitchen table while she prepared the food. Nick arrived as they began their noon meal.

"Right on time. I wondered if you ran into a snag somewhere."

"Hi, Aiden. No. Ted's trailer sits further away from the connection than I expected. I found more pipe, and he's hooked in now."

"He'll be thrilled. How many more sites are on your list?"

"Four. Duke is dropping by later today. Kiki and I need some help." He gives the dog an indulgent pat before she scurries around Stella's feet, begging for a snack.

Stella obliges. "Here you go, little one. Hard times in the truck, eh?"

"Do you plan to give my girl the weekend off, Aiden?"

Aiden glances at Stella and nods. Information shared with Nick isn't a problem.

"The morning proved interesting. Neither the old couple nor the hippies shed any light on the matter—but we think River and Saffron were customers of Vic's."

"More worthless details," Aiden mutters.

"We're off to meet Donamae Kutska after lunch," Stella states.

"The goat farmer?"

"Yes, and a shirttail relative of the former owner and builder of Raspberry Farm."

"And the old barn revealed no revelations yesterday." Aiden grunts while he reaches for a banana muffin and continues munching on a carrot stick. "If Angus didn't kill Vic Staples, where did the murderer go?"

His voice sounds whiny and annoys Stella. She wonders why he focuses on the quickest solution at the start of each investigation, although she knows he often says the most obvious answer turns into the right one.

"Did they hide on the property?" Nick chooses a cranberry and bran muffin while he keeps his eyes trained on Stella.

Her shoulders heave. "We haven't found a spot yet. If the murderer spent time at Raspberry Farm with Vic, he was familiar with the area. To complicate matters, they could have arrived separately, although no one noticed another vehicle on the road. Once we complete our first interviews, a thorough search will be necessary."

"Face facts, Stella." Aiden reaches for his mug of tea. "Angus is our perpetrator. You don't believe the truth because of Hester."

****

"Maisie. Maisie. Climb out of the lady's car." A frail woman dressed in grey sweats lunges toward Stella and wraps both arms around the chest of a brown and white goat the size of a golden retriever.

"What the hell?" Stella reacts before she thinks.

"Don't mind Maisie. She's my greeter." Donamae manoeuvres the goat out of the way and extends her hand. "You must be Detective North's better half, Stella. I'm Donamae. Pleased to meetcha."

Despite the goat, who nibbles on her running board, Stella wiggles out of the Jeep and shakes hands as Aiden's sedan pulls into the yard. "Nice to meet you, Donamae. Here comes the good detective now." She turns her attention toward Maisie. "May I pat her?"

"She'll be your friend for life, but I can't guarantee she won't climb into your car. She goes into town with me in my Bronco. Refuses to stay home." Donamae cackles while Aiden struts across the grass. "There are ten more, but I adopted Maisie first and I've kinda treated her like a dog." She turns her attention toward Aiden. "Good afternoon, Detective. Come on inside the house. Can I make ya tea?"

"No thanks," Aiden answers right away, with one eye still on the goat. "We finished lunch a half-hour ago. We want to discuss Raspberry Farm."

"Yeah. You said on the phone. No, Maisie. Stay on the porch. You behave now." She pops the goat on the nose with gentle authority.

Her small cottage twinkles and shines. From the outside, one might assume two bedrooms and a bathroom upstairs. The main floor has a kitchen, an eating area, and a living room. A closed door at the end of the hallway suggests another available space.

"Let's sit in the front. I don't git much company." She points to a French provincial brocade sofa, circa 1950, which has seen better days. Stella assumes letting a goat inside your home might affect the quality of the décor.

"Mrs. Kutska."

"I'm not married, Detective. Please, call me Donamae. Poor Angus. He's the closest I've got to family."

"We understand the earlier owners of Raspberry Farm were relatives."

"Right. My father and the man who built Angus' house, Klaus, were first cousins. He emigrated in 1940, after the war started. He came straight here with his wife and cobbled together the place himself." She glances out the front window. "He worked as an accountant in Germany but left in a hurry."

"Why?" Although the history of the original owners of Raspberry Farm isn't relevant, Stella asks.

"Cousin Klaus hid people and moved their money out of the country. He thought someone told authorities, so abandoned his business, home, and possessions to come here." She stares into the yard again. "Hard times. I can't imagine."

"You and your parents emigrated as well. After 1945?"

"No. No one wanted Germans in 1945. We came here in 1935, when I was five years old. Dad said he'd rather be a dirt farmer in Canada than stay in Europe. Although the world didn't predict how dangerous the war ended up bein', he moved us here before politics got out of hand. Klaus settled here because of Dad."

"Were you aware of the upstairs secret room, Donamae? Hester noted she discovered the room when she cleaned."

"Klaus believed the fightin' was gonna spread to North America. He wanted a place where he could hide his wife and children, if they ever gave birth to any. I heard there was a hidey-hole, but never knew for sure."

"Could Angus kill Vic Staples, in your opinion?" Aiden has asked the obvious but risks a yes or no answer.

"He's a sweet man, but he's got mental problems, gets upset easily, and can be unpredictable." Her expression is conspiratorial. "I help as much as I can. Between you and me, I'm not convinced a woman will be good for him in the long run. Lotsa pressure. Angus is happy when the world involves him and his potatoes."

"Was anyone on the road Sunday, after eight?" Aiden's tone suggests he has low expectations of a positive response.

"Angus' truck drove past around eight o'clock. I gather the goats for the night then. Didn't notice no one else afterward."

Stella pauses before she asks her last series of questions. "How did you meet Luther Greene? Angus said you told Luther he owned a place where someone might store a boat."

"Easy. I sell goat's milk to Luther for his little boy. The child's allergic to cow's milk. He used to be sick until Luther discovered the alternative. As for the boat, he suggested a friend needed a spot. I'm not on the water side, but I knew Angus had a rundown barn he doesn't use anymore, with access to the cove."

"How did you meet Luther?"

Donamae dips her head and flutters her eyelashes. "I attend funerals. Don't judge me. Funerals are my hobby, and funeral sandwiches are the best."

CHAPTER 7

Maybe A Woman?

Seated at the table and fuelled by a near-empty coffeepot, a crisp knock ushers in the first day of their season. Nick rushes through the living room while Stella makes a fresh brew.

"Guess who I found," Nick proclaims, as Merrilee Wild and Paul Morgan appear at the kitchen door.

"Good morning, you two. Paul," she admonishes, with a tease, "you don't need to wait for an invitation to come inside."

"Hi, Stella. Right, but Merrilee here," he jerks his thumb in the young woman's direction, "insisted we be polite."

"One time, eh Merrilee? Welcome, both of you. Sit. I expect Eve and Duke soon, and then our first meeting of the 1982 season can begin. Excited?" She smiles at each staff member. "Coffee, juice, toast?"

"Yes, yes, yes," Paul sputters.

Merrilee lifts her hand and acknowledges the offer. "Not for me, Stella. Thank you. I ate breakfast at home." She glances at her cotton skirt and baggy sweater. "I apologize for my attire, but I expected to clean the reception room today. With minimal use since October, the place could do with a spit and polish, correct?"

Stella frowns at her faded and frayed jeans. The McGill University hoodie she dragged on needs a wash. "You're fine, Merrilee. And yes, we'll do office housework."

"What's the plan for me, Nick?" Paul squirms on his chair while he reaches for the toast.

Nick leans back, crosses his legs, and nods his thanks when Stella sets a fresh cup of coffee at his elbow. "I made a list of jobs for you, Eve, Duke, and me, too."

"I love doin' site prep. And you opened five new seasonal spots, right?"

"Correct," Stella responds. "Merrilee and I will review the regulars and specific requests. I expect a busy week."

"Anybody home?" Eve's sunny voice reverberates through the main floor.

"In the kitchen, Eve. Welcome. Welcome." Stella's neck relaxes the minute Eve arrives. Although a measure of nervousness accompanies training a new staff member, she knows Eve will absorb any slack and do whatever's necessary. "How did school work out for everyone?"

Paul frowns. "I did okay. Alice did good, though."

Nick and Stella glance at one another. They both miss Alice's steady hand.

"University was great. Right, Merrilee?"

"Yes, Eve. I passed my courses, the same as you. Ready for next year with new tortures." She nods at Stella. "I expect my position at Shale Cliffs to be a welcome reprieve. I need the break."

Stella senses Merrilee experienced struggles at school, but this isn't the venue for questions.

"Howdy, folks. Time to git crackin'." Duke bends and lifts Kiki off the floor while he stares at the brown bread sliced on the counter.

"Toast?" Stella doesn't miss his expression.

"Don't mind if I do. How's everybody been keepin'? You must be the new one—Merrilee, right?"

She extends her hand. "Pleased to meet you, Duke. You've been here a long time, I hear."

"Eve's been talkin'. My friend here," he grins in the girl's direction, "never says nuthin' bad," he teases.

"Never." Eve sips her coffee while she stares at its rim.

Nick and Stella exchange glances again, and Nick begins. "Okay, everybody. Here's the story. The park opens a week from today. The seasonals, and we host fifty this year instead of forty-five, will no doubt require help when they hook into the sewer for the first time. Paul and I can manage, but Duke, I'll want you on standby. The rigs left here over the winter are done. I cleaned their systems and prepared them for the summer." He stops for a gulp of his now cooled coffee. "Eve, as you might expect, the bathrooms need a deep cleaning from top to bottom. With the water on, don't forget to pressure test the taps and toilets. If you notice low flow or leaks, call me right away. I did the washers and dryers three days ago. We're ahead of the game."

"I didn't know," Stella notes.

"You've been busy with Hester and Angus. I never found a minute to tell you." He waves his hand at her. "No big deal." He refocuses on the staff. "We'll start with a good cleaning of each site and deliver both a fire pit and a picnic table. A check of the water and electrical connections is next. Paul, if we need more tables, there's time to make a few before Friday, although I expect we're okay. Stella, how many regulars coming this weekend?"

Her shoulders sag. "Getting the attention of the folks who booked and confirmed a site can be a challenge. Friday will be busy with locals, but campers from further afield roll in anytime." Her eyes widen. "And I've scheduled fifteen of the thirty-five overnight sites for the holiday. A good beginning for the season. Let's hope we don't get rain." She turns and faces her assistant. "Merrilee and I need to organize. I'll make an updated list of the seasonals and where they are with their payments." She stands. "We'll open a fresh new reservation book."

"Okay, everyone has their assignments. Back here for a break at ten?"

Stella nods. "There will be muffins. Lunch is salmon salad bunwiches on homemade rolls—thank Nick, you guys—veggies, and chocolate chip cookies." She gathers dishes from the table.

"They've given us our orders. Let's go." Duke places Kiki gently on the floor and leads the troops.

With the kitchen emptied but for Merrilee, Stella fills the sink with soapy water.

"Let me dry," Merrilee offers.

"Thanks. Once we're tidied, I'll show you where I store the cleaning supplies and you can start. Straightening out the paperwork for my seasonals and the pre-booked over-nighters will be my top priority. I want a cheat sheet for you, in case I can't be here next Friday."

"Rumour suggests you're involved in the Vic Staples investigation."

"How did you discover that tidbit?" Stella frowns.

"Not directly. Eve suspected because of Hester Painter. Angus Raspberry is her boyfriend, right?"

"Yes." Del Trembly, Eve's grandmother and Hester's aunt, must share information with the relatives. "I hope the case doesn't interfere with opening weekend."

****

CBC Radio mumbles from the kitchen. They work in companionable silence for an hour. Coffee time fast approaches. She suspects Merrilee will help. So far, Stella has made a fresh paper spreadsheet for the fifty seasonal lots, with name, contact information, and how much they deposited in advance. She created a column for balances owed and a spot for payments received. Tables and spreadsheets give her pleasure. Thirty guests paid in full for the season. The others sent deposits and Merrilee must collect the difference.

She purchased the best reservation book she's ever found at the new stationery store in Port Ephron late last year. Each page has fifty lines, and she has associated each line with a lot number on the first page for the fifty seasonals. She dated the following pages and assigned lines to thirty-five overnight and multi-night stay lots, and fifteen spaces for tenters. They charge two separate prices—one for a three-way serviced lot and one for a tent site with water access. She has added in any current reservations. Most travellers pay upon arrival, but many send cheques over the winter. Merrilee can pencil in the entries, enabling adjustments when or if guests move to different sites for any reason. She hates inky scratches everywhere. She mourns the loss of Alice as her assistant for the umpteenth time today. Alice had a gift. If a party of four or five trailers wanted sites side-by-side, she always made the shuffle work for everyone involved. She hopes, with guidance, Merrilee will develop similar skills. She'll review the ledger with Merrilee in due course. The poor girl has enough to keep her busy in reception today.

"Hello!" Trixie's voice rings out through the house. "Are you home, Stella, or out somewhere in search of a perp?"

The unmistakable guffaw reverberates off the walls as her sister rounds the corner and fills the office doorway. Trixie always makes her presence known. "Hi. Want a drive in my new car?"

"Oh, Trixie, I'm sorry. Today's the first day for the staff and with an inexperienced administrative assistant to complicate matters—another time?" She attempts her best pout. "Let's go look at what you bought. You took long enough to decide."

They trot through the living room, Trixie on her platform heels. She's worn a leather miniskirt and white angora sweater, her signature style statements, along with glass earrings in the shape of feathers. A sequined clip clasps her strawberry blond curls. Stella notes her current attire once more. Despite the necessary sanitation jobs on the schedule for today, she disparages her personal lack of effort.

"What do you think?" Trixie pushes open the veranda screen door while Stella steps out in front of her. Parked in the driveway, beside her ancient Jeep, and with one wheel in a flower bed, sits a red 1982 Chevrolet Camero Z28. "*Motor Trend*'s Car of the Year for 1982," she exclaims. "Well?" She nudges Stella in the ribs.

"You needed a new vehicle. The VW Microbus didn't owe you another mile, but a Camaro might flaunt your newfound wealth?" Stella hopes she doesn't sound jealous, phrasing her statement as a question. She and Nick bought Trixie's shares in Shale Cliffs on January 1, 1982. Trixie purchased a stunning renovated Craftsman bungalow five minutes away from the park and now the Camaro. "Val's opinion of your choice?"

"Don't be a downer. Val supports whatever I do." She pauses and moves closer. "He's a good guy most of the time—and he loves my car." She touches Stella's arm.

Val Reguly and Trixie became involved before his sister, Mallory Gorman, died. He works as a caretaker at the old Presbyterian Church, now the Community Hall and Playhouse, and the new Presbyterian Church, too. "Take me for a ride when the rush is over. Once the staff fall into a routine, I can break away."

"Okay. We need to discuss Brigitte's wedding shower. Here we are on May 14 and the big day is June 26. A party for Brigitte at my place. Good idea?"

"Sure. I'll help." Stella loves her niece, and is smitten by her great-niece, Mia. They will make a sweet family with Carter Stephens, a partner in a local law firm. Brigitte operates Yellow House, a children's reading centre and bookstore for children and adults. They live in the spaces not available to the public. Brigitte has come into her own with a force not expected. "When do you want the get-together?" She runs her hand along the back of the plush and creamy leather seats.

"Will May 30 work? Sunday afternoon? I remember the rush of checkouts, but most are gone by noon, right?"

"Brigitte comes first. Let me know in advance what you need from me, okay?"

"Understood. You're involved in the Vic Staples case?"

"Yes. Everyone's gossiping. Angus is no killer, though."

"I imagine Hester's apoplectic." She nudges Stella again. "Rumour suggests the woman's invested."

"Poor Hester. She's upset."

"Shall I tell you a tidbit of information Val mentioned after the murder happened?" She continues without waiting for a reply. "He's in and out of the town office often because of his work at the hall. He said the receptionist or secretary, Tyna Derhay, dated Vic, but the romance didn't end well."

"Are you sure?"

"Val knows her. I thought she might be someone you could interview." She nudges Stella for the third time.

Stella interprets the behaviour as affection.

"I've seen you operate." She lifts her hands into the air. "You'll make stupid statements and analyze how a suspect answers or evades, or explains, or whatever."

"Do you think a girl named Tyna, from the town office, murdered Vic Staples?"

"Stranger stuff has happened in Shale Harbour. Now, I must go. I'll call you if I want your help and will give you lots of notice." She holds the rail while she navigates the veranda stairs. At the bottom, she turns and squints. "Shall we share a shower gift? She doesn't need much, but I thought we could buy them a down-filled comforter. The old house can be frigid in the winter."

"Good idea, Trixie."

Tires spray gravel when her sister peels out of the lot.

Show off.

Back in the office, she retrieves the completed paperwork and wanders into reception. Merrilee has washed the floors, baseboards, and desk unit. She's organized the shelves and placed the brochures and maps within easy reach for guests. "Ready for the list of seasonals and my new reservation book?"

Merrilee twists her wrist and examines her watch, which has a gold band. The face shines black with a diamond for the twelve.

Stella's not sure she's ever seen such a stunning timepiece.

"The staff will soon be back for their break, Stella. We can review paperwork once everyone's left and after we tidy. I believe I could eat a muffin." She lifts her bucket, mop, and supplies, turns on her heel, and marches toward the storage room behind the pantry.

The girl might work out, Stella muses.

****

"People on the veranda are asking for you, Stella. I suspect they aren't campers," Merrilee whispers.

Saturday dawned with the promise of the sun. The staff is assigned. Merrilee and Eve conspired yesterday, and today the former arrived in dungarees and a soft shirt, prepared to help Eve in the flower beds. Stella sat at her desk and reviewed cost estimates, loan payments, future expenses, and general budget scenarios. Then her assistant knocked on the office door.

"Who are they?"

"Hester and Angus," comes a familiar bark through the screen. "May we enter the premises and talk?"

Stella stands. "We're fine, Merrilee. You go back outside with Eve. These folks are my friends."

"Unusual," she mutters. "Shout if you want my help."

"Angus. Hester." Stella rushes out of her office. Gaunt and troubled faces stare at her. She's concerned as she assesses their demeanour. "What's happened? Coffee? Tea?" she sputters, while she settles in a chair across from the couch where she encourages them to sit.

"You spoke with the neighbours but never told us any information, Stella. You promised," she accuses.

"You're right. I thought I'd wait for more details, but I can share what little we've discovered to this point. No one observed anyone on the road after eight o'clock except for when your truck whizzed past on the way home from your dinner with Hester, Angus."

"No normal person could walk the shore at high tide." Hester pats Angus on the knee, as she clutches her canvas bag in her lap.

"When Vic arrived at your farm, Angus, was there ever anyone else who drove in a second car? I remember you said Vic had someone with him on one occasion, but the man never spoke, and you didn't see his face. And other times? Maybe a woman instead?" She remembers the name Tyna Derhay.

Angus shakes his whiskers and glances at Hester before he begins. "Vic was with the other fella in the yard once, and no extra vehicle, truck, or car. If someone drove along the road, at least one neighbour would notice. They're a nosy bunch."

When Angus hesitates to say more, she asks, "Do you have a theory?" The warm air around her weighs heavily while Angus musters his courage. His communication reticence has challenges in such pressured circumstances. Her mind wanders back to the women of the G-plex and the many complicated revelations.

"Vic felt alive."

"What?"

"Explain, Angus." Hester nudges him.

Hester repeatedly touching Angus distracts Stella. The woman has always shunned overt acts of affection and rarely showed tenderness—at least until now.

"When I drove in the driveway, and his truck was sitting in the yard, I went into the barn and touched his neck. His body was warm. I thought he was hurt, but he had no pulse. His vehicle felt cold. When the ambulance arrived, they said rigour mortis hadn't started."

"Rigour begins after three hours. He was obviously at the farm and then out on the water for a while if his vehicle was cold. His boat sat high on the ramp but wasn't cleaned, and he liked his skiff spotless. He never left seaweed on the propeller. Angus and I," Hester turns and her eyes twinkle, which becomes yet another surprise for Stella, "talked the case over and we think the murder occurred near the time Angus arrived home. I suspect the perpetrator found themselves stuck on the property because of high tide, and they didn't want to be seen on the road. They needed a place to hide and wait for the water to recede after midnight. Then they could slink back into town."

"A long slink," Stella mutters. "And where in God's name did the person go? The police used enormous lights and searched everywhere."

Hester shudders. "You are the investigator. We depend on you." She reaches toward Angus and fumbles for his hand.

"Okay. I understand. Right now, the evidence which implicates Angus amounts to basic circumstances." Angus buries his face in his collar. "You arrived home soon after Vic died. We talked with River and Saffron, the Wigglesworth couple, and Donamae. None of them saw anybody on the road but you. For those with a view of the beach, they didn't notice activity near the water, either. If someone walked the shore after midnight, your five neighbours were in bed, or they paid no attention."

"Can we search the barn, Stella? You and Detective North did your best, but you need my help."

"I'm not convinced he'll allow admittance soon, Hester. Let me talk to him. We should interview the residents who live on the road again, with a focus on the shoreline." She stands. "I expect the staff will arrive for coffee and a muffin any minute. Stay. I'll put on the kettle."

Her friend frowns, but Angus nods his agreement. "You run a great park. My folks admired your parents and the work they did. Does your father still live at the manor?"

Shocked by Angus' show of interest in the outside world, the thought crosses her mind Donamae might be wrong. He can discuss more than potatoes. "Dad makes his home at Harbour Manor, yes. He has dementia but enjoys his life. He understands and accepts his condition, and I'm grateful." She stands. "Come into the kitchen while I set out food for the crowd. We made blueberry muffins and cranberry-lemon ones, too—Jewel's recipe."

The veranda door squeaks open. "Don't worry, Stella. The hinge is on my list. Hi, Hester. Hi, Angus. Will you stay for coffee?" Nick bustles toward the stairs.

"Tea, and I guess Angus decided we will." A semblance of delight crosses Hester's face when she acknowledges Nick.

As they make their way into the kitchen, Paul, Eve, and Merrilee tumble into the house. They wait their turn by the bathroom door while Nick gallops upstairs. Duke appears with Kiki moments later. After introductions, in the crowded and sunny space, everyone sits around the table while the staff regale Angus, Hester, and Stella with stories of crooked fire pits and picnic tables beyond repair. Should she worry about the state of the park right now? Never.

Chapter 8

The Season Has Begun

"I've plowed through the toughest part of the job, Stella." Nick leans into her shoulder while he carves the ham she baked earlier in the day. She'll use the leftovers and stock the fridge for staff lunches. "I think we're ready."

She absorbs his essence—the kindness, strength, rock-solid support, and musky, warm scent of him—and turns.

He places the carving knife and fork on the platter with care before he takes her in his arms.

"I miss you when the place is busy, but tonight—you and me with no interruptions." She knits her brows and peers into his eyes. "You ate lunch in record time. Was there a problem somewhere?"

"Don't worry. Trouble with a valve in the pump house, but I keep replacements."

"Magic, my love. You are my magic." She turns toward the stove. "Vegetables are ready. Let's have a quiet dinner."

Once seated, with Kiki fed and in her kitchen bed, they toast each other with chilled white wine and review the park jobs done and near completion. Eve and Merrilee tidied and mulched the garden beds beside the office. The indispensable Eve aerated the lawn around the house, too. Their public facilities work—no more repairs necessary for now. "We'll enjoy a profitable year if the equipment stays in one piece, Nick. I scanned the books and we're in good shape if the weather holds and the tires don't fall off the truck."

After he chews a bite of roasted potato and dabs his lips, he answers. "No need for you spending the summer concerned an unforeseen disaster looms. We can use the extra money I stuck in the bank for calamities." He reaches across the table and pats her hand. "Enjoy the season, for God's sake."

"Thanks," she mumbles. "In a poor year, I wonder how we'll pay the bills, and in a good year, I save any surplus we make for fear of surprise shortages around the corner." Her chest heaves.

"My nest egg is your nest egg. Remember? Relax, okay?" His eyes glisten with emotion.

"Oh, Nick. How did you happen?"

"An ad in the paper for a maintenance worker." He reaches for another slice of ham. "You didn't know what your future held in store for you," he chortles.

Indeed.

"I hate to admit, but I'm curious. The wheels of justice have halted, from where I sit."

"Aiden called earlier. I suggested we talk with the Wigglesworth couple and the hippy pair, River and Saffron, tomorrow. They both live on the water side and when we met with them before, we didn't focus on the beach."

"Wasn't the tide high when Staples died? Is there pie?"

"Yes, and yes. I bought a pecan pie from the hotel—in the pantry."

He pushes his chair away from the table and clears both his dishes and hers. "You sit still. I'll handle dessert. Tea?"

She nods. "I asked if we could drop into the town office and visit with a woman named Tyna Derhay afterward. Trixie told me that Val said Tyna and Vic Staples were a couple, but the affair fizzled."

"Did she ever turn up at Raspberry Farm? Was she Vic's partner in his import and distribution business?"

"Possible, I guess. Angus reported he never noticed any female out at his place, and no vehicle besides Vic's truck. He wasn't in the yard and on watch every moment though, so possible. High tide times change over days, and Vic's visits matched the schedule. I asked Aiden if we could explore Tyna's association with Vic." She reaches for the plate, which must hold a quarter of the pie. "Big," she admonishes, but doesn't offer the dessert back for a smaller piece.

"Too good, right?"

She scoops a forkful and chews before she changes the subject. "Do you know Evan Fleguel, Nick?"

"Yeah. He's an engineer for the town—and Port Ephron, too. The guy's capable enough. Came out here and inspected our sewer system. Not too chatty, as I recall."

"Fleguel is Jesse and Hermione Wigglesworth's nephew. The old man uses a wheelchair, so Hermione runs the place. We noticed Evan there when we visited earlier. He helps them in the garden. She said he's indispensable."

"Retired and disabled. With no kids, or none nearby, they need someone to pitch in." He stands and turns toward the sink. The smell of Palmolive wafts around the kitchen as hot water pours from the tap. "We discussed the complications of childlessness when you and Aiden worked on the boarding home case. We decided Brigitte will be our support person, and you suggested we could share her with Aiden, as I recall."

"Correct. I did. Man, what a miserable investigation."

"Enough murder for one day. Let's finish here and take a walk around the park. The sun doesn't set for another hour. Let me show you the fruits of our labours. You've been stuck inside."

"Correct, again, but I organized our paperwork and calculated summary projections. If we avoid a hurricane, I'm optimistic."

They wash dishes in companionable silence, leash Kiki, don jackets because the wind refuses to abate, lock the door, and begin their meander around Shale Cliffs. Nick unhooks the dog. She trots ahead, stops, turns to check on their progress, and runs along further before she repeats the process.

Nick may be a safety net, but she'll be happier after they see consecutive profitable years, and a light at the end of their bank loan tunnel. She hugs his arm tighter. He snuggles her into his side. Another three days before they share Shale Cliffs' bliss with the public. Stella loves her life right now. Nevertheless, the money challenges remain.

****

"We must be certain no one witnessed someone along the shore." She's bundled into the passenger seat of his police-issue sedan. "These interviews won't take long, Aiden." She senses he has bigger concerns on his mind. "Donamae has no view of the water from her place, which eliminates the need for a visit with her."

"No problem, Stella. You're right. Loose ends."

When they drive into the Wigglesworth yard, they see River and Saffron seated on the deck with Jesse. Hermione comes through the open doorway as Aiden parks. "Our interviewees assembled themselves together. How convenient."

"We can ask our questions and make one trip do before we visit the town office and Miss Tyna with a 'Y'."

"What?"

Aiden turns and smirks at her. "When I called and told her we wanted an informal interview, she reminded me that her name is Tina, but spelled Tyna with a 'Y'."

"Okay," she answers. "Whatever you say." She waves at the group as she opens the car door. "Good morning. Detective North and I are pleased you're together. We still have questions related to the night of Vic Staples' murder." As she mounts the stairs and reaches the deck, everyone turns in her direction. She caught the tail end of a gun discussion, where she sensed a cautionary tone from River when he addressed Hermione. Maybe the older woman suggested target practice and River didn't appreciate the idea. Who knows? Not their issue today.

"Our focus is on the beach right now," Aiden begins. "You live on properties with views of the shoreline. Did anyone wander past, or cut through your yard toward the road, near eight in the evening?"

Hermione stands. "Detective North. Ms. Kirk. We spoke of this the other day. You asked if we noticed a person or persons on May 7, and we did not. Besides, how could someone manage the shore and the cliffs at high tide?" She pats her hair. "Perhaps your perpetrator found themselves caught in the water and drowned. Maybe a search for another body would be wise."

He turns to River and Saffron and asks, "What about you folks?" while he shoves his notebook back into his pocket.

River chuckles and wraps an arm around Saffron as they cuddle on the rattan settee. "My girl and I were pretty busy, Detective."

Once in the car again, Stella remarks, "Why do the words cult and collusion rattle through my mind? I think they have blown us off."

The engine turns over, and he slams the enormous sedan into reverse before he replies. "They are evasive, but cult?"

With a reception desk and a flip-up counter where employees can enter and exit, the Shale Harbour Town Office sports typical mahogany mill work from the 1950s. Stella suspects the young woman with the auburn curls, green striped top, and yellow plaid skirt is Tyna with a 'Y'.

"We scheduled a meeting with Tyna Derhay. Detective North from the RCMP and my community consultant, Stella Kirk."

Snap, chew, snap. She chomps on a wad of gum as she makes her way toward the counter. "I'm Tyna. Myrtle," she hollers, "gotta take my break. Back in ten."

An older woman, huddled over a pile of file folders, lifts a hand in a limp wave.

Tyna leads them into a lunchroom, swallowed by cardboard boxes. A table stands in the middle with a complement of four chairs. A small worktop leans against one wall. Stella surmises she could touch a stack of cartons from any of the seats.

"Don't forget I'm Tyna with a 'Y', Detective." She points her finger toward Aiden's notebook. "I knew Vic—well." Her green eyes widen.

"You were involved with him until lately, Tyna. When did you split?"

"Two and a half weeks ago. I discovered he ran with bad people."

Aiden leans forward. "And your reason for such a conclusion?"

"He lived at my apartment most of the time but stayed out at all hours, comin' home soaked and twitchy—awful nervous. He never told me why. I asked too many questions, and he went out one night and didn't come back."

"Friday, May 7?"

"Oh no. A week before he died. He came into the office the next day and said he planned on staying at his old rooming house from then on."

"Did you ever go with him when he stopped by Raspberry Farm?" Stella's not sure she will trust the answer.

"I don't know Raspberry Farm. I understand you found him on their property, but I never heard of the place before." She glances at the door. Her face pales. "My break is over in a minute. Are we done?"

North stands. "Thank you for your time, Ms. Derhay. We appreciate you taking a moment out of your workday."

"Was your split with Vic amicable, Tyna?" Stella remains unconvinced.

"Nope. I spat tacks and said stuff I regret now he's dead." Her curls swivel as she peers at them before she glances toward the open door once more. "You think I lost my cool and killed him? Are you serious?" She tilts her hip and places one hand on her waist. "I can find a new fella—lotsa guys in Shale Harbour."

"Where were you the night he died, Tyna?" The ultimate question requires asking, although Stella doubts her involvement.

"At home. I watched TV and called my mom in Halifax."

"Okay." Aiden turns and nods at Stella. "We'll be on our way, and thanks again."

On their walk out of the office, they meet Evan Fleguel. Stella wonders if he hovered near the lunchroom door while they interviewed Tyna. "Hi. Evan Fleguel, right?"

He doesn't speak, although she knows he sees them.

"You were at your aunt and uncle's the other day—the Wigglesworths'?" Evan frowns.

"At the Shale Harbour site today, eh?" Aiden's question doesn't cause the engineer to slow his pace. He turns on his heel and trudges toward an office at the back.

"Not a people person," Stella remarks.

"When I interviewed him in relation to the graveyard case, he often acted like he didn't hear a word I said. Rude. Let me buy you lunch."

"I told Nick I'd be home for tea. I've time for a bite."

They arrive at Cocoa and Café before the noon crowd. With their coffees in hand, and the specials ordered, Aiden mumbles, "Rosemary's become a problem again."

Stella holds her breath. Aiden's wife has spun around the revolving door of mental health institutions most of her life. She fixated on Stella for months because Stella and Aiden were an item in high school. Rosemary believed Stella couldn't work with Aiden without being involved in a personal sense. Thanks to Mary Jo, Stella knows Rosemary has good reason to mistrust her husband.

"Can Toni not control her?" Rosemary stays with her other sister, Toni Carr.

"She calls Cavelle's office a dozen times a day. Poor Cavelle. When you run a business, you must answer the phone—and you don't want to change your number."

Farley Tompkins owns the company. "How does Farley handle this complication?"

"More sympathetic. He appreciates her circumstances. Grey Cottage Realty hired an administrative assistant who takes most calls. Cavelle says she answers after the new girl or Farley has screened the caller. Farley covers lunch hour now instead of Cavelle, which I understand is a sacrifice for him. He hates the phone."

"And Toni and Mary Jo?" Stella expects they harbour little sympathy for their brother-in-law.

"I asked them not to give Rosemary my home number, and she can't find an unlisted one on her own."

"What do you plan to do?"

He sips his coffee in silence while she watches him.

"Avoid her. Rosemary isn't good and I've exhausted my patience."

****

The air is electric with anticipation as Stella and Nick tidy the kitchen and Merrilee assumes her post in reception. Friday morning has dawned crisp and clear. The sun will warm the earth and dry the dew-laden grass in no time. Many seasonals don't respect the two o'clock check-in rule. They consider themselves above such details. Cloris and Duke left at eight and opened the gate. They were off to help Mildred Fox move into her trailer. They must have passed Buddy McGarvey and his bulldog, Bell, on the road because now she hears Merrilee cooing with Bell. She hands the tea towel to Nick and scuttles toward the noise.

"Hey, Buddy. Welcome home. And you too, Bell." She bends and pats the old girl as Kiki rounds the corner, nails clicking on the hardwood. The two dogs sniff and mumble. "Meet Merrilee Wild, Buddy. She's my new assistant. Alice has moved out into the great wide world. Merrilee, let me introduce Buddy McGarvey. You've met Bell."

Before Merrilee answers, Kiki barks, and both canines tear into the living room. "Hi, Merrilee. Please to meetcha." He takes a step forward. "I'll grab Bell. Sorry."

"No problem. I don't believe Nick set your trailer for summer."

"Came early. Doin' the deed today."

"Okay, but when you're ready to hook into the sewer line, check with us first. Nick will meet you at your site and lend a hand. Did you purchase hoses and a valve?"

"Yup. We're in the big time now, eh, Stella?" He drops a stack of bills in front of Merrilee. "Count the money. Make sure I don't cheat ya." He snorts when he laughs. "Let me find my pooch."

After a quick glance at Stella, Merrilee counts Buddy's fee. He follows Stella into the living room where the dogs are curled on the sofas across from one another, in a Pomeranian / Bulldog standoff. The season has begun.

Ted Metcalfe and Lily, his companion, arrive thirty minutes later. Stella runs out to greet him. Lily, as usual, remains in the car. Nick has opened Ted's unit for the season.

"My work here is done. I might make cookies," she teases her assistant. "Here comes an unfamiliar unit. You don't see many Airstreams. Expensive." She rubs her thumb and forefinger together. "I'll stick around while you check them in." Stella leans against the frame of the door, which leads back into the house.

"Good morning! Welcome to Shale Cliffs. Did you make a reservation?"

"Yes. I'm Gavin Kershaw and the gal behind the wheel of the Malibu is my wife, Erica. We're from Halifax and reserved a space for the summer."

Merrilee opens her book, with a calmness which surprises Stella, and runs a manicured nail across the page. "Here we go. Our records show you've paid in full, Mr. Kershaw. I'll circle your site on the map." She nods to Stella.

"Nick will lead you into the park and explain the services. Circle the garbage bin and the laundry facilities, too, Merrilee. Give me a moment, Mr. Kershaw." She leans toward the guest and extends her hand. "I'm an owner, Stella Kirk. My partner, Nick Cochran, will come over on the cart right away."

"We're excited to start our summer at Shale Cliffs. First time staying in one place for a season. We've travelled in the past, but I've taken a local engineering contract and expect to be busy for three months." He pauses. "And call us Gavin and Erica. No need for formalities."

"Okay. Meet my assistant, Merrilee."

"Nick, will you escort the Kershaws to their site and help them, if necessary?"

"Sure. Duke can pick up the chore once he finishes with Mildred." He wipes his hands with a cotton kitchen towel. "On my way."

Duke and Cloris managed Mildred Fox until mid-afternoon. Stella carried her tea and walked along toward Mildred's once she thought Merrilee could manage on her own, and while the staff assembled in the house for a break. As expected, she finds the old girl perched on her plastic basket-weave chair, both caftan and awning flapping in the brisk but warm gusts.

"I hear your investigatin' a new case, Stella. Murders follow you wherever you go." Her familiar cackle breaks in the wind.

"Somebody killed Vic Staples, Mildred." She sits on the edge of the deck

Paul and Nick built for her last year because they were afraid she might fall through her rotten one.

"The guy who found the bones in Mallory Gorman's hole?"

"Correct. The killer hit him with a crowbar in Angus Raspberry's barn."

Mildred sips whatever she has in her stained Mel Mac cup and stares beyond Stella's shoulder at the water and land in the distance. "You folks heard Vic ran drugs, right?"

"For God's sake. Why are you aware Vic Staples sold drugs, Mildred?"

She snorts. "Can I be questioned by the good-lookin' Detective North?"

"I expect he'll be here on Sunday, along with his new girlfriend, to open his trailer."

"Cavelle." She grins. "Don't look so surprised. Everyone else in town has heard, too. Won't end well, if you git my drift." She sips again. "Can't blame a girl for checkin' Detective North out, though."

"Tell me your information about Vic, my dear. I can organize a visit with the detective after you share your secrets with me."

"Will I go to jail because I smoke weed for my arthritis?"

"Whew! I hope not."

"Vic had a bag delivered to me every once in a while. I can't afford much. No need to worry now he's dead. Dope works better on my aches and pains than booze." She hoists her cup. "Not gonna quit the lemonade, though." Her guffaw dances on the breeze.

By the end of the day, Stella lost count of the number of check-ins they managed. Merrilee did a stellar job. Eve worked hard in the yard and Paul trimmed bushes. Duke complained of exhaustion but took newcomers to their sites until dusk fell. On to tomorrow.

CHAPTER 9

Trust Can Be A Challenge

A flash of blue zips past her office window as Stella reviews reservations. Aiden and Cavelle have arrived in the park. Aiden said a family from Ontario rented his unit. Today, he'll connect services, clean, and work on any unforeseen issues. She glances at her watch. Coffee time. Once the staff appears for their break, she'll wander along to Aiden's site. He hasn't confirmed their plan for Tuesday. Forensics finishes in the barn tomorrow, she assumes.

Paul and Eve tromp across the living room floor. Duke and Nick are close behind. Kiki runs in circles and barks, forsaking Stella's lap for more active and exciting company. "Coffee's made," Merrilee shouts from reception.

Stella peeks into the office and sees her assistant studying a stack of registrations. "Will you stop for a muffin?"

The young woman's shoulders lift. "No, but I'll bring one back here when I find a moment. We booked a family group, scheduled for next month, and they called again because they want their sites side-by-side."

"Need me?"

She shrugs. "Let me try by myself first. You can check my work before I return any calls, okay?"

Her new assistant has gumption. "Good idea. Run and grab a snack. If you stay here in reception instead of the kitchen, I'll do a walkabout and stop at Aiden North's trailer to see if he and Cavelle need Nick's help with the septic."

"Okay. Back in a jiff."

Once alone, Stella peruses the reservations. A quick assessment suggests Merrilee will experience no problem when she adjusts sites for their weekend guests. Stella decides to keep quiet and give Merrilee a chance to discover options for herself. The park bustles. Most of the seasonals checked into their spots on Friday and Saturday. She expects those from further afield to roll in later. Curtis Walsh and Elroy Brown are nursing their seventeen-year-old Winnebago Brave from northern Ontario. They called and suggested they wouldn't arrive for another week. Stella enjoys this couple. They are a colourful and reliable addition to any gathering during the summer.

"Pumpkin muffins are my favourite, Stella. Did you make them or are they Nick's creations?"

"You can thank me." She turns. "I'll grab my coffee and be off. We'll go over your solutions once I'm back." In the kitchen, Stella visits her staff while she wishes she could give Nick a quick kiss. Rules are rules. They decided "not too much affection" in public, so she tells the assembled masses she's off to Aiden's trailer and hurries out.

Despite the welcome but unusually warm spring, the air off the water carries a bite. She dips her head and sips her drink on the way along the road. Aiden's unit sits near the bank. She turns right at the last crossroad, where she can see him focused on his septic connections. Cavelle must be inside.

She waves her hand and hollers "Hello" above the wind. Aiden glances toward her and Cavelle appears at the screen door.

"Hi, Stella. Easier than I thought." He squints at the hose. "Success is near. Tell Nick he's an excellent teacher. Busy weekend?"

Cavelle comes outside and sits on the deck with Stella.

"Oh yes, but Merrilee, my new assistant, fits in well." Stella winks at Cavelle. "I'll report to Nick you'll help folks who can't connect their sewers by themselves," she shouts to Aiden.

He ignores her tease and continues to work at the back.

"Are you two okay?" Stella watches Cavelle's face.

"Challenges, my friend. Lots of challenges. Rosemary calls me at the office—often. Thank God Farley hired a receptionist. I don't answer the telephone anymore. Farley covers her lunch break."

"Farley understands, I gather."

"Oh. Aiden told you." A thoughtful frown clouds her perfectly made-up face. "I'm not surprised. Rosemary doesn't know the house number yet, but one day, I suspect she'll disappear out of Toni's sight and make a beeline for Shale Harbour. I worry she'll appear at the door of Grey Cottage Realty when

I least expect her."

"Hard way to live your life, Cavelle." Aiden rounds the corner before Stella can ask what the plan is when Rosemary materializes at the house or the real estate office, for she no doubt will. "Must go help Merrilee. She's juggled sites for next weekend, and I promised I'd review her work before she confirms with the guests. Are we still on for Tuesday and a last search of Angus Raspberry's barn?"

"As far as I know. Forensics finished and found no new information. I don't want Angus and Hester inside, by the way. Not yet."

"You'll upset Hester."

"At least they're both trustworthy," he mumbles.

****

She walks into the house via the veranda entrance and hears her assistant on the phone.

"I will give Stella the message the minute she returns. She's out in the park. She'll call you back right away, Mrs. Carr."

Here we go. Stella trudges toward reception. Mrs. Carr is Toni Carr, Aiden's sister-in-law and the person with whom Rosemary now lives. "Hi. Did I hear you say I should telephone Toni Carr?"

"Yes. Here's the number. She sounded flustered."

"Normal status for Toni. I'll use my office."

"Stella. I'm glad you're there." Toni's breathless voice rattles along the line. "A realtor expressed interest in Rosemary and Aiden's house. We need to speak with Aiden, but we can't find him. Is he with you?"

"Not with me, Toni. He and Cavelle are here to open the trailer. Shall I tell him you want him to contact you?"

"No. We'll drive over and discuss the issue with him in person." She continues in a whisper. "I realize Rosemary has bothered Grey Cottage Realty. Please tell Aiden we're on our way and convince Cavelle she should disappear for an hour. Okay?" Her voice wobbles. "I can't cope with the drama, Stella. Aiden makes me cross. He should know better by now."

"Oh, my." Stella wants no part of what she suspects will be a troublesome exchange. "I'll let them know, Toni. You realize the wise decision is a message for him, or a suggestion he visit you in Port Ephron."

"Right," she replies, sarcastic and annoyed. "Tell me information I don't know. We'll be at the park in thirty minutes. Thanks for your help."

Against her better judgment for an extended list of reasons, Stella stops at reception and lets Merrilee know she'll be back soon, before she sprints toward Aiden's lot once again. She finds the couple perched on the steps, enjoying their coffee in the sunshine. "Sorry, you guys. Toni and Rosemary are on their way."

Aiden opens his mouth, but she waves her hand in his face.

"Let me finish. I tried to suggest she not make the trip to the park, but she refused to listen. I gather there's interest in your house in Port Ephron. Rosemary insists you discuss the issue now. Toni suggested you," she turns toward Cavelle, "come with me and avoid further upset." She studies her friend. "You are always welcome."

"No matter, Stella. She'll see Cavelle's car parked right here."

"Why should I disappear? I'm not the villain here."

There's the fact you moved in with the woman's husband. "I expect Rosemary sees the current circumstances in a different light, Cavelle, but the offer stands. If you leave while they're here, come to the house." Before they argue, she turns on her heel and sets out the way she came. As she walks along the road toward home, she glimpses Toni's Mustang over the rise. They must have located a telephone closer than Port Ephron or Shale Harbour.

****

Hester wasn't happy when Stella called yesterday and told her to expect yet another search of the crime scene. Hester's determined to examine the barn herself but will abide by the rules. Aiden wants one last go without what he considers the troublesome interference of family and friends. Stella doesn't understand why. Forensics has done their job. He knows Hester has the best of intentions. She suspects he still thinks Angus is their perpetrator and Hester might inadvertently, because she would never contaminate an area on purpose, jeopardize the investigation.

Aiden's police-issue sedan is parked in the yard when she arrives. Angus and Hester sit on the steps while Aiden leans against the railing and pets Orion. Angel, Hester's spaniel, curls half on Hester's knee and half on the step. Hester stares at her shoes. As she approaches, Stella realizes dialogue has reached a standstill. "Good morning, everyone."

Both dogs run and greet her—with more enthusiasm than she can credit the three humans. Aiden nods. Angus lifts a beefy hand in salutation. Hester ignores her approach.

"Okay. Okay. What's the matter?"

"You people need my expert assistance," Hester pouts. Her expression is unattractive.

"As I told you on the phone, we will go through the barn one more time and after the police review any fresh evidence gathered, the place becomes yours again and you'll be able to do whatever you want."

"You people," she repeats the word people with a distinct slur, "missed a clue and I am the only person capable of exonerating Angus."

Aiden's shoulders heave. "Listen, Hester. Angus remains a suspect. I appreciate your cooperation. You understand, one of you could have gone into the barn and planted an item which implicates someone besides Angus, without the knowledge of authorities, meaning me. Forensics took their pictures. Stella and I want another review." He grimaces in the morning light. "We note your annoyance. You're not under arrest, Angus." He pats the man on his broad shoulder. "Evidence gathered is circumstantial and relates to when you arrived home and what you found." He glances at Stella. "We've interviewed your neighbours and Vic's work mates in the town office. We'll explore his living arrangements as well." He refocuses on Angus. "Trust us."

"Trust can be a challenge when people think you're guilty," Hester mumbles.

They wander around the barn again. Stella taps her foot on every floorboard, in the faint hope of discovering a loose one. No luck. Aiden stares at her, confusion on his face. "I thought someone might have hidden under the floor, Aiden." She answers his unasked question.

"The perpetrator would still be here," he mutters in response. "We assigned staff in the yard for days. I don't think a person hid anywhere in here unless Angus helped them escape. No one allowed him near the barn. Remember?"

"Angus didn't kill Vic Staples." She delivers the sentence in a flat monotone, despite her best effort. She slides the heavy door open and steps onto the rocks. With the tide high, waves lap in rhythmic quiet not five feet from the barn's wall.

"Water rose as far as here the night Vic died." She points at the line of seaweed. "No one left via the beach unless they hid for a period, especially with the yard full of lights. Members were here overnight and for days afterward." She closes her eyes. "I don't understand." She turns and finds him with his back against the roughhewn wall.

"Before we go, shall I share the story of our visit with Rosemary?"

"Yes. Cavelle never appeared. I assumed all went well."

"Not so much. Cavelle left for a walk along the cliffs. She said she thought she'd jump." His complaints continue. "Rosie's in a state. My sympathies are with poor Toni." He pauses and peers at her. "Not enough for me to take back the reins, though. We've got a buyer for the house. Toni engaged a lawyer and if I make an appointment and sign the papers, the deal is done."

"Are you happy with the decision?"

He smirks. "Fifty percent of the proceeds will haul me out from under a significant mortgage. Cavelle has offered to assume ownership of half the new house, but I'd prefer not."

Stella remembers Mary Jo's cautionary tale of Aiden and his philandering history. "No commitment, Aiden?"

His eyes widen. "Slow progress is my preference for now. Rosemary threatened Cavelle—the reason she left the site. Rosie's in her typical spiral. She didn't mention you once, I'm happy to report."

She notices his strained smile. "Great. Rosemary has turned her sights on Cavelle, and I should be relieved. Aiden, you must protect Cavelle. I've said as much in the past."

"Understood. Once I sign the papers and we sell the house in Port Ephron, I'll start the divorce process."

As she nods silent support, she wonders if Aiden will follow through, and what Cavelle expects.

****

Butter tarts. Trixie asked her to contribute a batch of butter tarts for Brigitte's shower today. She has heard from neither Aiden nor Hester since Tuesday, which has been a godsend. The park has been busy. Out-of-town seasonals arrived in droves and, on Sunday, reception always hops with weekend checkouts. The last task she needed was a request for homemade baked goods. She nods her satisfaction at the rectangular cookie tin stuffed with waxed paper and cradling twenty-four of the tasty and indulgent sweets. She used her mother's recipe, which involved butter and maple syrup. What Trixie wants, Trixie gets.

"Merrilee, I'm off to my sister's for lunch, followed by the bridal shower. Do you need any help before I go?"

"No, Stella. Lunch will be a pleasant break, though. Busy morning."

"Sundays are. Ask Eve to cover for a few minutes so you can eat in peace. Pull any cards for sites due for check-out today. Nick or Duke will take a tour around the park and touch base with folks scheduled to leave."

"Okay. With the registrations pulled, Eve or I will be prepared when they pop into reception." She turns toward the cabinet beside the counter. "Thanks, Stella."

"Sorry, I didn't mention my trick sooner. You've done such a fine job. I forget you might need a hand."

Her assistant blushes. "Have fun at the party. What did you buy for your niece?"

"Trixie and I bought her a down-filled comforter. Yellow House can be chilly through the winter."

"Nice. Have fun," she repeats.

****

"I thought you'd never show. Our lunch is ready." She's breathless, unlike her normal contained self. "I want to eat and clear away the dishes before guests arrive. Good grief, Stella. She invited fifteen friends. With Cavelle, we're nineteen now. I appreciate your help."

"Hi. Thanks for the invitation." She pats her sister's hand when Trixie reaches for the cookie tin. "You'll be fine. The house shimmers, Trixie." Her sister bought a renovated Craftsman redone by a former boyfriend, currently in jail. When Trixie sold her shares in the park to Nick and Stella, she purchased the home of her dreams. While she dated Russ Harrison (AKA Harry Russell), she fantasized about her future role as lady of his manor. Little did she know she'd fallen in love with a professional hit man Stella and Aiden later caught. Hard times for Trixie, but life can change, and this is a prime example.

A slight nod acknowledges Stella's compliment. "Come into the kitchen. I thought we could sneak a few of the tea sandwiches." Trixie lifts the lid off Stella's donation. "What did you bring?"

"You asked for butter tarts."

Val appears in the doorway. He'd already put on his jacket. His eyes narrow when he sees Stella. "I'm off. I'll find chores to keep me busy after the service. Don't want to be underfoot here at home."

"He helped me move chairs around earlier. I told him he could stay."

"I was told to make myself scarce," he corrects, with a nod to Stella before he leaves.

"What's the matter? Are you two on the outs?"

Trixie glares. "Your thoughts first imagine a fight? No. Did you know he went and bought hearing aids?" She flaps her hands at Stella. "Sit. I made tea. Grab a sandwich." She drops the tin of sweets in the centre of the oak kitchen table. "I don't need to repeat every sentence I say. He doesn't have to watch my lips anymore when I talk."

"He had a hearing test?"

She flops into a chair in disgust. "Do you think? Yes, Stella, he took a hearing test. He booked one in Port Ephron and didn't tell me. I stopped at the place last week and they showed me the units and how they work. They stick inside your ear. I'm embarrassed—involved with a guy who wears hearing aids. Jeez!"

They finish their lunch as Brigitte arrives, flustered but eager in a white dress with layers of flounces, huge red earrings, and scarlet platform heels. She resembles Trixie more with each passing day.

The shower was as traditional as Stella expected. The girls made Brigitte wear a paper plate over her soft curls, with ties affixed under her chin. With every opened present, they taped the ribbons and bows on the top of the plate. The result was an absurd bridal hat worthy of Minnie Pearl's envy. They played recollection parlour games. Each guest provided the bride-to-be with a piece of advice. Finally, they passed the bouquet in a game reminiscent of musical chairs. Trixie gave out prizes—and wine.

As the guests make their goodbyes, Stella and Cavelle reconvene in the kitchen. They both volunteered to help Trixie tidy up after the party.

"What a bunch," Cavelle giggles. "I think I'm too old for their foolishness. Did you see the lingerie presents? I tried not to blush, but my goodness." She giggles again.

"Ah, the young-uns play different," Stella answers, in her best country vernacular. "You're still in the throes of new love. Why are you embarrassed?"

"I guess, once you reach our age, liaisons change."

Stella smirks. "Don't make assumptions, my friend." She retrieves two wine glasses off the table behind them, so Cavelle won't see the pink flood her cheeks.

"How many years between you and Nick? He's nine years younger. Right? I gather you manage." She returns Stella's smirk. "On a more serious note, I expect Aiden will pop the question soon."

"Aiden is still married, Cavelle." She struggles to prevent surprise and annoyance from infiltrating her tone.

"I know. I know." She groans. "He says the house is all but sold, and he's been in touch with a lawyer. The one stumbling block is Rosemary refusing to sign divorce papers."

"He won't ask you until after he has her signature, I suspect." She recalls Aiden's sister-in-law's comments again. "Be patient, okay? Rosemary is a force."

Chapter 10

Assess For Yourself

"You didn't, Hester." Stella gripped the phone.

"I will show you how I expect someone else hid on the property when dear Angus returned from his pork dinner at my house. I borrowed Jacob's Polaroid camera and took pictures."

"Pictures? Why? Forensics gathered hundreds of photographs at the scene."

"Do you remember the secret side entrance into a pantry at Paulina McAdams'?"

"Aiden and I discovered how Farley entered and exited her home while the neighbours were none the wiser. Yes. Brigitte maintains the exit in case of an emergency—the original reason for the door."

"There may be an underground room—well, not a room, but perhaps a hidden location—beneath the barn. Rocks appear out of place. Come out and assess for yourself. Aiden should be here, too. I won't explore further unless you're both on the property. Stella, tell Aiden he must bring his own police-issue camera."

"How's Angus?" She muffles a smart-ass remark about Hester instructing a detective. She can surmise any potential response.

"Not good, since you ask. He leaves the house and wanders the perimeter of his potato fields. He spends time in the other barn oiling machinery. When he doesn't wander or oil, he sits on the back steps with the dogs." Her voice hushes. "He's depressed, Stella. We must find the real culprit. Days pass with no sign of a solution."

She closes her eyes. Poor Angus. "Why not try a distraction? Let Jewel cook you dinner. Visit with Jacob."

"I've tried. No interest. Planting has started and now he'll spend more time on the land or in the machine shop. I'm worried, Stella."

"Come for a meal with us at the park."

"I already said he won't be interested. Will you contact Detective North?"

"Don't go anywhere. I'll telephone Aiden and call you back." She disconnected and called Aiden.

"Shale Harbour RCMP."

"Detective North, please. Stella Kirk.

"One moment."

"Hi, Stella. Are you calling to offer the same message my bosses delivered an hour ago—the investigation into Vic Staples' murder meanders along at a snail's pace?"

"Good morning, and no. I've called because Hester's found what she believes to be a clue, although I can't attest to value."

"Explain, Stella."

"She claims she's discovered a spot with disturbed foundation rocks, which she thinks might mean there's the possibility of a hidden room under the building."

"Describe what she found."

"There are pictures, but she insisted she didn't investigate further because she wanted you at the farm with a police-issue camera."

"Great," he mutters, impatient and churlish. "What does she expect I'll find?"

"A place where someone hid when Angus drove into the dooryard." No need to mince words. "The fellow who built the house and barn possessed a penchant for secret rooms because of his war-time experiences." She pauses. "Let's look at what she found."

"I don't know."

"Your superiors want progress on the case. If she's discovered a place where someone hid, assign forensics. Vic and a partner used the Raspberry property as a base for drug deals. They might have stashed product under the barn and there will be traces." Before any pause provides him opportunity for an argument, she instructs, "I'll meet you at Raspberry Farm today. Mondays are quiet here in the park and I can put off my month-end until tomorrow."

"Mondays are bedlam here. Besides the regular weekend high jinks, I've been called out over an incident which occurred last night in Port Ephron."

Her breath catches.

"No need for the pair of us. An assault. Once I interview the victim, I'll pass the case to another officer, who can't be there now."

"Shall I tell Hester we'll come tomorrow?" She hides her disappointment, but he has other cases between the two communities.

"Yes. Meet you at one-thirty. Both she and Angus should be present, but they need to stay away from the scene, particularly the barn, until we arrive."

"She won't be happy."

"I can't be at her service day and night."

"Understood, but the investigation has dragged on for twenty-four days and no results. Angus isn't in a good place."

"You know, my boss mentioned the same twenty-four days. Gotta go. Leave a message to confirm." The line goes dead.

Great. Now I must tell Hester we won't be over until tomorrow. She glances at the bills and receipts scattered on her desk before she makes her way into the kitchen in search of coffee, silently hoping Merrilee has taken on the task.

"Quiet in reception?"

Merrilee busies herself assembling muffins on a glass plate which once belonged to Dorothy Kirk. Stella acknowledges the pang of loss she feels when she connects with an item of her mother's. The house bulges with family possessions. Such emotions crowd out current thoughts regularly.

"Oh, yeah. I expect two rigs from out west later. I thought I'd give the kitchen a good clean after lunch." Her eyes question the decision and Stella's response.

"I'm swamped in my office and then off to Raspberry Farm tomorrow afternoon. Whatever you think is best is fine with me. Cranberry muffin day," she notes, while she examines the plate and its contents. "The staff should be in soon. I need to make a call, but I'll take one with me." She reaches for a napkin.

"I can deliver your coffee in a minute."

She nods her appreciation and returns to face her cluttered desk and telephone, supported by the sweet scent of cranberry and lemon.

"Hi. We'll be over at one-thirty tomorrow afternoon. Aiden requested you not survey or picture-take at the site of your suspicions again until he arrives."

"Is Detective North assigned a case more important than the removal of the shroud of controversy which hangs over Raspberry Farm and poor Angus?"

"An assault in Port Ephron. Nobody died. He will assess and hand the file to another officer." She swallows her impatience. "One more day won't hurt. This could be a break for Angus. Remember when you found Deena Finch's duplicate master key? Aiden appreciates your skills, Hester, but he has other responsibilities." Sometimes, logic and flattery work.

Her groan reverberates along the connection. "Stella, I must be brutal in my honesty. Detective North possesses insufficient motivation to solve our case. Vic Staples dealt drugs and his death garners no enormous loss for the people of Shale Harbour—not the same as Paulina or Lorraine. If we don't discover the identity of the actual murderer, Angus will live with veiled accusations the rest of his life, even if he isn't charged."

Stella, shocked, begins a stuttered response.

"You don't agree, and you said you'd help us," she continues, "but the police, Detective North in particular, guide your work. When you arrive, I expect to take charge. The case of Vic Staples' murder gets solved even if I must act alone. Until tomorrow."

For the second time, the line dies in her ear.

****

The next morning, she discovers Duke on the veranda with his back toward the screen. She expected him to barge inside, help himself to coffee, and eat more brown bread toast than any man his size should consume. "Are you okay, Duke? Come into the kitchen for breakfast."

"Not interested, Stella. I unlocked the gate earlier. Do you need the golf cart? I'll take a run around the park, make sure nothin's goin' on."

"I'm not using the cart now. Shall Kiki go with you?"

"Next time. Back later." His tread weighs heavily on the veranda stairs. He never turned to acknowledge Stella through the screen.

"No ride for you, I guess. You can come with me when I do my rounds." She bends and pats the Pomeranian, who prances at her heel.

"Security is upset," she announces. Merrilee, Paul, and Nick sit at the kitchen table with coffee, juice, and the ever-dependable brown bread.

"He wants a dog, Stella." Merrilee does her best to clarify Duke's behaviour.

Nick reaches for Kiki and hauls her into his lap. "Not my dog."

"No. He's pining for another dog because he's given Kiki away. He said he misses a pet in his life."

"Cloris won't be pleased," Stella mumbles, between gulps of fresh coffee. Today, Merrilee chose Irish cream, and the scent tickles her nostrils.

Merrilee warms to her audience. "Duke and Cloris are on the outs because Duke wants a dog. He mentioned, yesterday, how he's moved into his own trailer because she said if he wants another canine, he can sleep by himself."

"What did you say?"

"Not much. I have a suggestion, though. Once he gets back, I'll tell him my idea."

The sound of Eve's scooter on the gravel foreshadows her presence in the kitchen. "Hi, everyone. Great day to garden. Where's Duke?"

"Off for a run around the property. He'll be here soon. How are you?"

"Good. Busy over the weekend. Today should be quiet. I'll plant those annuals you bought, Nick." She sits before she reaches for the juice and toast.

"Since we're all here except for Duke, I'll share my list of tasks for the week. Stella, will you be nearby?" Nick defers to her side-gig before he lists their workload.

"Raspberry Farm later today and I expect interviews within the next day or two."

After she returns to her office, and Eve, Paul, and Nick leave for their various jobs, Duke tromps through from the veranda straight into reception. "Any coffee left, Merrilee?"

"Yes. I saved a cup for you. Listen, there's a potential solution for your pet problem with Cloris."

"Cloris and I will be kaput if I buy another pooch, but I sure miss takin' care of one of my own."

He sounds mournful. Unusual for Duke. Stella listens as Merrilee lays out her idea. "I wish I could own a pet, too, but not when I live by myself and I'm away each day. Not fair. Not even for a cat."

"Means goin' without," he grumbles.

"I volunteer three evenings a week at the animal shelter in Port Ephron. I handle after-supper walks for four dogs each night and walk for two hours in total. Good for them and good for me."

"You volunteer at the Port Ephron Animal Shelter," he repeats, his tone skeptical.

"Yes. I wish I could take every dog home, but knowing I can spend time with them whenever I want gives me no end of pleasure. May I introduce you? An option?"

"Might give your notion a whirl. Thanks, Kiddo." Coffee forgotten, he turns. "I'll be back after I talk with Cloris."

Stella leaves her office and peeks into reception. "Aren't you the problem-solver?"

Merrilee beams. "I hoped he'd take the bait. The shelter desperately needs more walkers. I sometimes manage two dogs at once. Each pooch requires a half-hour."

"I'm interested to hear how his discussion goes with Madame." She winks.

Duke returns as Stella prepares for her morning golf cart ride around the park.

"Movin' into Cloris' rig again, Stella, thanks to our girl, Merrilee. Gonna register at the animal shelter as a dog walker and donate a bag or two of food, too. Merrilee said they're signin' on more volunteers."

"No more trouble in paradise for you, Duke. I'm back in thirty minutes. Will you eat lunch with us, or at Cloris'?"

His grin stretches from ear to ear. "Spendin' my break with my honey," he says, as he saunters toward reception. "Need a quick chinwag with Merrilee."

****

She sees no sign of Aiden when she approaches the house at Raspberry Farm. No Angus, either. Hester crouches on the back step, a dirty apron over her green cardigan; her arm around Angel. Her expression doesn't reflect a woman who might be the reason the case against her lover breaks.

"Hi." She leans over and ruffles Angel's silky ears as she notes Hester's glum countenance. "Where's Angus?"

Hester points an earth-stained finger toward a field further along the road. "He's planting potatoes. A farm cannot wait until law enforcement finds convenient opportunities to investigate."

Admonished, Stella refrains from any form of justification and sits beside her friend. "Aiden will be here any minute. I'm early, although you didn't notice," she teases.

"If you seek to be praised each time you are *not* late, expect to be disappointed," comes the unexpected and fractious response.

Stella takes a moment and regroups. "Okay. What did you find? May I review the pictures?"

Hester places a stack of Polaroid photos, protected from the bright light by a brown manila envelope, in Stella's hand. She stares into space while she hugs her dog.

"Tell me what I should note."

"Thicket and prickles cover the far side of the barn, which you can't see from here. The undergrowth looks disturbed. I imagine the police walked around the perimeter and assume they didn't examine the foundation."

"Possible." Stella studies each image. She sees brush and supports—not much else.

"Inspect the stones. Note the rock out of place." She turns toward Stella and meets her gaze. "I did not, and I repeat, did not, touch the support structure, but my theory suggests the crooked stone, along with one or two others, is loose. The mortar looks missing."

"Mortar crumbles in old foundations."

Hester's eyes snap with their annoyance. "But the fellow who built the barn before the Raspberry family purchased the property expected the need to hide people, right?"

Stella appeases the woman's frustration with a nod. "When Aiden arrives...."

"If Detective North graces us with his presence, perhaps we find out. Did you tell him he needs his police-issue camera?"

"I did." She expects no improvement in Hester's mood at this rate. "Are you and Angus okay?"

"Stella, as you should understand, an alliance with our mutual challenges requires effort to maintain. Our joint focus remains consumed by Angus' avoidance of a murder charge. Each day, current circumstances erode our plans."

Reaching across the dog, she touches Hester's shoulder. For two seconds, her friend doesn't pull away.

"Here he comes now," she grunts, as she stands. "And a mere fifteen minutes late." She glances at Angel. "Stay."

Hester strides toward Aiden's sedan, with Stella following close behind, somehow feeling as if she's taken Angel's place.

"Thank you for coming, Detective. I'm sure you have more important tasks. The investigation of Vic Staples' murder must rank low on your priority list."

Her tone is caustic. Aiden squints at Stella and squares his shoulders before he replies.

"Tough morning. I understand from Stella you did a survey and took pictures. Is Angus here?"

"Where's your camera? You used one at Deena Finch's apartment."

He reaches into the car and retrieves the unit loaned out by the forensic department and points the device in her direction.

"Angus went out on the land. Work must be done when there's fine weather. He said he'd return for tea. First, I will show you the photos I took. Afterward, we can decide the accuracy of my theory." She looks at Stella. "Please fetch the envelope we left on the back step."

Stella does as she's told, although the word "fetch" grates. Hester states her truth with no attempts at varnishing. She sees issues as black and white, but Stella has never judged her behaviour as disrespectful or overbearing in any way one might describe as intentional—until today.

Aiden stands with his back toward the sun and studies the photographs. "Let's walk round and examine the spot, shall we? Were the brambles flattened by our staff?"

"From the house, we can't see that side of the barn, and there's no reason to be there—no reason for any disturbance on our part. I checked and other areas of the property with similar vegetation have minimal damage from police inspections—visible, but not as crushed as this area." She places her hands on her hips. "The rear door of the building stood open with the boat half inside, if you remember." She starts her walk toward the structure. "Someone rushed out the water side and crawled behind the stones."

Stella and Aiden lag. "She's more cranky than normal today, or does she have a beef with me?"

"You're the culprit, Detective North," Hester spits. "You were late, but worse, you have done little for Angus." She pauses. "I possess excellent hearing."

Once they reach the far end of the barn, Hester steps aside and points toward the stone in the foundation which appears askew. "There are three stones with no mortar. They are side-by-side, so I decided I'd take the pictures. You may disagree, but the rocks could be movable." She stands straighter. "I did not touch them. I borrowed my brother's camera."

Aiden snaps his own photographs. "I should call forensics personnel, but let's look more closely first."

"As we did at Paulina McAdams' and Deena Finch's, Detective." Her dry tone projects forthrightness without emotion.

"Here, Stella." Aiden has ignored Hester's disparaging remarks. He offers her the camera. "Now that I've documented what we found, I'll move the one crooked foundation rock."

"I can ask Angus for his help. He isn't too far away."

"No, Hester." The detective dons gloves. "A suspect can't aid in the examination of a murder scene." He drops onto his haunches, grunts, and leans forward. "We'll speak before I leave, though."

The stone moves with unexpected ease and falls on another one, wedged and partially hidden in the grass. Aiden digs for his flashlight, buried in the bottom of his jacket pocket, and shines a light inside the hole.

"What can you see, Aiden?" Stella asks but expects the answer before he replies.

"Someone could hide in there. Look for yourself."

Both women kneel, although Stella's knees don't appreciate her effort. She peers into the space.

In Stella's estimation, two people could lie side-by-side, pull the foundation rock back into place, and stay hidden. "Not comfortable, but if a person or persons needed to disappear in a hurry, we've found the spot. What's that?"

"Touch nothing. Vic's drug stash is in here. I'll radio Moyer and he'll send the team out as soon as possible. We'll need the drug squad from Halifax now." He leans forward again. "The stones on either side are movable, too. Did Angus ever mention this area, Hester?"

"No, Detective. Ask him yourself. We surmised, since the night Angus discovered Vic, that the perpetrator somehow hid on the property, out of sight of Angus and the investigators. They couldn't escape via the shore without significant risk. Vic Staples' murderer was obviously aware of this secret room behind the foundation, and crawled inside until the last police officers assigned were those stationed in the front yard. Once the tide receded, they travelled along the rocks. Whoever was involved understood the dangers."

"You've given your theory considerable thought," he responds with guarded admiration.

Before they return to the house, Aiden takes more photos. Angus saunters up the drive while they make their way back. Hester rushes toward him and shouts how they found a secret hole under the barn. Both dogs run and bark, circling their legs and risking an upset. Stella watches him hold her shoulders while she talks. The gesture is intimate. Hester calms.

Aiden sits in his sedan after a brief exchange with the couple, where he assured Angus that progress would happen soon. He praised Hester and told them not to worry. Neither replied. She hears him on the radio when he reviews the circumstances with Sergeant Moyer. She expects a team to arrive within the hour. When Aiden climbs out of his car, after his exchange with the office, she's seated on the rear bumper.

"We may have a breakthrough. Hester can be remarkable, Stella, despite her personality."

"Agreed. And your forensics folks?" She barely conceals her annoyance and doesn't expect any response in their defence. "Once they arrive," she continues. "Let's re-interview Luther Greene. He must know more than he's shared. Since we suspect someone availed themselves of an opportunity to avoid detection and hide contraband, I want to assess his reaction."

"Okay." He pauses. "And I appreciate your insinuation that the place wasn't properly cleared."

"Angus and Hester are out of patience. She told me he's depressed, and the lack of progress has affected their rapport as a couple. They need more action."

"Okay," he repeats. "Before the team arrives, let's check the barn floor again. Our murderer could have dropped into the hole from inside the building."

"I checked every board, at least twice, but sure. Will you call Luther?"

"Nope. We can surprise him at work."

While Hester and Angus remain at the house, they wander through the outbuilding once more until the approach of multiple vehicles disturbs the silence. No boards are loose above the underfloor secret room. She's not surprised.

CHAPTER 11

Nerves May Be In Play

"The sooner we're finished, the better, Stella. My boss expects me to follow up on the assault case. I bet Luther knows more." His unwieldy police-issue sedan swings wide as Aiden navigates the back driveway into Royalty Funeral Services.

"We missed tea. Where are we headed?"

"If we drive into the yard the same way as the garbage trucks, we avoid Otto King. Good idea?"

"They deliver the bodies through here," she notes, but appreciates potential avoidance of the clammy handshake and condescension of the owner.

"I don't want Luther on the wrong side of his employer because we've stopped and asked him questions again. King cut him a break after the Mallory Gorman issue, and we could inadvertently jeopardize his parole."

Luther Greene, Otto King's second in command, saunters out of the garage. His chiselled good looks, paired with deep blue eyes and a bodybuilder's physique, haven't changed in the six months since she's seen him, but Stella notices subtleties. Luther's shoulders slump and she can make out lines on his otherwise handsome face. He presents as a man with much on his mind.

Aiden reaches him first and extends his hand. "Afternoon, Luther. May we ask you a question or two related to Vic and his little side business?"

"Sure." He squints at Stella. "Hi, Stella."

"How's your son?"

"Good. Good. Timmy lives with me now. His mother left for better prospects out west. The court said I could take care of him."

"Big job—a single dad when you work full time."

The young man nods. "Mr. King helps. Timmy can come with me on days when the business has no appointments. He's in daycare and preschool, otherwise." He swipes a lock of sandy hair off his brow. "No chance for myself anymore—not even a haircut. He keeps me busy." The dark circles around his eyes tell the tale.

"We won't be long. Will you talk to us about Vic Staples' drug dealing situation?"

"I suspected. Who asks to store a boat near the water for random night runs when the tide's high? I didn't ask questions. I approached Donamae Kutska to see if anyone out her way owned a suitable building, as a favour for a friend. She told me Angus Raspberry, and I passed along his name and location. No more."

Stella watches his body language. Although he acts both helpful and open, he repeatedly turns toward the garage door.

He's afraid or worried Otto will appear, she surmises. "Did Vic work with a partner?" She didn't mention how Angus saw someone else with the victim on at least one occasion.

"Who knows? Vic lived at a boarding home. He fraternized with shady characters." His eyes widen in a display of forced enlightenment. "You should interview his fellow boarders. They might have been involved."

"Thanks for your time, Luther. We wish you the best with your little boy." Aiden shoves his hands in his pockets before he turns toward the car.

Luther's voice borders on a whisper. "Listen, I didn't hang with Vic. I couldn't risk my parole and my son's security. You realize I want to help you?"

"Yes. If you recall anyone who might stand out as a friend of Vic's, someone he trusted, call us, okay?"

"I will, Stella. Thanks."

Back in the car, as Aiden drives them to the station so Stella can retrieve her Jeep, she repeats Luther's words. "The kid stays on the right side of law enforcement. He parents his child, despite the difficulties—which were written on his face—and keeps out of trouble."

"His life is a struggle, but nerves may be in play. Shall we interview residents at the boarding home where Vic lived?"

"Sure, although I can't shed any light on location or ownership."

"I'll ask Moyer to find out the details and tell the person in charge we want a few minutes with each fellow after supper tomorrow. I suspect most of the men who board are labourers, and they won't be available until later in the day."

"Okay."

"I plan on a trip out to the park in the morning to fix the fridge door in the trailer. I have banked time that I might as well use. Let's review the people on the boarding home list and the forensics report; perhaps find a guy a cup of coffee?"

"No problem." She frowns. "Luther Greene didn't work with Vic Staples, let alone kill him. He did Vic a favour when he connected him with Angus, but he's not involved. Too much risk with his little boy." She nods to herself. "He learned his lesson when he helped his Uncle Hector and appreciates the second chance. What's the old expression? 'No good deed goes unpunished'. Poor Luther must feel caught in the crosshairs of our investigation."

He pulls the car into a parking spot behind the detachment, stops, and turns. "Problem, Stella? I can tell by your face that you aren't happy."

"Almost thirty days have passed since Angus discovered Vic Staples dead in his barn and we've made little to no progress. Poor Hester found a potential hiding place, and not to sound critical, but you're off work tomorrow morning because of a fridge door?"

"Listen. I'm under tremendous pressure. You understand, right?" With both hands clutched on the steering wheel, he glares at her. "Stella, Rosemary and her sisters occupy one corner of my life, Cavelle's in another, and my bosses are on my tail day and night. Let's interview Mildred Fox tomorrow morning. I told the staff I'd be off the clock, which means there's no need for them to learn my whereabouts. Doesn't mean I can't work."

Stella remains unimpressed. If his personal life is unmanageable, he should reassign Angus' case, take real time off, and harness circumstances. "Aiden, at the risk of repetition," she rests her fingers on the door handle, "straighten out your issues. Angus and Hester are suffering. This murder must be the priority, even if someone else takes over for you." The sound of metal against metal grates. She winces. "Your car needs a service, too. I'll see you tomorrow for coffee."

With her patience tethered to her manners by a thread, she exits his vehicle and walks toward hers.

****

She finds Nick, Duke, Kiki, and Cloris seated on the veranda when she pulls the Jeep into the parking lot at four-thirty. In the distance, she notices Paul with the grass trimmer. Eve toils with her back to the house, while she weeds a garden bed further away. Time to quit. "Hi, folks." She waves as she exits her vehicle. "Don't get up," she motions with her palm. "Merrilee still in reception?" She starts her ascent.

"Yes. She said the front was busy," Nick replies, as he holds Kiki's harness and waits for her.

"Three new rigs pulled in after lunch. I escorted 'em each into their spots. Everybody's happy." Duke pats Cloris on her knee. Her eyes narrow, but she doesn't move his hand.

Cloris stands with a grunt. "Must organize supper. My man ordered rosemary scallops done on the barbecue and they've been in the marinade for two hours."

"I'll start the grill, sweetie." Duke jumps up and locks his arm in hers. "See ya'll later." He pauses long enough to ruffle Kiki's fur. Cloris glowers.

With no idea what to prepare for an evening meal, Stella slumps into one of the wicker side chairs and closes her eyes. "Did you take anything out of the freezer, Nick? I must admit, and I'm sorry, but food never crossed my mind."

"Well in hand. Burgers and salad, ready when you are."

"Wonderful. You're relaxed." He rarely sits around during the day.

"Strange, and I don't want to jinx us, but our systems are in good shape. I expected to spend most of my days troubleshooting sewer issues, but our investments are paying off, Stella. For once, no problems."

"Wonders never cease." She's almost too tired to appreciate good news.

"Here." He offers her the dog. "You hold her, and I'll go find us a beer." He chuckles. "The staff will leave soon. Merrilee's suggestion is going to cost us."

"What? I don't understand." She watches Eve and Paul clean and pack their tools.

"Three evenings a week, we'll cover Duke's final rounds. He said he'd lock the gate when he returns from the animal shelter."

"Not a problem. We often do a walkabout in the evening, and I need one tonight."

****

After the staff left for home, and after a scrumptious supper where she described her visits to Raspberry Farm and Royalty Funeral Services, they set out for a trek along the streets of Shale Cliffs RV Park. As regularly happens, she advised new guests they're welcome at reception any time. She answered their questions: Where do we dump our garbage? Where is the overflow parking? May I hang outside lights? Can we check out later in the day? She and Nick answered each query with patience. Although outlined on the back of the park map, people rarely review the rules—the reason she likes personal introductions with new visitors. Trixie says she courts trouble, but she sees the process as prevention. Her sister has hated the business since they were children. No surprise she happily sold her shares to Nick last year.

They find Mildred Fox asleep in her chair by a smouldering campfire—her favourite pastime.

"I'll wake her, Nick. Aiden will be here tomorrow for a visit."

"Old, but not deaf," she mutters, before she opens her eyes.

"Good, my friend. You're not passed out, at least," Stella teases.

"Never you mind. I can hold my liquor." She struggles while she rearranges her ample rump in the orange basket chair—its role a perpetual endeavour to keep her off the grass. "What did you say about the handsome detective?"

"Aiden told me he planned to stop by his trailer tomorrow and visit with you afterward. He wants to hear how you became involved with Vic Staples."

"May I put more wood on your fire, Mildred?" Although the current situation produces smoke, and the neighbours will complain, Nick doesn't point out the obvious.

"Sure, Hon. Grab what you want from under the rig. Can't keep the stuff dry, but I do my best." She turns her attention back to Stella. Her tone adopts a more serious inflection. "Am I in trouble for smokin' pot for my arthritis?"

"No, Mildred. He assured me he's interested in what you can share in relation to Vic's enterprise."

"Okay." She settles into her chair. "Tell him I'll make him coffee."

As they leave, Stella whispers into Nick's sleeve. "He'll need a warning to avoid her motor oil brew."

They discover Gavin and Erica Kershaw stretched out in lounge chairs by their fire. Gavin jumps to his feet when they stop in front of the thirty-one-foot 1981 Airstream Excella. Stella can't take her eyes off the rig shimmering in the firelight. Each window sports a blue and white striped awning. The unit resembles ones in those RV brochure photos, except without the Florida or Arizona backdrop.

"Hi, you two. Questions or concerns? You've met my partner, Nick Cochran."

Nick steps forward and shakes Gavin's hand. Erica doesn't move from her chair. She and Stella wave an acknowledgement instead.

"We're fine. Love the place. Right, Babe?"

Erica's response lands somewhere between a nod and a furrowed brow. Her opinion of camping is not in alignment with her husband's, for sure.

"How's the project progressing?" She shifts from one foot to the other. Erica makes her uneasy and she can't pinpoint the reason.

Gavin, happier with talk related to his work, launches into the description of a new subdivision Shale Harbour's developing over the summer. From what Stella understands, the location of the expansion is near where Earlene Marigold built her four-plex. She surmises Borden Fisher, of Fisher's Contracting, will jump at the prospect of more building.

"Three months to complete layout, water, sewer, curbs, gutters, and pavement. We'll be home after Labour Day, right Erica?"

"We'd better be," she grumbles, before she nods at Stella and forces a smile.

"Can I ask you guys a question? You must know everybody in the area."

Nick chuckles. "Not me. Stella was born here and lived in the park. She's the one who knows the townsfolk."

"Okay." Gavin warms to his topic. "Evan Fleguel, the town engineer, is my partner in the project. Shale Harbour added my contract because he works in Port Ephron, too, and the fresh development will be too much workload. He lives in Shale Harbour, right?"

"Not sure, Gavin. Why?"

"The bugger's never around. I call the Port Ephron office, and they can't find him, either."

"Don't cause a fuss, Gavin. We're here for the summer. Never mind Evan." Erica's tone, laced with impatience, only serves to encourage her husband and he continues despite her pout.

"Is he an acquaintance or friend? Is he lazy? Is there a family problem?

The guy has no manners. Even when we work in the same office, he walks away while you're still talking. Any ideas?"

"I don't know the man, Gavin. I learned he helps his aunt and uncle—the Wigglesworths. Confront him and ask your questions directly. Best advice I can offer." Stella refuses entanglement and won't say too much in front of people she hardly knows.

"Oh, well." Gavin waves a hand and glances back at his wife. "New job jitters, I guess. We love the park, Stella. We're content here. Appreciate the hospitality."

"If you need help of any kind, don't be a stranger." Nick places Kiki on the ground and they saunter along the road toward the house. "Hard start for a temporary contractor when the permanent employee takes advantage of you right off the bat."

****

"Good evening. Shale Cliffs...."

"I'm late, but I want to ask you an important question." Trixie's voice pushes through the telephone line with a gasp.

Nick and Stella were curled on the sofa in front of the television. The news will be on in ten minutes. She never calls after nine o'clock. "Why the whisper? I can barely hear you."

"Val's asleep on the couch and I'm in the kitchen. He won't notice me anyway, but I want a private chat. Did I tell you he got hearing aids?"

"Yes, Trixie. You told me. What's the matter? Are Brigitte and Mia okay?"

"Too many questions, Stella. Everybody's fine. Did Brigitte decide where she'll buy her wedding gown? I can't remember the name of the fancy store in Halifax."

Stella pauses before she replies. "Trixie?"

"Listen," she huffs her displeasure, despite the hushed tone. "I can't remember who Brigitte finally hired to order her dress. No big deal. We visited a hundred places."

"Hope," Stella states, in as patient a voice as she can muster. Hope Carlyle owns a weaving shop across the street from Yellow House. Few people are aware of her accomplishments as a seamstress. Stella commissioned a red velvet Christmas frock from her for Mia. After she shopped at more bridal boutiques than Stella thought existed in the area from Shale Harbour to

Port Ephron to Halifax, Brigitte turned to Hope. Reluctant at first, because she's always reluctant, Hope took on the task with relish. Brigitte opted for a plain sweetheart neckline, with off-the-shoulder tulle sleeves, and a full skirt. The gown is an older design, reminiscent of the 1960s. Stella suspects Hope appreciated Brigitte's simple, yet elegant, choice. Specifics fly through Stella's brain throughout the silence at the other end of the line.

"The weaver is making Brigitte's dress. Are you sure?"

"Trixie. Don't you recall? The three of us went to her house and picked a pattern. Brigitte bought the fabric. I worried because the styles were old-fashioned, but Brigitte acted thrilled."

"Wait a sec." Tears filled the spaces between her words. "I couldn't remember."

Stella can hear her fumble for a paper and pen. "What are you doing?"

"Wait a second, I said." Her timbre holds an unfamiliar edge. "I'll copy what you've told me. I can't forget again. She asked if I could check on her dress and I forgot the name of the store. I figured you might tell me."

Stunned, Stella repeats the information focused on Hope and adds the woman's phone number. Stress may be the culprit, but not remembering Brigitte's seamstress, who lives across the street from her daughter's business and residence, is unnerving. The wedding date is twenty-five days away.

"I use a notebook and a calendar. I bought both to keep in my handbag. We're busy. I have trouble organizing." Her words are breathless and clipped. She puffs between sentences.

"My agenda sits at the ready on my desk, Trixie." Stella focuses and keeps her voice calm. "Everyone needs help now and again, especially when overwhelmed. Do you need any other details?"

Trixie warms to Stella's offer. "I'm sure Brigitte sent the invitations, right?" She titters. "Do we expect a crowd? Planning the food takes time."

In a sudden moment of clarity, although Trixie is a mere forty-two years old, Stella's thoughts drift to her father. "Grab your notebook. Ready? Brigitte invited fifty guests. She contracted the hotel and they're catering the reception. She made the arrangements with Eugenie Charlebois and Pepper. Your task is to find the perfect dress."

"Oh, I bought a gown. The price will be secret because I don't want Val to know how much money I have, but the fabric is cream coloured—don't wear white at someone else's wedding. The bodice plunges." She gushes, "but not too much, with sequins around my boobs and ruffles along the bottom. Very chic."

Stella grimaces while she pictures a sparkling mermaid-style dress on the mother of the bride. The last characteristic one might use when describing her sister is chic. She doesn't want Trixie outshining her daughter, especially for the wrong reasons. Brigitte has exhibited infinite tolerance with her mother's cravings for attention over the years, but her wedding day will be a different story. "Do you need more information tonight?"

"No," she whispers into the phone. "Thanks. Can I call you again for help?"

"Yes." She grits her teeth before she asks, "Any other details you've forgotten, Trixie?"

"Nope." Her haughty tone tells the tale. "I'm fine. Stressed because of the wedding and confused sometimes. That's all." The line disconnects—usual behaviour.

Before she returns to the comfort of Nick, she assesses Trixie's memory lapses. Her only real comparison is Norbert. When Stella returned home to help with the park, she found her father traversing from one day into the next by rote. The business had deteriorated around his ears at a steady pace after her mother died. He sometimes forgot to eat. He became a person with parts missing and the circumstances scared her more than managing alone. Trixie sounds similar, and she hopes the stress of the wedding has caused her current status, which will fade once the celebration ends.

CHAPTER 12

Kinda Like You

"Anybody home?"

Stella turns away from the kitchen counter when she hears his voice. "Come in. I'm out here," she bellows.

Aiden, dressed in blue jeans and a denim-coloured shirt, eyes the empty coffeepot from the doorway.

"I'll brew more. The staff started work five minutes ago. I didn't expect you this early. Have a seat." She points toward the table before she wipes a pile of crumbs off the counter. "They make a mess in the morning. Merrilee shouldn't face the remnants of breakfast every day. The poor girl has enough chores." Stella swipes the counter again with her sponge and drops more crumbs into the garbage before she fills the pot with water and reaches for a filter. "Won't take a sec."

"No problem."

He digs in his shirt pocket and pulls out a folded piece of paper.

"Forensics did their job, for once," he announces, with a thrust of his chest. He flattens the page on the table. "They found weed, white powder, and a flattened disc which might be a battery. They haven't determined usage, but perhaps one of those fancy hand-held calculators, or even a watch."

The smell of hazelnut wafts throughout the kitchen as the coffee pot gurgles. "Do we suspect a person with a fancy, battery-operated watch or one of those new mini-calculators, hid under the barn at Raspberry Farm?" She can't keep the sarcasm out of her tone as she repeats his phrasing.

"Vic stored product in the same space. Forensics said they found a significant amount scattered, as if a bag spilled."

"I assume none of his boarding home buddies own high-end watches or mini-calculators, Aiden." She's puzzled. The information provided makes little sense. "I understand you want your fridge fixed and there's a mountain of paperwork on my desk. Here's a plan. I'll wander along to your trailer in an hour, and we'll visit Mildred. You come for lunch with the crew and afterward, we can review boarding home residents."

"Moyer says the house is on Birch Street."

"Trixie might be familiar with the place."

"Okay. Give me a solid sixty minutes with the fridge door. I'll probably ask Nick for his help. I'm not very good with repairs."

"No problem. A word of advice. If you arrive at Mildred's before me, don't drink her coffee."

"Whatever you say." He rises and turns toward the living room before he exits via the veranda. "See you later."

Once settled in her office, comfortable because Merrilee doesn't need her help, she calls Trixie. The phone bleats six times before she hears a breathless, "Hello."

"Are you okay?"

"Fine. Fine. Behind. Val left before seven and I'm due at Yellow House by noon."

"Well, my clock says nine-thirty, my dear. Why are you flustered that you'll be late?"

"Someone has stolen my blue striped blouse."

Stella closes her eyes and steadies her breathing before she continues. "You told me a month ago you donated your blue striped blouse, along with a bunch of other pieces, to the women's shelter in Port Ephron. Did you deliver a bag of clothes for them?"

"Good grief! I did. But why give away my blue striped blouse? I loved that blouse," she whimpers, in a manner Stella finds unfamiliar.

"You told me how the buttons pulled around your boobs and you burst out of the front when you were at lunch with Cavelle. Remember?"

"Are you sure?" She whimpers again. "Alright. If you're certain, I'll stop my search and rescue mission and choose another. Gotta run."

"Trixie. I called you. Remember?" *Avoid the word "remember."*

"What? Did you? Okay. What do you want?"

"We've heard of a local boarding home—not one that caters to the elderly—where Vic Staples lived. I think Aiden mentioned the address is

Birch Street, around the corner from Grey Cottage Realty. Are you familiar with the business or the location?"

"Sure. I went to school with the owner, Etta Graney. She lives in a big old farmhouse—Yellow House, but rundown. After they'd been married for three years, an accident killed her husband, if I recall. She took care of his parents until they died and left her the house. No money for expenses. The place looks as if the roof could collapse any minute."

"And her family?"

"When we were in school, she was poor—poorer than us."

Offended by Trixie's assessment of their childhood, she inserts, "We weren't poor."

Ignoring Stella's response, Trixie prattles on. "Never noticed a mother in the picture. Her father took care of her until she married somebody Graney the year we graduated from high school. Her dad died or moved away a long time ago, Stella."

"Etta has been on her own since the age of eighteen, then."

"Yup. Keeps boarders, and a motley crew they are, too. I told Brigitte, when she was younger, to stay clear of those fellas because I didn't trust them. I may be wrong, though. Can't remember what I had for breakfast."

"Your memory seems pretty good today. Thanks, Sis. Wear your pale-pink oxford cloth blouse with your skinny jeans. Your big blue crystal earrings are perfect," she advises. "And those platform sandals."

"No need for fashion advice from you," Trixie grumbles.

"Funny, eh? Better finish my books and not be late. I'm due at an appointment with an old lady and a detective."

"Etta and I are the same age."

"No, you've misunderstood. Aiden's at his trailer and we're meeting with Mildred. Thanks for the information regarding the boarding home, though. I couldn't help Aiden with any details."

The phone clunks in her ear. Trixie disconnects. Stella pours another cup of coffee, spends valuable time with her ledger, reviews what's on the menu for lunch with Merrilee, and begins her trek along the main road toward the cliffs and Aiden's trailer. The wind whips off the water today, which lowers the temperature the further away from the house she walks. She sees Nick and Paul in the distance. They're straightening an electrical post that someone bumped with their truck. Earlier, Duke reported they helped the same driver extricate a fire pit ring from his wheel well. The time has arrived to invest in indicator flags, so people don't drive over the tractor rims the park uses for fire pits. She makes a mental note to discuss the idea with Nick when they talk next. Neither man notices her wave.

Aiden's trailer door stands open. She hears him swear.

"Ask Nick for help after lunch." She peers through the screen.

"Glad you're here. I've reached my limit. Let's go see Miss Fox."

"If you can find her behind the smoke," Stella replies.

****

"Hey, Mildred. Early in the day for a fire." She flaps her fingers in front of her face, dissipating the offensive air which wafts around her nose.

"Sit up wind, Stella. Grab a chair off the deck. Hello, Detective," the elder simpers.

Aiden nods, holds his hand to halt Stella, and makes his way toward two ancient basket-weave lawn chairs.

"Will you describe your affiliation with Vic Staples, Mildred?"

"Big word, but yeah, I'll talk. I wondered if the handsome detective was cross, though," she whispers. "Heard an awful lot of swearin'."

"The consequences of a useless attempt to fix the door on my fridge. You hear quite well," he notes, while he places the two chairs on the grass away from the smoke.

"Not bad for an old gal. Now ask your questions. Stella told me you're not gonna haul my ass to jail," she cackles. "Coffee?"

Stella refuses.

"No need for more morning fuel, but thanks, Miss Fox. Before we focus on business, I rented my trailer to a couple and their twin boys from Ontario— new neighbours for you."

Mildred sips her drink and nods. "Lotsa drama if you were out here with Cavelle Painter, and the wife rounded the corner." Her eyes challenge his.

"Agreed." He flushes slightly before he continues. "Now, Stella told me Vic Staples supplied your marijuana. Correct?"

She pauses and glares at Stella. "You're sure I ain't in any trouble?"

"Absolutely not, Mildred."

"Okay. I bought weed from Vic, but another fella delivered and rolled my joints for me."

"Can you describe the man who brought your stash, Miss Fox?"

"I didn't take to him." She looks at each of them and frowns. "He never talked."

"Tell us about this guy and his behaviour, Mildred. You're a people watcher. You've been helpful in the past."

"Tall and dressed nice."

"What does nice mean?" Aiden lifts a single brow.

"Kinda like you. Slacks, a shirt with buttons on the collar, and those jackets with the zipper men who work for the government wear—olive green."

"Okay. Good." Aiden blushes, as he touches the pocket of his beige jacket, a replica of the one Mildred described, except for the colour. "Now, the man himself?" Aiden encourages but doesn't push.

Stella leans forward. She understands Mildred appreciates her role as the centre of attention.

"Wore a ball cap, so I couldn't tell you if he's bald or not. Clean shaven. Fair complexion. Kept his eyes on what he was doin' and never," she points a crooked finger at Aiden, "never looked me in the eye. I didn't take to him," she repeats. "Rude beggar."

"Explain what you mean, Mildred."

"Didn't talk. Didn't listen. Walked away when I was talkin'. Vic contacted me whenever his guy could deliver my stuff. The fella stood in my kitchen, after I paid him, and rolled ten joints, but he never even exchanged the time of day."

"I don't remember noticing a man visiting you out here. Surely, I would have seen him once or twice."

"Only came to my senior's apartment. The summer's okay, but the cold and damp winters are hard. Can't say what I'm gonna do now." Her face clouds.

"Before we leave you in peace, Miss Fox, what else can you tell us you think might be useful?"

"He didn't appreciate my jokes. I teased, and he never even cracked a smile. I think I can be a hoot, but he didn't like my great sense of humour." She winks. "If I remember somethin' more, I'll get word to Stella."

Aiden locks his unit before they make their way along the park's main road toward the house. After lunch, they'll review the list of men who live at the boarding home before interviews tomorrow evening. Nick will help him with the fridge afterward.

They find Merrilee in the kitchen. Eve must be here already because Stella hears water running in the downstairs bathroom. She saw Paul and Nick in the distance, on their way from the machine shed. "You've been busy."

Merrilee, dressed in wide-legged blue jeans, a throwback to another era, spins on the heel of her sandal. "Good morning, Detective North." She points at the pile of sandwiches on a plate in the middle of the table. "You made egg salad, Stella, but I added a few ham and cheese, threw together a veggie platter, and scrounged for chocolate chip cookies from the freezer." She reaches in the fridge and turns with a flourish. "I prepared the strawberries, too."

Stella purchased two boxes on her way home yesterday but ran out of time to wash them. Although not local, and expensive, they sparkled in the store and somehow jumped into her arms. "Scrumptious, Merrilee. Thanks for taking care of the berries."

"Reception has been quiet. I wandered out to the gate for the mail and Eve took her coffee break at the desk so she could cover for me. Here's Eve. I hear Nick and Paul on the veranda."

"Sit, Aiden. I'll find the iced tea and we're ready for the masses." Once Nick stands in the doorway, Stella approaches and brushes his hand with hers. "Aiden needs a favour."

"And what can I do for you, Detective North?" He maintains a formal, yet casual air, as he sits at his place among the others.

"Hi, Nick. Everyone. My top hinge on the fridge door seems loose, and the seal isn't secure."

"Is the pin broken?" Nick reaches for the egg salad and gulps his iced tea. "I'll pop over later with a spare—shame to buy a new hinge." He takes a bite of his sandwich.

"Thanks, Nick. Stella and I will review our list of witnesses first. Okay?"

"Perfect. Paul and I have two table deliveries, and somebody drove over a fire pit again." He leans back in his chair while Eve and Paul shake their heads.

✳✳✳✳

As Merrilee covers the leftover sandwiches in plastic, Stella gathers dirty dishes. When the bells tinkle over the reception door, Merrilee's eyes widen.

"You run. I'll finish." She glances at Aiden. "We can talk while I tidy."

Merrilee rushes to her post. Stella hears her "Welcome to Shale Cliffs" salutation before she turns on the hot water tap and fills the sink.

"What did Moyer learn when he contacted the boarding home?" She stops long enough to interrupt herself. "I must relay a piece of information before you begin. Trixie attended school with the owner and gave me details which might be useful." She gathers more glasses and frowns. "I'm worried. Trixie isn't herself."

Aiden offers no comment.

"A story for another day." She repeats Trixie's details about Mrs. Graney. "Interesting, right?"

"Right." He pulls a folded paper from his shirt pocket. "The house sits on Birch Street. Cavelle told me. The landlady has placed no signage on the lawn or advertisements for roomers." He catches Stella's eye and grins. "Cavelle knows details on every property in town. At full capacity, the property supports four boarders. Since Vic's death, three remain. The owner, a woman named Etta Graney—Trixie's school chum—says Vic Staples kept and paid for a room even when he wasn't around much. The men who now rent spaces under her roof are Cam Keller, Wally Lavender, and Brad Masterson."

"Brad works at the fish plant. I remember him from when Trixie worked for them." She wrinkles her brow. "I think he asked her on a date at least once."

"The other two, Cam and Wally, are labourers for Borden Fisher. Anyway, Moyer requested Mrs. Graney tell the three of them to make themselves available tomorrow around seven in the evening for an interview with each man alone. She understands we want to talk with her, too." He folds the piece of paper. "I would appreciate your presence. Will the schedule work?"

"Sure. I expected as much. Shall we talk with Vic's employment colleagues as well? Since we've uncovered more information, we might squeeze another detail or two out of them. We should visit the town office and interview Tyna, Evan, and Shale Harbour's town manager, Philip Lewis."

"I'd rather contact Moyer and ask him to line up appointments at the detachment—more formal—more pressure. What do you think?"

"Let's plan on morning interviews, a debrief over lunch, and then meet at the boarding home for seven. I can be at the park all afternoon." She muffles a murmur of contentment.

"May I use your phone?"

Nodding toward the telephone on the wall, she offers, "Or the one in my office."

He opts for the office and passes Nick on his way around the corner. "Ready when you are, Aiden."

"I'll call the detachment. Won't be long."

Nick saunters into the kitchen and grabs a tea towel. "Let me dry while we wait for the detective."

She turns and admires his bronzed good looks. "You've started your 1982 tan." She touches his cheek. "You're developing those little white streaks in the corners of your eyes—the tiny creases where the sun doesn't reach. Time for your ball cap."

"Right after I help you with the dishes. What's the story with Aiden?"

"Instructions for Moyer to contact Vic's work colleagues for more formal interviews tomorrow at the detachment. After supper, we'll meet the three men from the boarding home, plus the owner." She leans against him. "Gives me the afternoon with you."

He presses back. "Gives you the afternoon with the crew," he corrects, "but I'll make your return later in the evening worth your while." He snickers into her hair.

"Ready when you are." Aiden repeats Nick's previous remark from the kitchen doorway.

"Okay. I left my toolbox on the veranda. See you, Stella." He runs a tanned finger along her arm.

A moment passes before the chills subside.

"Thanks for lunch, Stella. Tomorrow morning at the detachment—first interview will be at nine."

She stands in the living room and watches the two men leave. Despite the seven interviews scheduled for the next day, her thoughts settle on Trixie and Val. Stella turns toward her office and grabs the phone book, in sudden need of information from the business which provides hearing aids. The batteries in those units must be small if the contraption fits behind your ear.

"Good afternoon. Port Ephron Hearing Clinic. How may I help you?"

"Hi. I'm Stella Kirk, and I hope you might answer a few questions. Will you describe a hearing aid battery for me?"

"Yes, Ms. Kirk. They are chrome-coloured metal discs which measure one-quarter inch in diameter. We keep them in stock. Do you need batteries set aside?"

"No, but may I drop in and purchase a battery if I want a sample in my possession?"

"We can accommodate such a request anytime. Do you want more information today?"

"Not now. Thank you for your help."

Once off the phone, she drops into her chair. The disc found in the crawl space under Angus Raspberry's barn might be from a watch or calculator, but the item could be from a hearing aid. Val Reguly wears a hearing aid and knew Vic. Her sister has suffered the consequences of poor choices with numerous men in her life. Harry Russell earned the badge as the worst, but there have been others. *Will Trixie be in for another broken heart?*

$$\clubsuit$$

CHAPTER 13

Suspect Potential

"Thanks for scheduling me for the first interview. I asked the overnight call service, and they'll cover the town office until we finish."

"No problem, but I thought you worked with another older woman. Myrtle?" She and Aiden take their places. Staff tucked Evan Fleguel and Philip Lewis away in separate areas of the detachment. Tyna Derhay, who works as the receptionist in the Shale Harbour Town Office, has paired a yellow plaid skirt with a blue striped shirt, an ensemble resembling the one she wore when they first met—an obvious and unusual signature style. Stella's eyes hurt. Tyna's vibrant auburn curls shimmer brighter than when they last encountered her. She's wedged glitter encrusted clips into the mass and fiddles with a rough, red-lacquered fingernail while she talks.

"Myrtle's off." She sits straighter and squints at them. "What else can I tell you? I'll help if I'm able."

"Great, Ms. Derhay. We'll share information with you in the hopes you recall another detail or two."

Tyna tilts her face, resembling a robin listening for a worm.

Aiden continues. "We found a potential hiding spot under the floor of Angus Raspberry's barn where Vic Staples died. There was evidence of contraband and a metal disc which might be from a watch or calculator."

"Or a hearing aid," Stella interjects.

"Are you acquainted with anyone who owns a battery-operated watch or carries a small calculator with them?" Aiden ignores Stella's contribution.

Frowning, she turns her attention toward Stella. "Val Reguly wears a hearing aid, and he and Vic Staples were buddies. Lots of people own battery-operated watches. Phil Lewis carries a calculator everywhere. Evan appears deaf but doesn't wear a hearing aid. I can't think of any other details. Did someone evade the police when they hid beneath the floor of the barn?"

"We can't confirm or deny, Ms. Derhay, although we're convinced our victim had a partner. They stored drugs in the space."

"Vic and Luther Greene sometimes operated machinery together. He hung out with Evan and Philip, too, because he worked with them, and he spent time with the fellas where he lived. He knew Val, but I can't imagine any of those guys selling dope." She stops and runs her palm along a pleat in her skirt. "Honestly. Vic in the drug business." She shivers.

Stella sees her response as contrived. "No one else comes to mind, Tyna?"

"Don't you dare suspect me," she spits. "I wasn't involved in Vic's shenanigans. I knew about his sideline but stayed out of the way." She points her finger at them. "You won't pin his death on me." Her tone elevates. Her face flushes. "Do I need a lawyer?"

"Relax, Ms. Derhay. A lawyer isn't necessary. You're here because of your romantic entanglement with the victim at one point. Any more you can tell us?"

Tyna shakes her curls.

He stands. "I'll escort you out. Please keep our discussions private. Your confidentiality is of utmost importance for our investigation right now."

Her chin dips in a brisk nod. With a swish of yellow plaid, and a flash of glitter, she scuttles into the hall.

Before Stella assesses the tenor of their interview, Aiden returns and drops into his chair with a huff. "I'll write another note before we go see Philip Lewis, the town manager. He's in the conference room."

"I think she's a drama queen." Stella expresses her thoughts with surprising bluntness.

"She dated Vic, lived with him, and implicated how many men during her interview? Six? Tyna has suspect potential."

****

Philip Lewis sits at the oval table, dressed in a grey suit, and bent over a notepad when Stella and Aiden enter the room. He glances toward them, finishes his note, and says, "Good morning, folks. How can I help?"

"We need any details from you which might expand our understanding of Vic Staples and his contacts, Mr. Lewis. We're certain he worked with someone in his drug business." Aiden provided the man with similar information shared with Tyna.

Lewis acts aloof, even as an RCMP detective asks him pointed questions. Stella finds his behaviour mesmerizing. No, he didn't fraternize with Vic Staples. He lives in Port Ephron and has a family. His work in both communities keeps him busy. No, he isn't acquainted with any of Vic's friends, except Vic stepped out with Tyna from the office for several months. Yes, people wear hearing aids, but no one on his team. He wishes Evan used a full set, though. He's as deaf as a post.

"Listen. Did you meet with Gavin Kershaw?"

Now Philip's asking the questions. "How could he help us? He's a new employee." Stella doesn't understand, except his remark could be an attempt at deflection.

"The guy's a gossip." Philip shrugs. "I'm in and out of the office. I don't sit and chit-chat with employees. I maintain my distance. Vic lived in a boarding home. Talk with them," he advises.

"We're under control, Mr. Lewis. Thanks for your time. Please keep our discussions confidential while the department resolves the case. I'll walk out with you."

"He wasn't much help," Stella mumbles, when Aiden returns.

"Nope. His behaviour could be an act because he believes he's our prime suspect. Stays very close-lipped." Aiden winces. "Guys in positions of authority often avoid sharing their assumptions. He held back details. Handsome timepiece. Did you notice?"

"Oh, yeah. He yanked on his cuff after you told him we found a battery. One more interview before home. Both Tyna and Philip said Evan needs a hearing aid—or two."

****

Evan Fleguel, Shale Harbour and Port Ephron engineer and Hermione and Jesse Wigglesworth's nephew, bounces his knee and stares out the window of the office where he's sat secluded for the last hour. His back faces the door. He jumps when Aiden and Stella enter. "I've been here for hours."

"The clock says ten-fifteen, Mr. Fleguel. What does yours say?" Aiden challenges the witness.

When he turns forward and pushes up the sleeve of his lightweight golf jacket, Stella can tell he owns an old-fashioned wind-up watch. "Nice timepiece, Evan."

"What?" He sees her nod at his wrist. "Thanks. My late father's. The battery ones are more reliable." He readjusts his cuff. "Sentimental, I guess."

"Let's begin, Mr. Fleguel." Aiden has taken his place behind the desk while Stella sits on another chair angled sideways. "Tell us about your experience with our victim, Vic Staples."

"Vic? My experience?" His eyes widen as he surveys them. "He often hung around the Shale Harbour location. He worked on the graveyard expansion project. His job was garbage collection but could manage heavy equipment if our contractors were short-handed, and I requested his help."

"You and he were friends." Stella makes the statement while Evan faces Aiden.

"Pardon?" His head spins. "Friend? No, not a friend."

"Did you socialize? Go out for a beer after work?" Aiden tag-teams with Stella.

"Beer?"

"Evan." Stella uses his name, which ensures his attentiveness.

"Yes."

"Were you friends with Vic Staples? Did you go out after work or meet later?"

"No. Never." He gasps. "I don't socialize much. My wife doesn't like me to be late."

"Mr. Fleguel." Aiden follows Stella's lead. "Can you recall any of the people with whom Vic Staples chummed around?"

"Okay. Let me think." He stares at the light fixture on the ceiling. "Luther Greene, for sure. Remember the problems with the first grave in the expansion?"

They both nod.

"Anyone else?"

"I guy named Wally from the boarding house. He picked Vic up from the front of the office occasionally."

"You are the nephew of Mr. and Mrs. Wigglesworth." Stella leaves the statement open between them, on purpose.

"Yes. Yes. They are family and I help them when I can." As he becomes more comfortable, Evan contributes more details. "I came here in the summer as a kid, and I stayed with them. My folks were busy. I took a job in Shale

Harbour after college because I'm fond of the landscape."

"One might assume you possess an excellent knowledge of the coastline." Aiden comments.

"Stay off the beach when the tide is on its way to high. That's my advice. Real easy to misjudge and end your days stuck under the cliffs. Deadly."

"You've been helpful, Mr. Fleguel." He rises. "Your work awaits."

"What? Yes. Work."

****

The afternoon sped by. After a leisurely lunch where Nick, Paul, Eve, Merrilee, and Duke assembled in the kitchen for build-your-own subs, Stella jumped on the golf cart with Kiki and took a spin around the park. Although less busy until school finishes, Merrilee reminded her of new check-ins she could visit. She met with a couple from Florida and explained their garbage routine. She visited with Mildred for a few minutes but didn't discuss her impressions after the earlier interviews. "I will keep my opinions quiet for now, old girl," she said when pressured. She discovered a golden retriever enroute. Kiki was unimpressed although she remained on the machine. The other dog led her toward a fifth wheel, near Duke's trailer, at the far end of the property. She reinforced the notion, with his owners, that they are required to tie Griffin and not permit him to either run or mess on other sites. Many people think campground rules apply to others.

Merrilee presented her with tea when she returned home. She threw shrimp in a marinade and prepared a salad. She expected an evening meal free from drama—grateful for the break. Nick reported on the tasks everyone accomplished in her absence, and she regretted her promise to attend interviews later.

****

Etta Graney's old farmhouse on Birch Street has seen better days. The roof gives the impression the twenty-year shingles have been on the job for forty years. The lawn needs mowing and the flower beds weeding. Pale green paint struggles to stay on the clapboards. Aiden pulls the Caprice he drives when working in behind her. Three men sit in rockers on the porch. Two of them smoke. The other munches on an apple.

They climb the stairs and introduce themselves. "We'll meet with each of you after we interview Mrs. Graney. Stand by." Aiden takes charge. He opens the door and peeks inside. "Mrs. Graney?"

"On my way," the landlady shouts, from the back of the premises.

A tiny woman, who could be ten years older than Trixie, although they attended school together, rounds the corner. She wipes red hands on the front of a rose floral bib apron, which covers black slacks and a blue blouse. Stella notes her shoes—huge runners supporting swollen ankles.

"Good evening, Mrs. Graney. I'm Detective North and let me introduce my community consultant, Stella Kirk."

"Yes, we expected you. You're Trixie's sister." She acknowledges Stella before she glances at the front door. "The men were worried before supper, but I told them you wanted to look into Vic's background as part of your work." She unties her apron, creates a neat square with the fabric, and points toward the rear of the house. "I keep a private room on this floor."

Following her through a large kitchen and dining area, they enter an anteroom which mimics the size of Stella's pantry at home. Etta drags two chairs in with her. A single bed, a small dresser, and a rolled armchair, which reflects the condition of the dwelling and has seen better days, comprise the décor.

Before Aiden frames the interview, she asks in a frank tone, "Shall I discuss Vic?"

Aiden glances at Stella and nods toward the landlady. "Go ahead, Mrs. Graney."

"Please call me Etta. Vic Staples lived here for several years." She squints. "Maybe four. He became my ideal boarder because he stayed at his girlfriend's apartment but continued to maintain his monthly rent, regardless. His generosity put more money in my pocket. In the last weeks before his death, he moved back. He and Tyna fell out, from what I can gather."

"Were you aware of his side business?"

She indulges them with a sly smile. "His 'business', as you describe it, was difficult to avoid, Detective. Vic wasn't the sharpest knife in the drawer. You people never caught him, though." She maintains her expression despite the indirect criticism of the police.

"Did he hang out with anyone else in the house?" Aiden ignores her previous remark.

"He chummed with Wally. They often went to the hotel for a beer." She leans forward. "I don't allow any indulgences on my premises and the men abide by my rules."

"You've been in the boardinghouse business for a while now, Etta." Stella wants to explore what else she might share.

"Since my in-laws died. I must tell you, with the cost of living nowadays, the challenge is to pay the bills. I need another boarder. Three guests cover the expenses, but the fourth means there's money for extras." She scrapes a hand through her thin hair. "Tough times for poor people who live life on the edge."

"Thank you for your candour and your time, Mrs. Graney. We appreciate the opportunity you've given for us to interview each of your residents alone."

She jumps from her chair. "You can use my room. I'll finish a few preparation tasks in the kitchen for breakfast tomorrow."

****

They meet Brad Masterson first.

"Hi, Brad. Remember me?" Stella tries the casual approach.

"Sure. Trixie's sister. I heard she dated a hit man. She shoulda gone out with me instead." He doesn't ask where he should sit and slouches in Etta's armchair.

His dirty hair lays flat against his forehead. Worn neon-green flip-flops grace his feet and a grey sweat suit covers his pudgy body. His toenails are black and appear infected. *Hit man or not, Trixie made a wise choice when she avoided this fellow.*

"I'm Detective Aiden North. Stella and I are investigating the murder of Vic Staples. We wish to interview his associates."

"Didn't run with the guy and didn't appreciate what I saw. He wasn't around much. What else can I say?"

"Were you aware of his drug dealings?"

"Yup. Don't do drugs. I'd lose my job, and I need the money."

"Saving for your own apartment?" Stella probes.

"Nope. Gotta baby girl. She's the reason I avoid trouble. Vic Staples meant trouble. Wally and he were friends, and Cam sometimes tagged along, but not me." He sits on the edge of the cushion and clasps his hands between his knees. "I watch TV with Ms. Etta."

"Thanks for your time tonight, Brad. Will you send Wally in here, please?"

Brad heaves his bulky frame out of the chair. The slapping sound of his footwear echoes through the kitchen as he retreats toward the veranda.

"Not much help. Do you think he's hiding information?" Aiden whispers.

"No chance. He's told us the truth."

****

Although Wally Lavender works for Fisher Contracting as a construction worker, he presents for the interview in khakis and a green golf shirt. The thirty-year-old is clean shaven and illustrates the benefits of a recent haircut. His watch appears expensive and Stella wonders where the extra money comes from. Borden Fisher isn't generous in the remuneration department.

Aiden introduces them.

He shakes their hands and asks where they prefer him to sit. After he settles into Etta's armchair, he stares at Aiden.

"We appreciate your time. As we investigate Vic Staple's murder, we must interview anyone who came into regular contact with him. We understand you socialized with Vic."

"Correct, but rarely. When he lived at his girlfriend's, I collected his mail and we'd meet for a beer. Once they split, we dropped into the hotel more often."

Wally's demeanour reflects an open and honest man, although Stella remains skeptical. "Were you aware of his side business?" she asks.

"Not from him, but I heard rumours. I paid no attention."

"Nice watch," Aiden remarks.

He takes a quick glance at his wrist. "A gift from my girlfriend, Jill Sikes. She's landed a good job. No need to wind. Seems weird."

"Did you ever take a ride with Vic in his truck, perhaps out to Raspberry Farm, over on the point?" *He may well be Vic's partner, which lets poor Val and his hearing aid off the hook.*

"No. I own a beater to drive back and forth to work. I'd give him a lift when his pickup broke down. When we met at the bar, I most often walked." He stops and smirks at them. "Pepper's somethin' else. Sometimes I stay until they close and walk her home."

"Where were you the night of the murder, Friday, May 7?"

"At my girlfriend's place in Port Ephron. I'm there most weekends."

"Write her contact information on this pad and send Cam in. We appreciate your time, and I'll reach out to you again if we need more."

****

Cam Keller is the antithesis of Wally Lavender, although employed by the same company. Cam slinks into Etta's bedsitter and flops onto one of the kitchen chairs, still dressed in dirty work clothes. His boots are off and he's in sock feet—stained socks, with a big toe poked through a hole. He doesn't look at Stella, despite introductions.

"What can you tell us regarding Vic Staples, Cam?"

"Nuthin'."

"How long have you lived at the boardinghouse?" Stella's curiosity piques. He claims he has no information.

"Couple of months but avoided the guy. I'm not the social type."

"Duly noted," Aiden mumbles. "Were you aware of the drug sideline?"

"Didn't pay attention. I did ninety days for possession, and I wanted no part of what he was doin'. Nuthin' but trouble."

"Explain what you mean." Aiden sits straighter in the armchair.

"Vic was full of crap. Big talker. Figured he could do no wrong. No desire to have Vic Staples for a friend. Went out with him and Wally once or twice, but Vic was nuthin' but trouble," he repeats. "I could tell he was bad news. Wally liked him. I didn't." He taps his foot and glares.

"You're angry with Vic Staples." Stella makes the vague statement in the faint hope Cam will reveal more.

"Can't be mad at a dead guy, but I figure he got what he deserved."

****

By eight-thirty, they've thanked Etta for her hospitality, reminded each of their four interviewees to keep discussions to themselves, and returned to their vehicles.

"What do you think?"

"Not sure." She's in the driver's seat as Aiden leans against the door. "Wally's the best of the bunch in the suspect department. His watch tells the tale—and the fact he has a girlfriend who buys him expensive presents, but he still walks Pepper Ferguson home."

"He may be a two-timer, but smart enough to stay uninvolved. The others, even Etta Graney, are vulnerable somehow. We can ponder and talk tomorrow. I dropped Cavelle at her office before we met. I'm off to fetch her now."

****

Back to the park at last. The old house looms large against the indigo sky. An unintended, although contented, moan escapes her lips while she pulls the Jeep into a spot beside the veranda stairs. As she expected when she drove into the park, he meets her—one hand pushing open the screen and the other holding Kiki.

"Long day?"

"The first half dragged. The second longer. Glad I'm home."

"Wine?"

"Let me run upstairs and change." She kisses him and snuggles Kiki against her face.

Moments later, dressed in soft cotton pants and her Mount Allison University sweatshirt, she returns. They wait on the sofa—her loves. Glass in hand, she reviews the interviews with him. "Tyna Derhay began by throwing everybody Vic ever spoke to under the bus. She included Val Reguly because he wears a hearing aid." Stella strokes Kiki while she talks. The action soothes. "She said Evan Fleguel is almost deaf but doesn't wear one. She also implied Vic's friends were people who could be involved." Grumbling in frustration, she continues. "As for Evan Fleguel, he has obvious hearing challenges. He suggested Wally Lavender, from the boarding house, was in business with Vic. Wally wears a nice, battery-operated watch but wasn't the least perturbed by our questions. He admitted his friendship with Vic and said they drank together, and he collected the guy's mail."

"And the Shale Harbour town manager?"

"Philip Lewis? He complained Evan needs hearing aids. Philip wears a battery-operated watch and suggested we interview Gavin Kershaw because he's a gossip. I found his remark odd. I question when one person considers another a gossip."

"What about the other boarders besides Wally?"

"Etta liked Vic, and appreciated the fact he paid even when he stayed away for days. She's forever short of funds. I sympathize. She struggles with money. Her three roomers respect her and abide by her rules." She stops for wine. "Cam and Brad, the other two, weren't much help. Either could have been Vic's partner, but if one of them worked with our victim, he's a talented actor."

"You're exhausted, Stella." He touches her leg. "Tomorrow will be easy for me. Are you off again? I'll work inside."

"We're scheduled for re-interviews with Angus' neighbours in the morning. I expect little. We'll tell them about the room under the barn and see if the additional detail shakes out any memories or forgotten bits of information."

CHAPTER 14

Sorry For The Interruption

"Hester." With one ear frozen to the telephone receiver, Stella rests her chin in her palm. "Aiden and I are investigating as thoroughly as possible, given the circumstances. We're speaking with Angus' neighbours again today."

"Why? They haven't helped in the past." Her tone sharpens. "Your investigation needs to be finished. Angus lies to me and says he's fine. Not true."

"And you're angry." No harm in stating the obvious. "I'll ask Aiden if you and I can review the case. I expect a busy weekend here at the park, but maybe a meeting on Monday?"

"Out at my farm, Stella. In the vegetable patch. I still run my market garden. The work never ends," she grumbles. "Be there early."

The phone clunks in her ear. Fridays, particularly the afternoons, are hectic. She and Aiden will revisit the three properties on the road to Raspberry Farm this morning. Nick, Eve, and Paul are busy outside while Merrilee sings a soft melody in reception. She checks the clock on the kitchen wall. Time for another cup of coffee before Aiden arrives.

What does she expect from the neighbours? Donamae might possess more information than she's shared to date. She doesn't sense the hippies will cooperate, except on the surface. Hermione Wigglesworth troubles Stella. The woman's involved somehow. Although her husband struggles with communication, Hermione isolates Jesse from any level of exchange. She closes her eyes. *I should spend a minute or two alone with Jesse.*

"Anybody home?" The screen door slams.

"In the kitchen, Aiden."

"Ready?" He stands at the entrance.

"Coffee before we go?"

He nods.

"As for the interviews, I expect we're on a fool's errand, except for Jesse Wigglesworth. His wife never lets him contribute a full sentence. He has obvious problems, but no harm in trying."

The detective frowns as he reaches for the offered mug.

"Keep Hermione engaged until I can see what her husband says when she can't put her foot on his throat."

"Brutal but true. Miss Kutska first. River and Saffron next—a complete waste of time, in my humble opinion—and finish with the Wigglesworth couple. I'll ask her what they did before they retired." He swigs the last of his hot coffee. "Let's go."

****

They find Donamae Kutska, the second-cousin-once-removed of the man who built Raspberry Farm, perched on her porch swing. Maisie the goat has her butt balanced on the seat while Donamae rocks and waves. "I told your people when they called me, Detective North." She whispers in the goat's ear. "I can't help you."

Aiden slams the door of the sedan. "Good morning, Miss, ah, Donamae. Should I be afraid of your bodyguard?"

The woman laughs—an uproarious and open sound—a laugh Stella considers honest and without restraint.

"Maisie's nice, aren't you, old girl?" Stella approaches the animal, hand extended. The goat stands, moves closer, and leans against her hip.

"You wait here, Maisie." Donamae leads them into her kitchen.

Stella absorbs the pale pine floors, low ceilings, and notes the armless rocker covered in a blue and white scrap quilt and cuddled in the corner. A wood/oil combination Enterprise stove—a creamy compact unit—must be her source of heat in the winter, although Stella can sense warmth radiating across the kitchen right now.

"Take a seat at the table. I made coffee. Nippy this morning, so I fired 'er up," she gives a respectful nod to the Enterprise, "to clear the damp. I'll serve you cowboy coffee today."

"I love cowboy coffee, Donamae. We used the fireplace when the ice storm blew the power."

"Find a stove like mine." She pats the enamelled surface. "I considered gettin' rid of her, but I can't. I never worry about heat or makin' a cuppa when the electricity quits." She places two mugs of steaming black liquid in front of them before she grabs a tray with cream and sugar from the counter. Finished with her hostess duties, she sits. "Now, what can I help you with today?"

"We discovered a hidden space under the barn, above where Angus found Vic Staples' body. We wondered if you were aware of the spot," Aiden begins.

Donamae's eyes widen. "I told you before, I suspected secret rooms. The one upstairs made sense, although I had no direct evidence until you reported your discovery. Under the barn, eh? Well, good on the old fella. He allowed for anyone and everyone, I guess."

"Did Angus use the area?" Confronted with stronger coffee than she expected, she's reminded of her molasses-meets-motor-oil experiences with Mary Jo and Mildred.

"Don't be absurd. If Angus Raspberry had knowledge, you'd hear. The guy can't hide information. He's too honest." She takes a slug of the black concoction. "You folks wonderin' if the murderer hid under the floorboards until the tide went out? Grand theory, but the person woulda needed to understand the cliffs and tides so as not to take such a chance after dark. If they estimated wrong, could be trouble."

None the wiser after their visit with Donamae, they search for River and Saffron. After fifteen minutes, they find them at the community look-off between their property and Raspberry Farm.

"Good morning, folks. We expected you'd eventually see us here." River's arm wraps around Saffron's shoulder in a tight grip. They're seated on a worn bench with a spectacular view across the bay into Shale Harbour.

Aiden and Stella are polite with the couple. With no knowledge of hidden rooms, and less related to Angus Raspberry, River and Saffron contribute little more to the investigation. They bought their weed from Vic, the way Mildred Fox did, which appears as their only connection to the murder or the victim.

When they exit the car at the Wigglesworth home, Stella observes there's no need to be a rocket scientist to recognize an altercation when you see one. The words Stella hears when she opens her door are, "I don't care what you want." Hermione lords over Jesse, seated in his wheelchair. She and Aiden stand and watch Hermione shake her finger in Jesse's face.

Aiden slams his car door and they both turn in his direction. "Mr. And Mrs. Wigglesworth. Sorry for the interruption."

Hermione wipes her hands against her apron, glares at her husband, and bustles past his cumbersome chair. "Let's go through the side entrance and talk in the kitchen, although I'm not sure what help I might offer." She scuttles along the ramp from the front deck.

Stella glances at Aiden for confirmation before she turns toward Jesse. "I'll keep your husband company while Detective North provides you with the latest information."

"What? No need. He's fine out here. Come with me," she sputters.

"My colleague finds the repetition tiresome, Mrs. Wigglesworth. She'll stay on the deck with Mr. Wigglesworth."

With no plan at hand, Stella blinks her gratitude and turns toward the ramp.

"Good morning, Jesse. Fabulous seeing you. Lovely day." She touches his shoulder. "Hermione angry with you?"

"No more guns." He lifts bloodshot eyes.

"Your wife was an accomplished sharpshooter when she was young, I gather."

"Cleaning. Forgets steps. Gonna hurt herself, or me." He fidgets with the blanket across his legs. Stella straightens the folds.

"Do you remember the night Vic Staples died?"

He grits his teeth, an act which exposes dentures too big for his mouth. "Lotsa police."

"Before the traffic?"

"Nope. Evan came for breakfast, though. Borrowed our car."

"Pleasant visit?"

"Yup."

****

"Is the cottage rented, Merrilee?" She saunters into the office as her assistant hangs the key ring on a hook behind the desk.

Merrilee jumps before she faces her boss. "You startled me," she accuses. "They fell on the floor. No guests yet. What can I do for you?"

Her babbling strikes Stella as odd. She maintains her stance and crosses her arms. "Any news?"

"No, Stella. I expect a handful of checkouts and a quiet afternoon. And you?" Her fingers tremble while she tidies the stack of maps displayed at the end of the counter.

"Okay." *Why does she seem nervous around me?* "I'm off on a run about the park. I'll be back for coffee."

She returns an hour later and discovers Merrilee hanging the cottage key again. It must fall off the hook. Nick will need to install a bigger one.

The house drifts into silence once people enjoy a muffin and return to whatever chores are required of them today. She knows the flower beds demanded Eve's attention. Duke mentioned essential tasks for Cloris. Nick and Paul said the lawns need a mow. "I'll make lunches," she hollers toward reception.

Later in the afternoon, Nick suggests the two of them, along with Kiki, take a walk around the park. She isn't enthusiastic because she's completed a tour already today, but the pleasure of his company is worth the trek. Times are rare when they sit by the cliffs once the season begins and the lots fill. They sip their tea, discuss the amount of erosion which has occurred over the previous three years, and decide on moving the road back twenty feet next November. Leaving the decision with Mother Nature is courting disaster. The sewer service connections might present a challenge, but Nick thinks they can reconfigure the area with minimal movement required, thanks to efficient planning before the project. Her watch says four. They tromp toward home.

Stella makes for the side yard and the veranda entrance. Nick suggests they sneak through reception, an unusual choice. No Merrilee. The house remains eerily quiet. She squints at Nick. "Should I be suspicious?"

"Surprise!"

With a pumping heart, she scans the faces of her family and her staff. Val and Trixie lift their glasses in a toast. They each hold a beer. Carter hoists Mia into his arms. "Brigitte will be here in a half an hour, Stella. Happy Birthday!"

"Happy Birthday, Auntie Stel."

Stella races across the room and kisses her great-niece.

She can see Cloris and Duke, separated by a row of younger staff. Stella judges by their expressions they're pleased to be included, whatever the occasion. Cavelle and Hester linger by the screen door.

"Birthday! Today isn't my birthday, but any excuse for a party. What a surprise."

Merrilee steps forward. "We all felt you needed a shindig, despite not being the correct date. Sundays are easier." She glances at her watch. "Except for the check-ins." Her soft chuckle pairs with a knowing nod. "Call the affair an appreciation event, if you prefer."

With both hands poised on her hips in mock anger, Stella asks, "How does the cottage key fit into your plans? I knew something was amiss."

Nick winks at Merrilee, and Stella notices the exchange. "He whispers in Stella's ear. The cottage has a fridge, and we hid the birthday feast, so you wouldn't suspect."

Her eyes widen.

"We have one gift for you on behalf of the group, with Hester as the special contributor."

Hester steps forward. "The trunk of Cavelle's fancy car overflows with hosta and astilbe plants from my garden. Eve, we must give them air to prevent suffocation."

"I prepared, with Duke's help, perennial beds which line both sides of the lane on the drive toward the cottage." Eve shifts her weight from one foot to the other. "Hester and I will plant them while Merrilee and Nick organize supper."

"Come Eve." Hester extends her hand and Cavelle drops her keys into her sister's palm. "We must work fast, as I am famished, but these plants require an introduction to their new home at once."

Eve turns toward the group and waves, palms exposed. The screen slaps closed behind them. Stella stands, somewhat stunned, while Nick and Kiki follow in Hester's wake. Merrilee runs into reception when a fifth wheel pulls into the parking space by the door. Cloris pats Duke on the arm and announces, "Back in a jiff."

"Cavelle. Wine or beer?"

"Perhaps lemonade or iced tea, Stella. I'm the driver today."

"They didn't invite Aiden?"

Carter and Mia wander toward the veranda. Brigitte will arrive any time now.

"Merrilee planned your surprise with Eve and Hester. I'm chauffeur and nothing more. Lovely to be here, though." She smiles as she accepts a tall glass of iced tea and heads outside.

Stella, once alone, closes her eyes and settles her breathing. Before her heart rate calms, she hears Cloris and Duke.

"Out of our way. Kitchen bound," Cloris directs, as she pushes through. They each carry a platter of beef kabobs, ready for the barbecue. "I kept them in a stack in my fridge," she prattles on. "They look more appetizing displayed on the platters. Right, Duke?"

"Right, Love. Where's Nick, Stella?"

"He went out with the dog. I expect he followed Hester and Eve. Why?"

"I'll find him. He'll need my help."

Her frown begs the unasked question.

"Cake and potato salad, both at the cottage." Cloris explains. "Jeez. When we can't use your enormous kitchen, we require at least two others for the extra grub. Go catch him, Duke. Don't leave Nick without another pair of hands," she commands, before she turns her attention back toward Stella. "You were a stunned pickle."

"Excellent description. What can I pour for you before we join the crew?"

"Oh, I brought my own." She swivels a sling from around her neck and shoulder. Stella discovers a bottle of wine inside. "My little helper," Cloris snorts. "Where's your corkscrew?"

****

Exhausted from the spectacular afternoon and evening, Nick and Stella sat in the now quiet kitchen and enjoyed another piece of cake. With a lemon filling and an inch of boiled icing, Stella swooned over the mother of all angel food cakes when Merrilee first served the creation. She closed her eyes in pure bliss. Merrilee, with a measure of reluctance, admitted she made the confection—a triumph.

Before darkness fell, they walked the cottage path and appreciated, once more, the work of Eve and Hester. She never imagined such an edge along the narrow drive. Too many other priorities came as the obvious reason. They returned home and collapsed in front of the television.

Trixie and Val were both prickly tonight, she ruminates, as *The Nature of Things* slides into the national news. She settles beside Nick and reviews the evening while he focuses on current events.

Her sister arrived behind the wheel of her new car, dressed in a midi-length T-shirt, adorned with ten necklaces, her hair clipped into a contrived messy bun and her feet secured in platform heels only she could manage. She presented Stella with a gift certificate for a visit to the salon of her longtime personal hairdresser. She tucked the piece of paper into Stella's pocket while guests focused elsewhere—as if the act would be their little secret.

"Val drives me nuts," Trixie whispered. "Even with the damned hearing aid, he doesn't hear me. See him over in the corner, all woebegone? I still face him and grab his attention before I talk. I wish the word 'what' didn't exist." She slumped into the nearest chair.

"I'll go visit with him. He's said before how uncomfortable he feels in crowds."

"Right. Where did I leave my purse?"

Stella takes a breath. "You dropped your bag on the table in the kitchen before we barbecued the beef kabobs. Busy time."

Without a word, she jumped up and ran toward the back of the house.

"Hi. Alone?"

"What?" Val stared at her, his face blank.

"You aren't a fan of parties, eh, Val?" Stella sat beside him.

"Correct!" His voice elevated, as if she was a contest winner and her prize was being announced.

"I assumed your hearing aid would help."

"Not with bunches of people. Too much background noise. I adjusted the volume, but I can't hear you talkin' then, unless I see your lips."

"Val, were you a friend of Vic Staples?"

"Knew the guy—not well, but he worked for the town, collected garbage, ran the odd machine when they needed someone."

"Were you aware Vic dealt drugs?"

Val's eyes widened. "I'm not involved, Stella. I don't do drugs and don't sell them either."

She studied him carefully before she replied. "We found what could be a hearing aid battery in a crawl space under the barn."

"Not me, Stella. Stay home at night and watch your sister." He cracked his knuckles and avoided her eyes while he spoke.

"And the reason Trixie needs your constant supervision?" Stella feared his answer but asked.

"Honest to God, Trixie's losin' her grip. She can't remember where she's put stuff. The woman shouldn't be drivin'. Did she tell you she took a wrong turn in Port Ephron the other day and called me from a dress shop? I explained how to find the highway. I sure as hell won't be the one tellin' her to park her new car for good. We're not married. Trixie turns into a rabid dog when you mention her memory."

"Maybe Brigitte should discuss her issues with her."

"Somebody should. She's young. I ain't gonna devote my life to bein' a nursemaid for a woman who can't remember where she put her coat…or glasses…or tea…or…. Understand?"

****

Stella's dragged out of her reverie as the news reader announces thirty-thousand Israeli troops invaded Lebanon. The world is in a mess.

"I lost you in space, Stella." His eyes hold unasked questions. "The case?"

"No. Val and Trixie may not be a couple for long."

"They're having problems?" He leans closer, and lifts Kiki onto his lap, which gives room for his shoulder to touch hers.

"Val complained and bemoaned Trixie's memory loss along with the resulting daily challenges. Trixie focused on his hearing disability, even with an aid. I bet their relationship is on its last legs."

"Trixie acted okay when I was around."

"Yeah, she wasn't too bad tonight. Lost her handbag—the one issue I saw. Val complains she can't remember where she puts stuff—ever. He said he won't be her caregiver down the road."

"Harsh. Doesn't sound like true love to me."

"Trixie gripes because she says Val hears no better with the aid in his ear than he does when it's stashed in his trouser pocket. He claims amplification won't work when a bunch of people talk at once."

Nick touches her hand. "Not your problem, Stella."

"No. But Val wears a hearing aid and knew Vic Staples, although they weren't friends. He insists he didn't approve of Vic's side hustle and wasn't involved. I couldn't wangle a clear alibi for the night of the murder. I doubt if Trixie can remember any details related to the evening and Val's whereabouts." She leans back against the sofa cushion and closes her eyes. "Aiden will interview Val, and I'll plan on a discreet visit with Brigitte soon. I hope a family intervention doesn't become the only option."

🐝

CHAPTER 15

An Ill-Advised Circumstance

After a quick word with Jewel, and with a mug of her invigorating coffee clutched in her hand, Stella wanders into the backyard and Hester's vegetable and herb garden. She finds her friend squatting over a hoed row, while she drops seeds one by one in a straight line.

"Hi. You never stop. May I help?"

Hester doesn't turn. "No. Sit on the side, if the grass isn't too wet, and provide your report."

"My report?"

"I expect any information you and Detective North gleaned after your many, and might I add fruitless, interviews to be shared with me this morning."

"And you assume they're fruitless because…?"

With effort, she turns. "Angus has been under a cloud of suspicion for over a month. You interviewed his neighbours, Vic's work colleagues, and the boarding home residents, but are none the wiser. You've made no progress and won't admit your sister's love interest could well be the architect of your failures."

Stella sips her coffee while she plans a response, realizing she enjoyed the new Hester—the one more inclined toward social norms and who considered others—more than this redesigned older version. She's regressed, since the discovery of Vic Staples' body, into the previously accusatory and alienated Hester—the one who has trouble maintaining a two-sided dialogue. Now she's aloof and judgmental once again.

"Aiden said I could discuss the case with you, although he suggested the idea was inappropriate. He expects you're professional enough to separate the investigation from your partnership with Angus, if we communicate openly.

Correct?"

"Yes…and no. Angus and I want to plan our future. We cannot focus while suspicion of murder hangs over our lives—an ill-advised circumstance." She reaches for her seed packet. "I will maintain your confidence. Perhaps I can assist."

"What are you planting?" She hopes a discussion focused on the garden relaxes her friend somehow.

"To be precise, I am sowing seeds. The word planting suggests transplants, which I started indoors in the early spring and transplanted outside a week ago." She points in the general direction of a smaller plot beyond her current workspace. "I nurture many of my herbs inside the house, as you can see. You'll be on my doorstep in the fall, cap in hand, impatient to benefit from the fruits of my labour. Today, I'll focus on parsnips, pole beans, and carrots. I've added another row of radishes. They've done well from the first round, and I will pick you a bunch for your salads."

"Thank you, Hester. Nick and I love radishes."

"Can you make a radish rose?" Her back remains turned away from Stella.

"As a matter of fact, yes. Learned the art in home economics class."

Hester stands and moves in Stella's direction. "Although I never attended school, I experienced superior home economics training. Opal was an excellent teacher."

Also, her sister was an accomplished murderer. Stella permits Hester's comment to pass.

"You need your own herb garden, Stella. I could guide you."

Mid-morning sun warms her neck, and she wishes she'd brought her hat. "Shall we discuss suspects before you finish *sowing* your parsnips?"

"Yes. I'll sit here beside you."

"Let's begin with the solid evidence. In the crawlspace under the barn— the barn where Angus discovered Vic's body…."

"The spot I found," she interrupts.

"Correct. The spot you found. Forensics retrieved a battery, which could be for a watch, a hearing aid, or a calculator. They also found evidence of drugs. Our current theory suggests they stored contreband at various times and the perpetrator evaded police by rolling into the underfloor secret area from the access point outside the barn. He or she remained hidden until they deemed the shore safe enough and crept away at dawn."

"Your theory appears sound on the surface. Val wears a hearing aid."

"And one boarder, Wally Lavender, owns a fancy battery-operated watch, as does Philip Lewis, the town manager. In all fairness, Wally seemed too honest in the interview. He wasn't suspicious. Philip Lewis pointed us toward Evan Fleguel and complained with considerable annoyance regarding his unaddressed hearing disability. He suggested we meet with the new engineer, a guy named Gavin Kershaw, in Shale Harbour on a contract. He and his wife are guests at the park for the summer."

"Val?"

She closes her eyes before she answers. "Val's alibi seems vague for the night of the murder, but he swears he wasn't a friend of Vic's and insists he isn't involved in the local drug trade. Aiden can interview him and detail his whereabouts."

Hester grunts to her feet. "I require a cup of tea and a cookie. I suspect they will be ready to come out of the oven about now." She peers inside Stella's empty mug. "You need a refill." She marches toward the American Foursquare farmhouse, her home until Vic Staples' murder, when she moved in with Angus.

Stella follows in her wake.

While Hester scuttles into the downstairs mudroom and washes her hands, Stella finds Jewel busy with her little boy as they make chocolate chip cookies. "Hi, again. I made a fresh pot of coffee and put the kettle on for her highness. This batch will cool soon."

"Her highness?"

Jewel squints and whispers, "She acts the same as when I first came here, Stella. Givin' me lectures and instructions; expectin' the household revolves around her. I'm happy she's not here much except in the mornings, now. One of us drives her home by lunchtime. Angus drops her off."

"I'll talk with her if I can."

"Good luck." She places six fresh cookies on a green glass plate, pulls napkins from the cupboard, and sets the table. "She'll be back any minute."

"Ready for tea?" Jewel stands at the counter and reaches for the cord to the kettle.

"What didn't you understand? I said I wanted my tea." Hester had materialized out of nowhere.

Stella glances at Jewel before she pours herself coffee and sits.

"The men won't be in for coffee, Hester. Jacob said he and Ken were goin' into Port Ephron, home for lunch."

"Don't care." She grabs a cookie and munches.

With a precious friendship in the balance, Stella makes a statement with the hope Hester feels compelled to clarify. "Stress often causes a person to revert to old habits, even though they know their behaviour isn't for the best."

Hester pours her tea and remains silent.

"And your opinion, Hester?"

"Does your verbiage include me? I didn't realize." She flutters her hand at them, brushing away flies of disinterest. "I battle far more important issues besides social graces and people who misbehave. To whom are you referring?" She glares at Jewel and avoids Stella's gaze.

"You, Hester. I understand how the pressure of the investigation has caused disruption in your life."

She frowns before she turns in her chair and focuses her attention out the window.

"I remember," Stella presses forward, "during Lucy's murder inquiry, a different woman—one who refused personal contact and didn't partake unless asked the exact needed question. We've discussed how you've changed since then, but lately, not so much."

"Have I regressed in my attempts to become socially appropriate?"

Stella doesn't miss the challenge in her friend's eyes. "Yes. I want the new Hester back—the Hester with whom I can discuss the case and even ask for help. Right now, you shut me out."

"Me, too," Jewel pipes in from across the kitchen. "Kenny and Angel," she leans over and pats the dog, sitting beside the child and not near Hester, "want the new Hester back, too." Her barely negligible nod toward Stella doesn't fool Hester.

"You two collaborated on an intervention. I don't...."

Jewel interrupts, "You haven't been nice since the morning Sergeant Moyer called and told you Angus was at the detachment. We know you're upset. Everyone's concerned for dear Angus, but stop bein' cross, not talkin', and goin' in and out without even a 'by-your-leave'."

Hester pushes back her chair and stands. Her chin trembles. She approaches Jewel, bends, and lifts Kenny off the floor. "I'm sorry, little boy. Is Auntie Hester a mean lady?"

The toddler plants a wet kiss on Hester's cheek. Tears flow.

****

Cocoa and Café vibrates with activity as Stella mounts the stairs at eleven-thirty. She's due to meet Aiden at noon. From her observations, Andrew and Tiffany's takeout business has grown. They now advertise how they will make brown bag lunches for workers and picnickers alike. She nods with quiet satisfaction. The little café isn't the only success story on Main Street. The Harbour Hotel, Parlour Antiques, and Hope Carlyle's weaving shop each contribute to Shale Harbour's success as a summer tourist destination.

Tiffany wiggles her fingers in Stella's direction and points toward one of the minuscule bistro tables in the back corner. "Coffee?"

"Not today. An iced tea, or lemonade, please." Tiffany makes her own, both from scratch, and either drink will suffice.

"Lemonade on the way."

Stella uses the time before Aiden arrives to review her meeting with Hester. She hopes her friend's newfound awareness assists her to manage the current stresses impacting her life.

"Thanks, Tiffany."

"Someone joining you?"

"Aiden should be here soon, unless an incident occurred."

"I saw him ten minutes ago, on his way along Birch. When I empty the garbage, I enjoy a clear view of Grey Cottage Realty from the step," she inserts, as a means of explanation. "Fetching Cavelle?"

She shrugs. The purpose of their meeting is business. Cavelle's potential appearance would be inappropriate, but she swallows her opinion.

He bustles into the bistro, dishevelled and windblown. She waves.

"Sorry I'm late."

"No problem. Have you suffered a busy morning?"

"Once I find a cup of coffee," he twists his wrist in Tiffany's general direction, "I'll be fine. Want to discuss an issue with you, but case first. How's Hester?"

"Frustrated. Angry. Impatient. She claims we haven't completed a thorough investigation. She's fixated on Val Reguly."

Aiden accepts his brew from Tiffany and lifts a brow.

"Val wears a hearing aid and knew Vic, but insists they weren't friends.

I talked with him at the little family and staff party in the park last night."

"The one where I received no invitation." He raises his hand, preventing any unnecessary response. "Teasing."

"The guy didn't reveal a solid alibi or account for his whereabouts the night of May 7. Even if I asked Trixie, and I won't, she's unlikely to remember. You talk with Val and find the answer."

"Could he be our suspect?"

"No, but to distract Hester from the idea Val Reguly killed Vic Staples, we need his alibi."

"And alternate suspects?"

"Wally Lavender or Philip Lewis, both with their fancy watches."

"Listen. I'll complete interviews with Val, Wally, and Philip. You talk to Gavin, the extra engineer, and uncover any scuttlebutt. Philip says he's a gossip, right?"

"Correct. Let's order lunch and you can tell me about the other issue on your mind." She suspects Rosemary but won't lead him.

They ask for garden salads and fresh cheese biscuits. Once they're alone again, Aiden begins. "I've met with Rosemary and Toni twice in the last ten days. She's better, Stella."

"Any sign of Annette Funicello?"

"No. No. Toni says she takes her medication without supervision, attends her psychiatrist appointments willingly, and the sale of the house went through problem-free. She hired her own lawyer when the property closed, and I paid the bill. Easy."

"You said you've met with her?"

"Yeah. Twice at Toni's. We eat dinner and talk. Toni leaves us alone. We visit. I enjoy her company again, Stella."

"And Cavelle?"

He winces. "I haven't told Cavelle. I let on I work the odd evening in Port Ephron." He sips his coffee. "She's none the wiser so far."

"Do you want my opinion, Aiden?"

"I can guess what you'll say, but sure." He smirks.

"You made a commitment to Cavelle when you invited her into your home. Now you sneak around behind her back." She doesn't give a damn how accusatory she sounds.

"Rosemary and I are married," he replies, with thick sarcasm. "You understand, I've been sneaking around with my *wife*."

Stella studies his expression. Mary Jo described his past philandering behaviour; how he always returns to Rosemary's side the minute she shows any signs of recovery. Mary Jo knows her brother-in-law well. "Cavelle deserves your honesty, Aiden. You will break her heart."

He prefaces his next remark with a shrug. "She understood what might happen. I tried to see her before I came here, but she was busy on the phone. Once we find time for a serious chat, she can move back to the farm. Rosemary should be able to come and visit. If she likes my new place, she can re-locate to Shale Harbour whenever she wants."

A last gulp of her lemonade before her chair scrapes as she retrieves her handbag from the pine floor. "I'm finished." She avoids his eyes. "I'll pay my bill on the way out." As the tinkle of the bistro bells fades, she stands on the steps for a minute and gathers her thoughts before she visits Yellow House, where she must face yet another touchy subject involving the human condition. She jumps when Aiden taps her shoulder.

"What, Aiden? I'm off to Brigitte's."

"My status is none of your concern, you know. I wanted you to be aware of the lay of the land in case Rosemary moves to Shale Harbour."

"Why should where she lives affect me? You claim she's cured," comes the accusation.

"Not cured, Stella. Managed," he adds, with exaggerated patience.

"I don't want her anywhere near me, Aiden. You do what's necessary. Now, I told Brigitte to expect me. Let me know how your three interviews go."

****

As she crosses the street, she blinks away the sting of tears forming at the corners of her eyes. Fears for Cavelle, and anger toward Aiden, assume a back seat when her niece answers the door.

"I'm glad you're here, Aunt Stella. I want to discuss Mom with you—in confidence," she murmurs, her gaze focused on the floor.

"Funny. Your mother is the reason I called."

"Come into the kitchen. I decided not to open until two o'clock today. I took Mia for a practice run at daycare."

She follows Brigitte through the living room and dining room, both used as bookstore and children's library space, into the large family room and kitchen addition at the back.

Stella's brow furrows. "I thought you wanted to keep her home with you or with Trixie until next year, when she'll be five and start kindergarten."

"Yes, and no." Brigitte turns from the counter where she's plugged in the kettle. "She can't begin until after her fifth birthday—in January 1983." She nibbles her lip. "I'm nervous now when Mom minds Mia."

"Tell me more." Stella's heart beats. The heat of a flush warms her cheeks, but she won't mention the reason for her visit until she hears more from Brigitte.

"Mom forgets she said she'd babysit. She doesn't bring Mia back home at the time we decide. Once I called and she said she forgot Mia was with her. I jumped in the car and roared to her house." She pours hot water into the pot.

"No problems, I gather."

"Frightened the life out of me. When I arrived, Mom had Mia dressed in her coat. I asked her what happened, and Mia said Glammy took a snooze while she played in her room. Mom shrugged the whole situation off."

"Your mother's memory has become an issue, Brigitte." Stella pushes forward. "Val, last night at the party, told me she often forgets. He also noted she couldn't remember how to access the road home from Port Ephron, and she shouldn't be behind the wheel."

Brigitte sets the teapot on the table and turns back toward the counter for cups. Both drink chamomile tea without the addition of sweetener or milk— they're set. "I'm relieved you understand. Carter and I talked the problem over. We need a strategy. Between us, and you and Val, we should keep a better eye on her. As for Mia, the daycare option is available on my open days until she starts school in January."

Do I mention Val's attitude? Not now. "A family intervention is the first step, Brigitte. Her car's an issue. Mia is another, although resolved until she discovers the measures you've taken. Trixie will be cross. She needs a visit with her doctor." Stella frowns into her teacup. "You might be required to assume her financial responsibilities."

"Val can manage her money."

"They aren't married. Appreciate my bluntness. He shouldn't access her finances, except household expenses."

"You're right." Brigitte's strawberry blond curls bob. "Mom accused Val the other day. She said he stole cash out of her wallet. I told her the idea was crazy. Bad choice of words, I guess."

"Trixie isn't crazy. Trixie suffers from memory issues, a problem not diagnosed often in people her age." She swallows. "Uncommon, but accusations happen. I don't imagine Val has stolen from her, but paranoia can manifest as a symptom."

"How do you know, Stella?"

"I spent hours in the library after I moved back here with your grandfather. I checked out a dozen books on dementia and learned whatever I could in a short period. In the end, I felt confident our best choice for him was placement at Harbour Manor."

Brigitte closes her eyes. Tears wet her cheeks. "Mom could go to Harbour Manor, right?"

"No sugar-coated answer, kid. Nursing home may happen, but not tomorrow. Dad managed the park even though his disease was advanced." Stella touches her fingertips while she continues. "First, she must see the doctor, get a diagnosis, and then change her behaviours—driving, for example. You should become her Power of Attorney. Carter can explain the exact process."

Soft sobs dribble from her niece. "Aunt Stella, I've been wishing Mom's issues would disappear after the wedding. I hope she's under stress, or sick, or depressed. I want her behaviour to be curable."

"Me, too. On the upside, she could stay in her present state for years. The progression of dementia, if the doctor diagnoses her, as he probably will, can be slow." She leans across the table and touches Brigitte's hand. "If she understands and cooperates, life may not be a challenge for a long time."

Brigitte's shoulders hunch while her body sags into acceptance.

On the trip home, Stella hopes the investigation into Vic's murder wraps up before long. She expects family complications will absorb her time going forward.

CHAPTER 16

Stella Avoids The Bait

Someone parked their truck and trailer near the guest entrance. Faint mutters come from reception. Nick and the other staff are out of sight. No squeals and fingernails on the floor from Kiki. She peeks into the front office. Her assistant waves while she describes different available sites to a man of significant vintage. Stella glimpses the bob of silver curls inside the cab of the half-ton pickup before she wanders into the kitchen.

Four o'clock and supper isn't on the go—no stew in the oven, steaks in marinade, or pork chops ready to grill. Nick's been busy. She remembers he mentioned Paul and Eve on yardwork today and he'd asked Duke to help him unblock a sewer line. Fun. A plan for scallops with herbs comes to mind, so she rummages in the fridge. She locates them before she starts the white wine and rosemary sauce. Once satisfied, and while they chill, she washes a bowl of new potatoes, lifting her eyes from the task at hand when Merrilee taps on the door frame.

"Didn't want to startle you. They were the last of the expected arrivals. The evening won't be busy now." Her staff departs for home at five, but reception remains open until eight o'clock.

"Cute outfit." Merrilee's capri pants coordinate with her blouse. The motif around the neck reflects the colour of the trousers.

She pats her top. "Thanks. Not new, but perfect for office work on a warm day." She watches Stella putter at the counter. "You understand that if you share your supper plans, I can start preparations for you." Her mother hen tone percolates.

"True." Stella halts the flow of cold water on the salad greens and focuses on her assistant. "You pitch in at lunch, but an evening meal isn't in the job description, unless we plan a get-together. Nick has a handle on food most of the time, but today sounded as if the park had an emergency."

"Yup. They didn't come in for coffee and made a quick stop for a muffin after twelve. The plumbers were here, too."

"Oh, God. I can imagine the bill." She closes her eyes.

"No. Don't worry. The company admitted their mistake—a leaky valve not tightened enough at the time of installation. Don't worry," she repeats.

Paul and Eve appear at four-forty-five, grass-stained and sweaty. Paul has clippings stuck throughout the blond hairs of his tanned calves. He's been busy with the whipper-snipper.

"Any more needed from us today, Stella? We're too dirty to come further," Eve shouts.

Stella wipes her hands with a kitchen towel and walks toward the back door. "You two can leave whenever you want. I gather I missed a productive day."

"Duke assumed poop duty while we mowed," Paul chuckles. "I expect Cloris complained about the state of him."

Eve nudges him in the side. "Appreciated, Stella. I'm off and Paul," she nudges him again, "will wait on the veranda for Merrilee."

Within ten minutes, Paul, Eve, and Merrilee were gone. Nick materializes in filthy and foul-scented glory, chiselled, tanned, and handsome despite his current condition. "Straight into the shower for you, mister. Supper is under control."

"No kisses? You've been gone forever."

She sidesteps his fake attempt for a hug and grabs Kiki off the floor. "No smooches for him—not right now," she sputters and coos while she hugs the dog, who has remained clean despite the day.

Their barbecue lights with no problem. She skewers the scallops, pours oil into the cast iron frying pan for the smashed potatoes, and tosses the salad in Nick's homemade dressing.

"Where are you?"

"In the kitchen." She watches his face light when he sees her. More time with this man—the goal for tonight. She surveys her accomplishments. "Not a perfect plan to cook spuds in the house and scallops on the grill, but such is my life. Besides, Kiki wanted her dinner right away. Did you not feed her today?"

He trots toward the stove. "She ate her treats at lunchtime. Here. Give me the pan. We can barbecue these outside, too. Gather the rest." He winks at her surprised face.

Before she argues, he's in front of the grill. With two glasses of chilled white wine in hand, she joins him.

Nick regales her with septic stories at supper time. One includes Cloris' reaction when Duke tried to enter her trailer for his shower. Duke's love interest stood at the door and ordered him back to his own unit.

"Not to insert investigative business into our evening, Nick, but I need a wee visit with Gavin Kershaw again." She leans over and pats Kiki. "Will you two accompany me on a walk around the grounds?"

"Sure." Always ready to agree, he adds, "Let's tidy before we go."

The park hums. Kids are on bikes, grills smoke, music plays, air conditioners hum, and the leaves rustle. The tide is high. Waves crash against the rocks below. They find Gavin and Erica Kershaw stretched in loungers beside their Airstream. Stella assumes coffee or tea in their mugs, but she has known Mildred Fox for far too long to guarantee the contents of anyone's drinking vessel of choice.

"Hi folks. How goes the battle?" Her goal is a casual talk. Gavin knows she's part of the investigation.

His wife frowns, but Gavin jumps from his chair and approaches. "We're good. We enjoy your hospitality. Listen." He glances back and lowers his voice. "Listen," he repeats. "This is what I saw yesterday. I hoped you might show up on your walk."

"Sure, Gavin. What?"

Nick takes Kiki across the lane into an open lot.

Erica sits straighter in her chair. "Don't gossip, Gavin. Stay out of the mess."

"Please ignore her." He flicks a hand in Erica's direction. "Evan Fleguel must be involved in your murder investigation. I'm certain."

"Why, Gavin?"

"Every time I turn around, he's disappeared. I used my truck and searched for the town vehicle yesterday. I found him over at the funeral home in Port Ephron." His eyes widen. "The funeral home, for God's sake!"

"What did you do?"

"I watched. He didn't recognize me because I drive my personal pickup."

He points. "No signage. They pay me extra while I'm here."

She's uninterested in his financial arrangements with the Town of Shale Harbour. "What did you see?"

"Him and another guy. I asked Tyna who the fella might be, and she suggested Luther Greene."

Stella doesn't react. "Luther Greene and Evan Fleguel met yesterday?"

"Yup."

"Anything else?" She sees Nick, out of the corner of her eye, on his way back from his short walk.

"Nope." He shoves both hands in the pockets of his shorts. "But I figured my observation might be important."

"Thanks, Gavin. If you remember any other details, call. Every bit helps." She waves toward Erica, whose scowl proves difficult to miss, before she takes Nick's arm.

On their return, she mutters her response to Nick's unasked questions. "Gavin Kershaw has followed Evan Fleguel around. I bet he wants the guy's job."

The phone jangles as they tumble in the door. She runs to the office. "Shale Cliffs…."

"Will you meet me for lunch tomorrow? We should talk."

"Sure, Trixie. What's the problem?"

"I'll tell you over a glass of wine. Val worries me."

Stella's mind returns to her exchange with Brigitte, and Trixie's paranoia over money.

"At the café?"

"No. Too many big ears," she whispers. "The hotel. Noon."

"Okay. May I collect you?" One less day on the planet where Trixie's behind the wheel.

"Not on your life." The phone dies in her ear.

****

The Cocoa and Café station wagon, angled in front of the Harbour Hotel at five minutes to twelve, strikes her as odd. Stella settles the Jeep into a space nearby and wonders why Tiffany or Andrew Blair conduct business here at lunchtime rush hour. When she opens the screen door, she comes upon Andrew and Pepper, heads together, at the registration desk. One might describe Andrew Blair as a man of minimal stature. Pepper, from behind reception, looks as if she's perched on a box, although Stella knows she isn't. When they notice her approach, the discussion ends, and Andrew makes his goodbyes with unusual haste.

"Didn't mean to interrupt. Has my sister arrived yet, Pepper?"

"Yes. There's a group of managers from area fish plants booked. The front will be busy. She's in the back. Andrew dropped off two cheesecakes for me. My chef couldn't find the time."

"Sounds great," Stella replies, to the unnecessary information about reservations and cheesecakes, before she nods toward Andrew. "Nice to see you. Hi to Tiffany."

She finds Trixie in the dining room furthest away from reception. Stella stops at the door and watches her sister while she conducts what appears to be a serious dialogue with herself. "Been here long?" She squares her shoulders and makes as casual an entrance as she can muster.

"Half an hour. Why are you late?"

"You said noon. My watch shows noon."

"Eleven-thirty. I've waited and waited. Pepper!" she screams.

Stella expects the people two floors above can hear her. "Quiet, Trixie. She'll be here in a minute. She's serving other diners."

"I want another glass of wine," she states, her gaze fixed over Stella's shoulder through the private space doorway, as Pepper appears.

Stella twists in her chair and assesses Pepper's response. The young woman's blank expression reveals her thoughts.

"Right away, Trixie. And for you?" She turns her attention toward Stella and her wide eyes blink.

"Tea, Pepper. Any herbal variety will be fine." She winces. "Something calming."

"Chamomile and a white wine refill." With a swish of her ponytail, she's gone.

"Trixie. What's the matter with you? You were rude."

"The girl's been out in the hall, chatting up Andrew Blair, or vice versa, ever since I arrived. No wonder Eugenie Charlebois doesn't promote her."

A discussion regarding the owner of the Harbour Hotel and how she takes advantage of Pepper Ferguson's good nature must wait for another day. Stella pushes back her chair and crosses her legs. "Well, why did you call this tête-à-tête?"

"You told Brigitte I shouldn't babysit Mia anymore. She's registered my granddaughter in daycare, if you can imagine. I don't want my granddaughter in daycare." She huffs and accuses in one breath.

"Here comes Pepper. Relax." After they order the lobster salad, Stella attempts an explanation. "I never advised Brigitte. She told me her plan because she felt traumatized the day you forgot Mia."

"Accidentally," she shrugs. "I fell asleep on the couch. I promised her no more dozing on the job."

"And you've not remembered to pick her up from Yellow House."

Trixie sips her wine and pouts. "Twice. No big deal." She fiddles with the pearl button on the cuff of her blouse.

"Brigitte needs reliability, and you fill your life with other pressures. Don't concern yourself with Brigitte or Mia. She must adapt, eventually, to the idea that Mia will start kindergarten in seven months, and a new era begins. They might as well practise now as later."

Her sister munches on her salad. Her eyes remain focused on the Royal Albert Silver Birch dinner plate.

"Any issues at home, Trixie? Are you under strain that you haven't mentioned?"

"Val acts mad at me most of the time, and when he's angry, I'm flustered." She shrugs again. "I might ask him to leave because he isn't the same guy anymore."

"How so?" Stella appreciates Val's struggles with Trixie's memory problems. She also possesses a modicum of understanding about early-stage dementia. Stress often exacerbates the condition. In no time, the result becomes a pressure cooker for the family.

"He says my memory's on the fritz, Stella. He called me stupid the other day." Tears puddle and threaten her makeup.

"Oh, Trixie. How unfair of him. Let's be honest, though, between the two of us. When you recall Dad and how he acted before I moved back here, has your memory ever failed you in the same way? Can I help you cope?"

"I possess flawless recollection." She flicks her wrist at Stella. "I need less stress. And a boyfriend who won't steal from my wallet, and one who comes home at night and doesn't gallivant at all hours." She slugs the last of her wine and leans across the table. Fabric from her blouse rests on her unfinished lobster salad. "I should tell you that the night of Vic Staples' murder, Val never came home. I'm sure he spent the entire time out somewhere."

Stella's heart pounds. "Where could he have been, Trixie?"

"Val told me you asked him if he and Vic were friends, or if he was aware of Vic's drug business." Her eyes widen as if she's experienced a sudden consequential idea. "I bet he went to Raspberry Farm with Vic Staples and killed him before he walked home along the shore." She pauses and points her finger in Stella's direction. "And he wears a hearing aid, don't forget."

"Hard to fathom, Trixie." She won't encourage the concept with her sister. "Are you sure you're not cross with him and imagined he didn't come home on May 7? The murder happened over a month ago." She hopes Aiden uncovers a solid alibi for the guy.

"He could be your murderer, Stella." She snorts. "Not the first time I've slept with a killer."

****

The clock says ten past nine when Stella races through the living room and answers the phone. She, Nick, and Kiki were curled on the rattan sofa on the veranda, immersed in the soft June air. Perfect nights near the water are a gift. They discussed her lunch with Trixie. An explanation of her sister's behaviours said aloud made them seem more real.

"Shale Cliffs RV…."

"Hi. Home from Port Ephron. Long day."

"I imagine. Cavelle still with you?"

"She moved back to the Painter place today. Besides my domestic trouble, I completed phone calls, interviewed, checked alibis, acted as if I were a proper police detective, and enjoyed an extended lunch with my wife. Certain aspects went better than others."

Stella avoids the bait. "How did the interviews go?"

He murmurs unintelligible words before he begins. "Wally Lavender spent the weekend with his girlfriend, Jill, in Port Ephron. I checked the details. She's a social worker for the province, involved in child protection cases, and I don't suspect she lies. I'm confident in her statement, for now."

"Okay. I didn't consider he could be our guy. And Phil Lewis?"

"His wife says she moves heaven and earth to keep him home after work—the quintessential family man. He's a dead end."

"Any chance to connect with Val Reguly?"

"I talked to him once I came back into town. I sensed a problem between him and your sister."

"Could be." She won't share Trixie's accusations yet.

"He spent the night of the murder at his brother-in-law's."

"Did you check with Theo Gorman? Are you sure?"

"Yes. When I contacted Mr. Gorman, he confirmed Val was with him. He and Vic were in the sauce—not for the first time, from what I gathered. Val called Trixie and told her he couldn't drive home. Theo expected her to come to town, collect him, and retrieve his car the next day, but Reguly insisted she stay put, telling her he would return in the morning. The alibi seems straightforward."

"No chance Val and Theo are involved?"

Aiden scoffs. "Not strait-laced Theo Gorman, except for maybe the over-indulgence. One other curious detail, though."

She waits.

"When I called Philip, he told me he's encouraged council to fire Evan Fleguel because of his frequent absences."

"The idea matches with Gavin, who says Evan's never around, and he ends up stuck with the work." She details her discussion with the contracted engineer. "We need a visit with Evan's wife."

"Agreed, although we've never found a battery connection with him. Who knows? Maybe the battery has no relevance, lost months or years ago."

"Almost time for the news. Ten o'clock." She hopes she's provided sufficient encouragement for him to sign off.

"Don't you want the latest update on Rosemary?"

She closes her eyes. "To be honest, Aiden, no, but go on."

"Appreciate your support."

Sarcasm isn't his strength.

"Rosemary and I discussed my hope that she'll move in with me in Shale Harbour. She's open to the idea, but not right away. She told me she wants her independence, and we should date for a while."

"Sounds smart."

"Not her first time. My Rosie prefers the often-fleeting concept of 'in love' over the day-to-day humdrum of meals and cleaning while I work."

Although well apprised of his history, she asks, "Repeat performance?"

He chuckles. "Yes. I enjoy alternate female companionship when we live apart but invariably re-discover how Rosemary is, and forever will be, the love of my life."

The line between them quiets.

"Did you consider yourself to be the love of my life, Stella? Sorry you're disappointed. You might have been my first, but...."

With flushed cheeks and pounding heart, she struggles for breath. "Everyone needs to be the love of someone's life, Aiden, and I've chosen well. Nick is waiting for me as we speak. I hope you haven't hurt Cavelle beyond repair. She's a wonderful person."

"Cavelle requires work in the focus department. She puts her energies into her career and doesn't leave contribution room for an intimate partnership. She misinterprets the idea of a couple. I expected us to be a team, but Cavelle's a clear team of one." His tone accuses. "Life at the farm means Jewel handles her meals, her laundry, and various other home oversight requirements with superb efficiency."

"And you wanted her to perform those tasks for you."

Her scorn goes unnoticed. "Yes. And she's no good at the art of household management. She said we should hire a housekeeper, like that would ever happen."

"I must go, Aiden." She glances at her watch. "Schedule an interview with Mrs. Fleguel and tell me when and where. I'm happy to attend with you." She replaces the phone in the cradle and saunters back to find Nick in the living room.

He reaches out his hand and takes hers as she curls into his side.

"Have I told you lately," she mumbles into his shoulder, "that you are the love of my life?"

"You are my one and only, too, but what's the trouble?" He hugs her closer. "Can't be a murder investigation discussion with North."

"No. Not murder."

❧

CHAPTER 17

The Realm of Possibility

"Yes?" she squeaks, with the door open a crack. Dressed in a tattered housecoat wrapped across her emaciated body, her dark hair hangs in unkempt strands. With a pasty and mottled complexion, one needn't be a doctor to understand Jocelyn Fleguel isn't well.

"Mrs. Evan Fleguel? Jocelyn?"

"Yes," she repeats.

"I'm Detective Aiden North of the Port Ephron and Shale Harbour RCMP." He acknowledges Stella with a nod. "Meet my community liaison, Stella Kirk. We're investigating the murder of Vic Staples. May we come inside?"

"I prefer not. I feel sick and don't want visitors."

Aiden places his hand on the birch slab entry door. "We won't take much of your time."

The home is a three-level split, built within the last two years in a modern subdivision away from the water. Jocelyn leads them into a living room furnished with white leather couches and oak accent tables. A plush area carpet in a pale green oriental style pattern with tassels on either end covers the maple hardwood floor. Evan's sick wife perches on the edge of a coordinated chair and waits.

"We're sorry we've disturbed you, Jocelyn. I expect Evan's at work today?"

"No idea. He comes and goes as he pleases. I am not at my best. Stella, right?"

"Correct. May I be bold and ask about your illness?"

Her eyes dart between them. "No one knows. I visit doctors, but they can't help."

"Your condition has contributed to weight loss." Her frailness may be normal, but the statement encourages a response.

"I eat but lose anyway and I'm forever tired. I suffer from horrible headaches and my joints hurt. The medical system is useless." She taps her bare heel on the carpet and coughs.

Without permission from their host, Stella rises. "I'll fetch you a glass of water."

When Jocelyn lifts from her seat, Aiden raises a hand. "Don't get up, Mrs. Fleguel. Stella will go."

Garbage sits piled in one corner of the messy kitchen. The remnants of past meals, TV dinner containers, and leftovers cover the counters. She finds an unused glass in the cupboard and runs water into the sink filled with plates and bowls. Jocelyn's ferocious cough rattles throughout the space. Stella scans the room and sees two empty pill bottles with the labels removed, a wee brush which resembles a bottle brush suitable for doll dishes, a dirty ashtray, and unopened mail—in a heap on the chrome trimmed table. Drink in hand, she returns.

"Here she comes, Mrs. Fleguel. Relax and you'll be fine." Aiden glances at Stella, his eyes wide.

The water helps. Her cough subsides.

"Jocelyn, will you describe your husband's friendship with Vic Staples before he died?"

"Did he know Vic Staples?" She studies her glass.

"Can you tell us Evan's whereabouts on the evening of May 7?"

She maintains her focus on her drink. "He often spends the night at the Wigglesworth house." She lifts her face toward them. "Hermione and Jesse are his aunt and uncle. He stays late and sleeps in their spare room." She sits straighter but remains on the edge of the sofa. "They need lots of help."

"And you go with him?" Stella expects her answer will be an emphatic "no."

"Never. Mr. and Mrs. Wigglesworth aren't fond of me." Her chin drops further toward her chest. She refolds the front of her threadbare dressing gown. "Evan isn't sure why. Most of the time, I'm not well, anyway."

"Our information suggests you don't work outside the home, Mrs. Fleguel."

"No. Like I've told you, I'm ill." An edge of annoyance has crept into her tone. "My husband is a professional engineer and therefore I can avoid the job market."

"Children?"

"Not everyone in the world wants children." She leans across the open space and sets her water glass on the coffee table with exaggerated care. "Stella, are you a mother?" She sits back and crosses her arms, as if she's lost patience with her guests. "And you, Detective North? Do you live with a house full of little brats who compete for your time?"

The detective doesn't answer. "Mrs. Fleguel. Will you state your husband stayed at the Wigglesworth home on the night of May 7?"

"I don't keep a diary." She uncrosses her arms and reaches for her water once again.

Stella takes a chance on her next statement. "Jocelyn, Evan never wears his hearing aid."

"Evan struggles with his disability. He won't admit his faults, so avoids the aid. He said he broke the battery chamber when he worked the rototiller at his aunt's house."

Aiden stands. "Thank you for your time, Mrs. Fleguel. Sorry we didn't call ahead. I hope you're better soon."

"Nice to meet you, Jocelyn. Give our best to Evan."

Back in the car, Aiden turns toward her. "Good catch."

"If I acted as if we knew he wore his device, I expected she might relax and confirm. When I went into the kitchen for the water, I saw a miniature brush on the table. I've seen a similar version at Trixie's because Val uses one when he cleans his hearing aid. I took a chance."

"Smart. Now we know there's a possibility Evan lost a battery at Angus' barn. Another option. I'll drop you at the detachment so you can collect your Jeep."

"Evan's potential involvement with Vic could be because of Jocelyn."

Aiden frowns while he negotiates the big Caprice through the narrow subdivision streets. "Evan bought drugs from Vic." She pauses for effect. "Because of his addicted wife."

"I didn't smell any trace of marijuana when we were inside the house."

"Pills."

"What?"

"We could be on the right track. Vic imported other products besides grass, according to the evidence. Assume he met Evan because of weed, but she progressed to stronger drugs. Jocelyn Fleguel has a problem—skinny beyond belief, agitated, twitchy, tired, headaches, eats but doesn't gain weight, plus aches and pains. She can't be much above thirty. She has an addiction, Aiden."

"Okay. Let's schedule a formal interview with Fleguel on Friday. Will the date work for you?"

"I can meet then. Let me know a time."

****

Supper with Cloris and Duke in her trailer. She said no contribution was needed, but Nick found a bottle of white wine. She hasn't been near Cloris' 1978 Vanguard fifth wheel since she moved the rig from storage at the back of the house for the winter, into her lot in the park. Stella isn't sure what prompted the invitation for a meal, but she's curious about the fifth wheel. Duke describes her unit as posh, and Cloris as a stickler for order.

They walk along the main road, arm in arm, and make the turn at the second intersection. Cloris' rig sits at the far end, on the right. The edge of the trees forms her back view and with the elevation, she can see the water from her steps, regardless of what RV parks in front of her—a decent spot.

Unprepared for the landscaping, she suppresses a giggle and leans into Nick's shoulder as they approach. *Oh, no.* Duke mentioned Cloris worked on her gardening and he wished she'd requested Eve's help. Flower beds flank either side of her cement patio stone walkway. She asked permission and Stella never says no to her seasonals' requests, if they keep within their perimeter—and no vegetable gardens. Cloris has "planted" wooden tulips painted in bright colours, and plastic sunflowers where the petals spin in the wind. Besides her pathway borders, she's installed window boxes and filled them with silk ivy and fuchsia. The yard screams trailer park—an effect Stella has tried to avoid since she assumed the reins.

Cloris pushes open the screen door and yells, "They're here, Duke. Come help me. Hi, you two. We'll start the barbecue now. Admiring my work?"

Before she composes an appropriate response, Nick contributes with enthusiasm. "Lots of this style in Florida where the hot weather kills real flowers most of the time. Did you find your collection while you and Duke were south last winter?"

Stella can't help but appreciate how her love has side-stepped, with skill, the opportunity to answer the question.

"Right, Nick! When we were at my place, I decided artificial is the ideal worry-free décor for my lot. Glad you two approve."

Approve? No one approved, but whatever.

"Come inside." She moves over as they mount the stairs. "Welcome to my humble abode." She indicates the interior with her arm held wide.

The Vanguard's as posh as Duke described. She sees a leather sofa, dinette, a gigantic kitchen with every amenity, and an enormous bed situated up two steps from the main level. The bathroom access is off the bedroom. Emerald-green satin square-dancing outfits hang from the closet doors, perhaps in need of attention before their next soirée. Her vague knowledge of the culture and the accoutrements means she refrains from any remarks.

"Take a seat. Let's crack your bottle." Duke returned from the bathroom and reached for the wine from Nick. "Shrimp ready for the barbecue, honey?"

"Yes, John," she grumbles in response. "I invite guests and don't prepare food." She huffs her annoyance. "The potatoes are in the fire pit. They'll be cooked once the kabobs are done." She reaches into her ample fridge and pulls out a plate of shrimp and mushroom skewers.

Cloris scrambles down the steps onto the outside carpet, places the platter on the picnic table, grabs her oven mitt, and, with admirable dexterity, turns the potatoes. She clambers inside the trailer and puffs instructions. "Start now, John. The grill is hot. Where's my wine?"

Stella points at the side counter as Nick and Duke go outside.

"You and Detective North questioned Hermione and Jesse? Correct?"

"Your rule, if I recall from the past, says we don't discuss murder investigations around you, Cloris, but yes, we spoke with the Wigglesworths. They live on the same road as Raspberry Farm. We queried activity on the night of the homicide and the morning afterward—standard procedure."

"I know the couple well." She stops and places napkins and silverware on the dinette table. "After Jesse's stroke, Hermione engaged me as a caregiver, and I helped her with him." She glances at the costumes which hang in the bedroom. "We square danced in the same club back in the day." Her shoulders shudder. Melancholy clouds her eyes. "Jesse Wigglesworth runs deeper than Hermione gives him credit. He can't talk much, but he makes his point. If you interview him, pay attention." She claps a hand to her mouth. "John better not scorch my shrimp. John," she shouts, while her nose juts toward the air conditioner installed in the roof.

"Five minutes, Love. Check the potatoes and we'll be ready."

Cloris drags a bowl of broccoli and cauliflower coleslaw from the fridge and sets the concoction on the table, before she lumbers down the stairs again. Stella watches, safer on the couch for the moment.

Nick, Duke, and Cloris wrestle their way back inside, and dinner is served. While she enjoys lemon and garlic shrimp with mushrooms and a baked potato, paired with the best slaw she's eaten in years, Stella compliments both Cloris and Duke while her mind examines the idea of Jesse Wigglesworth in silent possession of additional information. Did Evan Fleguel really walk from town on the morning after the murder and borrow their car for the return trip home? Makes little sense. Hermione suggested her husband's remarks were the ramblings of an old man. Because of Jocelyn Fleguel, they now realize Evan owns a hearing aid which he may or may not wear. If he appeared at his aunt and uncle's because he'd crept along the shore from Raspberry Farm once the tide withdrew, Jesse's statement becomes within the realm of possibility.

"What?" She hasn't been paying attention.

"Busy summer. Has the new girl worked out?"

"Merrilee Wild? Better than fine, Cloris. I'm happy we found someone. No need for any guilt because you changed your mind. Wise decisions for everyone."

****

She's troubled and needs his counsel. Although a cup of tea on the veranda is a much better idea, poor Kiki spent the evening alone, and she must come first. "Shall we take Kiki for a walk before dark?"

"Sure. Let's review staff performance and discuss my expansion plan." He winks and lifts his hand in salute. "Only with Madam's approval, though."

Her breath catches. Nick's inheritance from his aunt burns a hole in his pocket. Not enough that he renovated the upstairs of the old house and turned the space into a modern primary suite. He purchased fifty per cent of the company from Trixie, too. What now?

She pats him on the chest. "Okay, big guy. I want to discuss Trixie, Rosemary, and the Staples case with you." She smirks.

He hooks the dog to a leash, since park traffic can be heavier after supper, and off they go. Arm in arm, the couple turns left at the first intersection, and strolls toward the far end of the property where Duke keeps his trailer. "You start," she encourages. "I have noticed no issues with staff. You?"

"You told Cloris how Merrilee has worked out. I agree. Paul appreciates the fact she drives him back and forth. She and Eve manage well when they're inside the house together on a rainy day. Agreed?"

"I worried I'd miss Alice more, but because of Merrilee, I'm okay." She leans into his arm while they walk. "I trust her, and she's calmer since she first started. Her nervousness made me uncomfortable for a while," Stella explains.

"Duke and Cloris work somehow. Funny couple, though." He peeks at her with twinkling eyes. "Duke seems happiest when a woman gives him orders."

"Aren't most men the same?" She unsuccessfully smothers her tease. "Now, more traumatic topics, Nick. I'm concerned my sister walks on the same path as Dad, but she's started younger. To be honest, I wasn't around much, and can't comment on Dad's journey. By the time I moved home, his dementia had advanced." She sees the concern in her lover's eyes. "Trixie claims she never noticed a problem with Dad. Brigitte worries and won't leave Mia with her anymore. She enrolled her in daycare until kindergarten begins in the fall."

"Stress for poor Brigitte."

"And, as an addition to our aggravation," she focuses on the ground, "Aiden has sent Cavelle back home. He's invited Rosemary to live with him in the house in Shale Harbour, but she suggested they take their time. They will 'date' for now."

"I'm shocked, Stella. He acted genuine with Cavelle."

As they turn the corner and begin their walk along the next road, she shares the information provided by Mary Jo when the Deena Finch case concluded. "I didn't tell you because I assumed she exaggerated."

"Aiden North, a philanderer. Honest to God, Stella, I never pegged him. I'm shocked."

"Rosemary won't make life miserable for either Cavelle or me, according to Aiden, but I expect he's wrong. His judgment is poor lately. He was sure one of the women from the bridge club killed Deena Finch. Later, he changed his mind and suspected her sister. Once we knew her son, a victim of long-term abuse, possessed opportunity, the case seemed obvious." She stops.

"Enough of Deena Finch. Now, he still considers Angus Raspberry our prime suspect in the Staples investigation."

"You don't agree."

"No. Aiden's lost his focus. Anyone with a hearing aid, a battery-operated watch, or a hand-held calculator could be our perpetrator. First off, Angus owns none of those objects and he didn't hide under the barn when the police came. He called them. I can't contact Hester because she wants a resolution and we've made little progress."

"Do you suspect someone?"

"I haven't put the pieces together. We met Evan Fleguel's wife today. Even though I have no experience with drug addicts, she resembled one."

"How?"

"Hollow eyes. Skinny. Dirty hair. Blank expression. Complained of poor health and how doctors can't help her. Evan also has a hearing aid which he doesn't wear. His disability explains the rudeness and appearance of being standoffish. He can't hear people when they address him if he isn't face-to-face."

"His wife could be on amphetamines, Stella. Lots of prescription use in the US before I left. Enormous problems. Physicians prescribed them like candy."

"I'm convinced Evan knows more. Maybe he accessed drugs from Vic for Jocelyn."

They pass Mildred Fox's dilapidated Cardinal. As usual, she's outside, in her basket chair snuggled by the fire, a cup of whatever at her elbow. They wave.

Nick whispers, "Hard to believe her poor unit stands up to the winter, but the trailer remains, with Mildred contented for another summer. I guess the adage that 'they don't make them like they used to' holds true."

"Come over for a minute." She waves a flabby arm wrapped in the red floral cotton of her caftan. "I gotta tell you somethin'."

"Sure, Mildred. Hi. What's on your mind?" Stella approaches. Nick and the dog remain behind.

"Remember, I described the guy who delivered my weed and collected the money?"

"Yes, I do. Do you recall information you forgot at the time?"

"No. Nuthin' important. I've seen a man here in the park who dresses like him, and Detective North, too." She cackles. "North's not the weed guy, in case you're worried." Her repeated cackles echo along the shore.

"Funny, my dear."

"The fella lives here." She jerks her thumb toward the road behind her trailer.

"Who, Mildred?"

"Don't know his name, but he owns a big fancy Airstream, dresses in a zippered jacket the same as the one who delivered my stash, and he has a grumpy wife. She goes for walks but doesn't wave or stop and visit."

On the trudge home, Nick mentions the idea of a future park expansion. Stella grits her teeth before she attempts enthusiasm.

CHAPTER 18

Continue Your Trust, Please

Fog-laden mist floats across the yard and brushes against her office window. Merrilee and Eve's soft voices drift into her space. Paul and Nick are at the machine shed and Kiki snuggles in her lap. The perfect day for bookwork. The phone jangles. She hears Merrilee answer with, "One moment, please." The light blinks and her assistant comes to her door. "A lady named Etta Graney is on hold for you."

"Thanks, Merrilee." She reaches for the receiver. "Good morning, Etta. What can I do for you?"

"Hello, Stella," her caller whispers. "I watch my guests when given the opportunity and, although I don't relish a loss of income, Wally Lavender and Luther Greene worked with Vic Staples. I'm sure."

"What's your concern, Etta?"

"Well…Luther and his little boy were over here last night. They sat with Wally on the back step and talked for an hour. Afterward, Wally came inside and called his girlfriend. He sounded worried. They were involved in Vic's business," she repeats. "My theory involves Wally and the recruitment of Luther since Vic died." Her voice flutters. "His girlfriend might be the brains of the group," she gasps.

"Lots of conjecture, Etta, but thanks. I'll discuss your concerns and observations with the detective. We'll double-check the information as soon as we can."

Wally Lavender has a rock-solid alibi, provided Jill Sikes hasn't lied. She's sure Luther isn't involved with the drug business. Why is Etta Graney in a lather? She answers the next interruption before Merrilee has an opportunity. "Shale Cliffs…."

"Angus and I wait in vain for your call every day, Stella. We need a progress report."

"Good morning, Hester. How are you?"

"Busy—with non-existent information." Her unveiled derision trickles along the line. "Come out to Raspberry Farm and I can make you coffee almost as tasty as Jewel's. I practise on Angus."

"Hester, we've established other suspects besides Angus, who *isn't* one." She adopts a stern tone and hopes Hester calms. "Try not to worry. At the time of the murder, you told me you trusted my help. Continue your trust, please."

"Detective North has his thoughts on other situations beyond the investigation. I don't mind sharing Cavelle's devastation with you. Ask her for lunch," she commands.

"Trixie spoke with her."

"Your sister has problems of her own."

"Explain?" Stella regrets her question while she waits for what is sure to be Hester's caustic, albeit honest, answer.

"Serious memory issues cloud her judgment, and she may well be in a relationship with a murderer for the second time in as many years."

"Understood, but Val isn't involved, Hester. He spent the night of the murder at Theo Gorman's house."

"Mr. Gorman might save his former brother-in-law with a lie."

"Hester, I disagree. I told you we have other suspects. Trust me, okay? You and I will visit soon. Say hi to Angus for me, and *trust* me," she repeats. "I expect I've figured out who killed Vic Staples, but the timeline, evidence, and witness statements are still unorganized. Be patient."

"For now." The phone disconnects in her ear.

"Detective North, please. Stella Kirk here." She correctly expected she'd find him in Port Ephron—closer to Rosemary and further away from any chance he might meet Cavelle.

"North."

"Hi. Port Ephron today?"

"Yeah. Lunch with my lady. Are we still on for tomorrow? We've booked Evan Fleguel and his lawyer, someone I've never heard of, for one o'clock in Shale Harbour."

"I'll come, but I want to report two pieces of information right now. They may prove important."

"Whatever. Go on."

She plows through despite her suspicion of his voiced indifference. "I spoke with Mildred last evening. She said a man in the park dresses the same as the guy who delivered weed to her on behalf of Vic Staples."

"Are you sure?"

Satisfied she's captured his interest; she expands her comments. "Mildred identified Gavin Kershaw. We've established Evan has a hearing aid, and he lost a part if we accept his wife's statement. He borrowed the Wigglesworths' car the morning after the murder and Jocelyn can't reliably confirm he spent the evening at home."

"You wonder if Evan Fleguel delivered weed to the homes of old ladies and rolled their joints for them?"

"Possible."

"Big chance for a guy in his position."

"If his wife needed pills, he might have helped Vic out for a better deal and to make more money for himself." She huffs her frustration. "Evan's movements are contradictory, and Angus Raspberry didn't kill Vic Staples."

"You've been talking to Hester, but I agree," he mutters.

Encouraged, she continues. "Etta Graney called me earlier. Her theory is Luther Greene and Wally Lavender are in cahoots. I don't imagine, for one minute, Luther Greene would jeopardize his custody arrangement and become involved. I told her I'd mention the idea when I talked with you, though."

"Call Luther and ask him. I agree with you, but we might as well hear his story. Wally Lavender has an alibi and a reputable girlfriend. Luther could handle Wally's dirty work for a fee. Call him and ask," he insists. "Shall we visit Wally at the job site later?"

"Sure. I'll meet you at the detachment at one-thirty."

Luther sounds out of breath when he answers the phone.

"Hi, Luther. I hoped you were at the funeral home. Stella Kirk here."

"Good morning. I recognized your voice. What can I do for you? Mr. King isn't in the office."

"No need for Mr. King. Detective North and I want clarification of information as part of our investigation into Vic Staples' murder. Describe your friendship with Wally Lavender."

"We're friends, go for a beer, talk baseball. I don't indulge anymore because of the boy. Babysitters are too expensive."

"You called on him last night."

"Mrs. Graney keeps an eye out."

"Your son was with you."

"Yup. Timmy's with me when I'm not workin'." He chuckles. "You wonderin' why I visited Wally?"

"Yes."

"His girlfriend's a social worker and she works with single parents and their kids. I needed Wally's help so I could see about subsidizin' my boy's daycare costs. He gave her my number. I can't make the payments on my salary. Wally suggested I apply for Vic's job and collect garbage. Workin' in town is easier and pays more, but Mr. King treats me good, and I owe him after the mess with my uncle." He coughs. "The pay isn't great until I finish my apprenticeship, though, but then I'll have a future."

"Why didn't you schedule an appointment with the social worker yourself?"

He chuckles again. "Hoped Wally could pave the way. I'm old-fashioned. There are advantages to havin' the right contacts. She called earlier, and she's comin' by today. Without Wally's help, the wait could be two weeks for a callback."

"Point taken. Thanks for being honest. I hope you can access subsidized daycare for Timmy."

Time for lunch. She expects the rest of her day will be a waste, too. Wally Lavender, despite his fancy battery-operated watch, isn't their perpetrator. Luther, Val, and Angus aren't involved, either. The field of potential culprits has narrowed. Although she'd happily confront her primary suspect right away, she respects the importance of the art of pacing. The minute the person becomes suspicious, they could leave town, or worse.

****

Aiden leans against the reception counter while she pulls open the plate glass entry door to the RCMP detachment. Moyer fidgets with papers. Aiden makes jokes Moyer obviously doesn't appreciate. His expression remains blank. Her sympathies lie with the sergeant.

"Hi." Aiden glances at his watch. "Right on time."

"I try." Because Aiden's behaviour often causes an unpleasant sensation in her gut, she focuses on dependable Moyer. "Good afternoon, Moyer. You're busy if the pile of files on your desk is any sign."

"Stacks of paperwork, Stella. You two havin' a talk with Wally Lavender?"

Stella frowns at Aiden, afraid they'll waste their time. "Your plan, right? You never said you changed your mind. He has a solid alibi, in case you don't recall," she mumbles under her breath.

"According to him and his girlfriend, but I'm still suspicious," Aiden justifies.

She relays her exchange with Luther. "Wally bought his drugs from Vic Staples, but he didn't work with the guy."

"Well, let's find out. He's at the new subdivision, past Earlene Marigold's fourplex. I called Fisher's Contracting earlier."

They see Wally pouring cement footings for a duplex. He hands his shovel over to another fellow in rubber boots and approaches the police-issue Caprice.

"Mornin', folks. Borden told me you wanted a word. Still haven't found out who killed poor old Vic, eh?"

"Not yet, Wally, but we're closer." Aiden opens the car door. Wally moves back as he gets out.

No law enforcement officer will sit lower than the person they question. Stella interprets his move and exits the vehicle, too.

"We understand your alibi, Wally. We need more details regarding you and Vic."

His shoulders heave. "I bought weed from him, but once I started seein' my girlfriend, she made me stop. She works for the government and says she can't stay involved with a guy doin' dope." He chuckles. "She's worth the trouble. I didn't buy from him in the six months before he died. We went for a beer, but nuthin' more. Luther Greene often came, too, until the court granted him custody of his boy. Now he's a full-blown single parent. My girlfriend's helpin' him."

"As he said," Stella acknowledges. "And pills, Wally? Vic sold hard drugs?"

"Sure, but not to me." Wally turns back toward the job site. "Are we finished? Cement can be particular with the weather and the time. We want the footings partly set before the rain starts. We were late because of the mist and now the forecast says wet by midnight."

"No problem, Wally. Thanks for speaking to us." Aiden opens the car door and drops into the seat. As he wheels around and off the job site, he sputters, "I still don't trust him."

Exasperated, Stella can hear the edge in her voice. "Did you notice how fast he admitted his previous dealings with our victim? No reluctance. No nervousness. Aiden, he isn't the murderer. I'm impatient for our interview with Evan Fleguel."

Aiden turns toward her. "An engineer, a man with a fancy house and a good job, dabbled in the drug business? Vic Staples ran with Wally, Luther, Cam Keller, and Brad Masterson—blue-collar workers with no prospects. They are far better candidates than Evan Fleguel."

"We decided Cam and Brad weren't involved. I'm sure Luther isn't either. He has a future at the funeral home and responsibilities with Timmy. Wally won't risk his relationship with his girlfriend, the well-paid social worker. They work blue-collar jobs, but with valid reasons for each of them to avoid trouble. Evan, no doubt, has a hefty mortgage and a wife who's sick. More pressure. When do we talk with him again?"

"Tomorrow at one o'clock. When I called, he said he's hired a lawyer because our investigation borders on harassment. He gave me a name, a woman, but I can't remember her details."

"Evan dresses in the way Mildred described, and I still wonder why he walked to the Wigglesworths' on the morning after the murder. His behaviour makes little sense. Jesse says he trudged out to their house, visited, and borrowed their vehicle. Evan claims the old man has lost touch with reality, although Evan's wife suggests he wasn't home. I won't be happy until his movements align. Now, I'm curious. Why the afternoon for his interview? We prefer mornings."

He faces her after he pulls the car into a space behind the detachment. "On a hot date tonight and expect I'll be late."

She turns toward him but remains quiet.

"I've planned a dinner here in Shale Harbour, at my home, with Rosemary. Toni will drop her off before she visits Mary Jo. I suggested Toni plan on a dark drive back to Port Ephron." His eyes widen.

"For God's sake, Aiden. Settle down. You're not a horny teenager."

"Jealous?"

His guffaws continue as she climbs into her Jeep.

****

"Fleguel and his fancy lawyer are in the conference room, Stella. Detective North said I should call him when you arrive." Moyer grabs the phone.

"I'm here," she shrugs. "I'll wait for him in the hall." She stands beside the glass window, which provides a view into the area where the pair sit. They face the hallway, but lean close together while they confer, and don't notice her. Stella makes a quick assessment of the scene. Dressed in khaki pants, a golf shirt, and a beige zippered jacket, Evan presents as the picture of Mildred Fox's description. As for representation, Stella has no clue who the woman might be. Her suit, briefcase, and bag suggest expensive tastes. Her haircut and blond highlights are courtesy of a high-end salon. She has flawless skin and faultless makeup.

"He's lawyered well. Her name is Courtney Abraham. She comes from the city, but her firm has an office in Port Ephron. I don't imagine she's cheap," Aiden mutters on his approach toward her.

"Here we go." Stella's stomach lurches. Although convinced of Evan Fleguel's involvement, Aiden isn't on board. She will exercise caution with her questions, although certain he bought weed and hard drugs for his wife from Vic. He was a customer in the same way Wally Lavender and Mildred purchased for themselves. His normal attire resembles Mildred's description of the man who delivered her cannabis and rolled her joints.

Stella enters first and extends her hand. "Good afternoon. I'm Stella Kirk, a consultant for the RCMP in the murder of Victor Staples."

"Courtney Abraham, solicitor for Mr. Fleguel. Nice to meet you."

"Detective Aiden North."

"Nice to meet you, as well." She turns toward Evan, who remained in his seat throughout the introductions. "And you've both met my client."

Aiden nods and motions to the chair at the corner of the oval table for Stella while he sits across from the pair.

Ms. Abraham slides a single sheet of paper to Aiden.

Silence settles while he reads.

After a minute, she interrupts. "My letter to the department—a request for no more interviews at home, at a police station, or at my client's place of employment without me present, including any visits with Mrs. Fleguel. I will now schedule and approve all contacts from law enforcement."

"Ms. Abraham, we decide the when and where of meetings. We can call before we come, but your clients must ask for your presence. We don't make appointments with lawyers."

Courtney brushes a strand of hair from her cheek and straightens her tight skirt. "I expect a judge would enforce my terms."

"Let's hope to avoid any issues, Ms. Abraham." Intimidation tactics carry no sway with Aiden. "Our investigation has revealed contradictions in Mr. Fleguel's statements from past interviews and discussions. Today is the time that we will sort those details." He nods toward Stella.

"Evan. Verification of your whereabouts on the night of May 7 has become an issue. Jesse Wigglesworth told us you walked into his yard on Saturday morning, May 8, and borrowed his car for the drive home." She squints. "Your wife claims you weren't at your residence on the evening in question and spent the night at the Wigglesworths' home after a day where you helped them in the garden. You insist you were at your residence."

He turns toward Courtney. She whispers into his ear.

"Jocelyn suffers under the cloud of an unknown illness, as you no doubt noticed, and Uncle Jesse endures the consequences of a stroke. He makes no sense most of the time. They're both wrong. I spent the night with my wife."

"Are you acquainted with Angus Raspberry or visit his farm?"

Again, he confers with Ms. Abraham, who whispers.

Stella wonders if he hears the questions in their entirety, or if he catches specific words and his lawyer provides the complete sentences.

"Never been to the place. I recognize Angus if I see him."

"Your wife uses cannabis and amphetamines which you purchased from Vic Staples." Stella lets her accusation rest like a dark cloud in the middle of the table.

"Ms. Kirk, can you prove such a statement?" Courtney touches Evan's wrist when he leans forward in his chair.

"We met Jocelyn. She complains of sickness, but her symptoms could result from drug use." She hopes he assumes they possess facts, which they don't.

Evan turns. His face flushes.

Ms. Abraham whispers in his ear again.

"You're no medical person. We thought her condition might be MS, but the doctors say no. Seems easier for them when they tell us what isn't wrong with her, but harder to find a diagnosis. Why would I buy her drugs, for God's sake?" He blushes and tugs at his collar.

"But you knew Vic."

"He worked for the town and ran machinery on job sites for me when we were short-handed—another guy on the crew."

Aiden's tone elevates. "Do you wear a hearing aid, Mr. Fleguel?"

Evan's eyes widen. Stella observes the squirm.

"No." He turns from side to side, pointing first one ear toward them and then the other. "As you can see, no junk in my ears."

"You own a device." Stella's bluntness matches the level set by Aiden.

"Tried, but hate the damned contraption—piece of crap, won't work, chafes my skin."

"Mr. Fleguel, we will give you a last chance before we compile your statement. You were at home the night of May 7 and did not arrive at the Wigglesworth property on the morning of the eighth, needing a ride into town. Are you satisfied with these facts?"

"My client has stipulated as to his whereabouts," Courtney interrupts. "Mrs. Fleguel's condition fluctuates, and she rarely recalls details. Jesse Wigglesworth proves unreliable most days. Once my client's statement is prepared, call me and I will deliver Mr. Fleguel for a signature." She stands, nods toward Evan, and steps out from behind the table.

Aiden reaches for the phone.

"We can see ourselves to the exit, Detective. Good day."

Once they leave, Stella spits, "She won't let him sign. He's lied, and she's aware, or at least suspects. Cloris told me people don't give Jesse Wigglesworth enough credit. She said he understands more than you might realize. We should talk to him again." She frowns. "And Evan matches the description of the fellow who delivered Mildred's weed."

"Evan wore a brand new jacket to the interview. The folds from the package were obvious. I hate those creases," Aiden scowls. "And how is Cloris mixed up with the Wigglesworths?"

"She provided caregiver help after Jesse's stroke. She told me we should pay closer attention. He's smart and understands but has a challenge expressing words. I want to talk with him again—and Hermione, too. I wonder if she'll cover for Evan. Hard to decide."

"I'll schedule a visit for Monday and collect you from the park."

CHAPTER 19

A Thankless Role

"Cavelle's here. She's a mess. Can you come over? Right away?"

Before Stella answered her kitchen phone after her staff departed to begin their day, she had expected the enjoyment of a moment's peace with a third cup of coffee. The herd would return for their break at ten-thirty and a walk around the park with Kiki was her plan. Now Trixie's on the horn.

"What does Cavelle want from me? Aiden's made his choice, and she must live with his decision, despite the cruelty." *Might as well state the facts.* "How long has she been back at the farm? Three days? Cavelle must accept the circumstances and move forward, Trixie. Everyone's been through a failed romance."

"Not you. My years of heartbreak are common knowledge, but not you."

Stella swallows a personal and private lump of disappointment. She appreciates Cavelle's pain because of an affair she experienced when she worked in the city, before she moved home and dealt with both her father and the park. She avoids any historical revelations. "Whatever. Are you sure you want me in the mix?"

"Yes. She's a blubbery mess and I'm not at my best."

"Okay. Give me thirty minutes." She races from the kitchen into reception, where she finds Merrilee behind the counter with Kiki on her knee. Although she knows her assistant heard every word, she repeats Trixie's request. Can Merrilee manage coffee break and start lunch if the office isn't busy? She'll be back by noon.

Merrilee, always dependable, nods her enthusiasm.

"I'll take Kiki outside with me and find Nick or Duke. One of them should mind her. You don't need her underfoot." She scratches Kiki's ears. The dog leans into her hand but doesn't move from her spot.

"I can keep her, Stella. She and I are buddies, aren't we, Baby Doll?" Kiki licks her finger.

On the way toward the parking lot, she meets Eve. "Please find Nick and let him know I've been called over to Trixie's for an hour and will be back by lunch."

"No problem, Boss. I planned on meeting them at the shop after a quick trip to the bathroom. I'll tell him."

During the five-minute drive, she considers her lack of surprise. Cavelle's a mess. No wonder. Earlier in the affair, she imagined potential consequences—Rosemary's threats escalating. Wrong. Until Mary Jo's revelations regarding Aiden's habits, she never saw Cavelle as the victim of a break-up.

Trixie answers the door and whispers, "I've never seen her this wretched. I'm afraid she might hurt herself." After a quick tug on her red leather miniskirt, she trots ahead of Stella.

Under-dressed in blue jeans and a sweatshirt—Saturday attire—and now worried for Cavelle's personal safety, Stella follows her sister into the small sitting room off the kitchen, a place most often reserved for family, particularly Mia. She sees Cavelle, rumpled and untidy. Stella smothers her shock. She didn't consider their friend capable of a state of disarray, regardless of the circumstances.

"Hi, Cavelle. Trixie called and said you asked for me." *Ask a question with an obvious answer.* "How goes the battle?" Without her signature thick layer of foundation and eye shadow, Cavelle appears ghostly and plain.

Blotches of redness rim her eyes. She brushes shed tears away from her cheeks while she gazes at Stella from her perch on a leather ottoman.

"Our friend needs an explanation." Trixie takes a seat on the edge of a recliner and leans forward. Her posture exposes ample cleavage beneath the white blouse. "I can't explain him to her. I'm not Aiden's colleague." She shakes her curls. "Help Cavelle understand. Sit. I'll bring coffee." She taps her way toward the kitchen in absurdly high heels.

"Why, Stella?" Cavelle whines. "I can't believe what's happened."

"Not your fault, Cavelle. You're collateral damage." She struggles with the information in her possession. Mary Jo's words echo, but she won't repeat them here. Aiden's admission he uses women and fills a void when Rosemary's mental health deteriorates can't be part of her explanation, either.

"You landed in the middle of a marriage which serially flounders. Aiden yearns for Rosemary to be a stable and normal wife. She isn't. He's often discouraged, but when a new medication or therapy comes along, he starts the process again."

"He said he loved me." She grabs a tissue offered by Trixie after she hands Stella a cup of coffee and reclaims her spot on the recliner. "I adored the way he treated me." She pauses. "I must admit, he struggled with the idea I don't keep house." She shrugs. "My personal weakness, I guess. Opal managed our home. Jewel came along after Opal—you two understand. I don't cook, clean, or do laundry. I assumed he understood I wasn't his housekeeper. I'd pay for hired help, but apparently, I'm an alien species because I can't mop floors or make bread."

"Cavelle. It is my considered opinion that Aiden yearns for a traditional marriage where his wife stays home and manages the household. Rosemary fills the role when she's mentally fit."

"Which isn't often, these days," Trixie mumbles.

Stella continues. "The minute Rosemary shows the faintest signs of competency, he runs right back. Although their personal history is none of my affair, you are likely not the first woman dropped upon Rosemary's return to the land of the sane."

"You mean he's lived with other women when Rosemary's in hospital?" Cavelle's eyes darken with anger.

"No direct knowledge, my friend. I suggest he wants his wife back when she's well."

Trixie leans across the space and pats Cavelle's knee. "Don't worry. You aren't alone. Val will get his walking papers right after Brigitte's wedding."

"What? Trixie, you're joking." Stella gasps, unable to suppress the shock in her voice.

Her sister's glare could frighten dogs and little children. "I'm sure," she huffs. "He steals from me, and I refuse to support his sorry ass anymore."

Without direct acknowledgement of Trixie's venomous remarks, she turns her attention back to Cavelle. "I won't give you advice, but I foresee no chance of a reconciliation. Forgive my bluntness, and I guess this is advice." She squints. "Move forward, not backward. And don't," she inserts as an afterthought, "jeopardize your personal well-being for Aiden North."

"And if Rosemary goes off the rails again, and lands in the hospital?"

Aiden won't pursue Cavelle another time because she can't manage his home for him. She's too focused on her career, but Stella avoids information shared by Aiden. "Run. Don't let Aiden take advantage, Cavelle. You are much too fine a person." *More advice.* She stands before she addresses Trixie. "Thank you for the coffee. We can talk later, but Val Reguly is a good guy, and he doesn't steal from you."

Back home, she decides another discussion with Brigitte will be in order, but with her wedding in twelve days, she'll avoid any potential conflict for now.

****

She stares at him, paying minimal attention, while he prattles. Aiden arrived for coffee and a case review as the staff departed for their various tasks. In desperate need of a trim, his white hair hangs across his brow. Both hands clutch the pottery mug. He slurps and chatters, twitches and squirms. Rosemary spent the weekend. Toni drove her into Shale Harbour and returned home to Port Ephron alone after her visit with Mary Jo. She was angry. Selfishly, he didn't care. Rosemary might move in with him soon, so Toni needs to get used to being alone again.

"Any contact with Cavelle?" She regrets the question the moment it escapes her compressed lips.

"The woman calls every five minutes." Stella hears the annoyance in his voice. "I unplugged my phone. Didn't want any interference with my weekend."

"Can't have interference," comes her deadpan response.

"Have you seen her?"

"Yes. On Saturday. Cavelle doesn't understand she performed a stopgap for you until Rosemary improved." Stella continues, albeit with an unsteady voice. "If you took time and explained your habit of seeking solace in between bouts of sanity, she might back off." *Temper your attitude.*

"Stella. Rosemary's stable right now. Cavelle filled the crazy space for the moment. I'm well done with her. Accusations, when not at an interview, don't become you."

Each word emerging from his face is more unbelievable than the last. She points a trembling finger. "Your behaviour toward Cavelle doesn't become you either." She swallows the urge to punch him. "More coffee? Let's discuss the case." *Deflection.*

He holds his empty mug aloft. She turns her back on him while she refills their cups, realizing she's missing the fortitude necessary to manage their partnership much longer. Relief clears a pressure in her chest when she accepts her truth. She'll keep her promise to Hester, then tell Aiden she's done. Hopefully, Essie Matkowski returns, and she'll be dropped off the hook from which she now wriggles.

"The murder of Vic Staples didn't involve Angus Raspberry." *State the facts as you see them.*

"Agreed, Stella. Let's focus on potential partners in Staples' business enterprise. Wally Lavender, Luther Greene, Evan Fleguel, Cam Keller, Brad Masterson and even Tyna Derhay are possibilities. Maybe the neighbours, River and Saffron?" He squints.

"Boarding home residents and Luther aren't involved, either. They each possess more motivation to stay clear of illegal activity. Wally respects his social worker girlfriend, Jill Sikes. Cam went to jail once and said he'd never take a chance and repeat his performance. Brad works hard so he can gain more access to his little girl. Luther's responsibilities as a single father colour every act he accomplishes. Tyna? They had a rocky split."

"We checked her phone records and spoke with her mother. She called Halifax from home at the time of the murder." I guess she's on the no-list.

"I bet on Evan Fleguel, Aiden. Jesse Wigglesworth's interview will be worth the trip. He's more astute than we assumed. I'll pay closer attention when I ask him questions. You can keep Hermione company."

After a quick check with Merrilee, they make the drive to the Wigglesworth property, on the road to Raspberry Farm. Vic Staples' murder occurred on May 7 and today is June 12. For Angus and Hester, time passes slowly. Hester's potential regression is possible, despite the gains she's made over the past two years. This case requires a resolution sooner rather than later.

As they motor along in silence, Stella studies the man beside her. Over recent months, light has revealed sides of him which have created unwelcome revelations for her. She always considered her friend and high school lover a patient person. Once they became reacquainted after he moved to Port Ephron, he admitted how he had spent his life battling chaos and the misfortune of mental illness in the woman he loves. She saw him as long-suffering, and frequently experienced pity for his lot. Mary Jo, in a private revelation after the Deena Finch investigation, shared his philandering side. Now, she's observed first-hand his behaviour with Cavelle Painter, and concludes she possesses little understanding of Aiden North.

Evan Fleguel killed Vic Staples. She's certain. Once she talks with Jesse, she'll make better arguments, and they can close this file. Her consultation services with the department will cease for good afterward.

"You're quiet," he remarks, while his eyes remain focused on the windshield.

"Contemplation. Perhaps, while we're at the Wigglesworth home, you could show an interest in her guns. Don't be the cop who will confiscate her arsenal—feign enthusiasm and give me time with Jesse."

"Right." He turns toward her and winks. "Now you're the chief detective. Giving me instructions?"

"As Hester suggests when she educates me on a certain topic—a thankless role."

****

They find River and Saffron seated on the patio swing sofa, keeping company with a bent and blanket-covered Jesse, huddled in his wheelchair. Hermione must be inside. They're expected.

"Good morning, everyone. Beautiful day." Stella climbs the ramp and stands against the rail where she knows Jesse, who stares at his lap, can see her.

Aiden follows and sits in the empty lawn chair near the swing. "Hello, folks."

"Visits from the police make me nervous," Saffron simpers, to no one in particular.

"They're here for a yak with Hermione and Jesse, my dear. No help needed from us." He stands. "We must be off. Hermione's made you coffee." He reaches for Saffron's hand and hauls her to her feet. "We'll visit later, Jesse. You keep out of trouble." He pats the old man's covered knee, and they make their way along the ramp, hand-in-hand.

Stella notices they're without a vehicle and follow a well-worn path toward the cliffs, which must become a shortcut to their property.

"I'm here. I'm here." Hermione surveys the deck. Her frown communicates volumes.

"Your neighbours left for home. They said they'd come back later." Stella takes the offered mug and reaches for a pitcher of milk. She squints at Aiden.

"Mrs. Wigglesworth, let's have a look at your gun collection."

She gasps. The jar of spoons rattles in her hand.

"Don't worry. I expect your paperwork's in order, and no one's been shot," he sputters.

Stella hopes Hermione doesn't notice his nervousness.

"I own collectible rifles you might appreciate."

"Perfect." Aiden stands, cup in hand, and follows her inside.

Stella hears a muffled, yet satisfied, snort while Hermione leads the way.

"Now we're alone, Jesse. Anything you need before we talk?" She isn't sure he's able to communicate with enough precision for any revelations.

He shakes his head and lifts deep blue eyes which meet hers. "Evan," he mumbles.

"Well, you're preceptive, Jesse. Will you tell me what happened the morning after Vic Staples' murder at Raspberry Farm?"

Deeply veined and arthritic fingers fumble with the blanket which slides from his knees. Stella sets her mug on the table and assists him.

Once secured, he holds both hands together. Stella assumes this is a fruitless attempt to avoid further trembles. He meets her eyes again. "People, Hermione in particular, act as if I'm stupid."

"Not me, Jesse."

"No, not you. Evan says I'm confused."

"Yes."

"Wrong."

"I agree with you. The reason for our chat."

"Talk with Hermie." He lowers his eyes again, as if the effort of lifting his chin puts a strain on his neck muscles.

Stella leans closer. "She might cover for him, and in the end, such behaviour could be bad for her."

His lips turn up at the corners.

She hears Aiden as he admires a gun Hermione calls a Savage. "Describe the morning of May 8 in your own words, Jesse. Take your time."

The clock in her mind ticks without mercy, but she won't hurry the man. He will tell her the story and she'll prevent Hermione's interference if the point comes when Aiden no longer successfully keeps her occupied.

"Evan arrived early that morning—dirty and twitchy." Jesse gasps for air but continues despite his struggle. "He said he walked here because he couldn't sleep and borrowed our car to drive back home." He stares at his hands, in obvious exhaustion from the words.

"Jesse, are you convinced he lied?"

Curved shoulders heave. "Evan takes pride in how he's turned out."

"And he wasn't?"

"He tracked sand. More work for Hermie. Blood on his pants and jacket. I see pretty good. The stroke didn't affect my eyes."

"Will your wife agree with you?"

"I've told you the truth She has no choice." He lifts a limp hand toward her. "She's scared. Evan helps on the property. We can't manage alone."

"River and Saffron are nearby."

Jesse sputters. "They're fun when we smoke weed. Not much good otherwise."

"You smoke dope?" Stella gasps.

"Since the stroke." His eyes twinkle. "Don't tell the cop."

"Not on your life." She pats him on the shoulder. "I'll find your wife."

She stands, leans against the door casing and waits until Hermione finishes her story about a shooting competition where she came in second and her father insisted that she performed the best of the contestants. "Crooked judges, Dad said. He couldn't help me, but he made sure everyone understood the win was really mine." Her lower jaw juts forward and emphasizes her point.

Aiden's brow furrows.

"Hermione. Thank you for the coffee. I appreciate your efforts. Your husband is a smart and insightful man despite his stroke and challenges. He has told me the true story of events the morning after Vic Staples' death."

Her face blanches, but she regains her composure. "Jesse doesn't understand the consequences of his behaviour, Stella."

"Consider other avenues of physical support here on your property, or a move into smaller premises, if what Jesse told me leads to charges."

"I'm sorry I avoided the truth. I can't be sure Evan murdered the Staples boy. He appeared here at sunrise with sand on his shoes and blood on his clothes. I loaned him my car. Later, River took me into town, and I fetched it while Saffron stayed with Jesse. We decided we'd avoid any revelations to law enforcement." She glances at the door. "But Jesse, despite my wishes, insists on the facts." Her shoulders shudder. "He likes you."

Back in Aiden's sedan, Stella details Jesse's interview and Aiden radios the station. "Moyer, send a unit. Find and collect Evan Fleguel. He could be in Shale Harbour or Port Ephron. Detain him—now!" Once off the radio, he turns toward Stella. "He was due in for a signature on his statement tomorrow. I can hold him for twenty-four hours and I'd better exercise my right before he telephones his Aunt Hermione."

By the time they reach Shale Cliffs, Moyer has radioed. They discovered Evan at home and a crew has been assigned to deliver him to the Shale Harbour detachment. Thoughts of vindication absorb her musings. Hester will appreciate her determination.

CHAPTER 20

Thin At Best

"Stella, Hester Painter on the line. Shall I tell her you're already gone?"

"No. I'll talk with her." With one foot out the door, on her way to the detachment, she doesn't need Hester's angst now. Although the case has progressed, she feels the time isn't right for suspect revelations. She straightens her shoulders, prepares for the onslaught, which is Hester, and grabs the receiver. "Hi. What can I do for you this early on a stellar Tuesday morning?"

"I want a face-to-face with you and Detective North as quickly as possible—today. A development transpired and both of you should hear from me, because Angus won't enter the police station for fear he'll experience a second arrest," she gulps.

Her shoulders heave while she harnesses her patience. "The RCMP isn't interested in Angus, Hester. I've emphasized repeatedly, he's no longer a suspect. We've identified other candidates. I can't reveal the details. Trust me. What has happened?"

"Not over the phone. Angus brought me home. Will you fetch me and drive me into town?"

"I'm due for a meeting with Aiden for an interview at ten-thirty." She squints at her watch. "If we go right away, he might meet with you for a few minutes beforehand, as a personal favour. I can't deliver you back to the farm until after I finish at the detachment."

"Sitting alone, composed and patient over in the café, I will drink my tea and wait for you. Tiffany does an adequate job with English Breakfast tea. Perhaps after you complete your work, we'll enjoy lunch."

"We'll see how the first half of the day goes, my friend. I'll be at Painter

Farm in ten minutes. Be ready."

"Stella, Stella," she declares. "When am I not ready?"

The phone clunks in her ear.

What additional information could Hester possess? She can't imagine.

"Good morning, Sergeant. Please connect me with Aiden for a moment."

"Sure, Stella. I'll put you right through. Aren't you expected here soon?"

"Correct. An issue's grabbed my attention."

"North."

"Aiden. Hester called. She wants a conflab with us before our interview. She claims she has information but won't discuss specifics over the phone."

"Crap, Stella. This is an important meeting today. I'm not sure floundering around in Hester Painter's world before we meet with Evan Fleguel is ideal."

"Understood, but I told her she could steal fifteen minutes from your schedule."

"Are you my appointment secretary now?"

She hears an expulsion of air as he exhales his annoyance.

"I guess we can spare her some time. Better be good."

Police may hold Evan until noon without laying charges. Hester must make her point regarding her "development" with haste. The woman draws out an explanation and expects her audience's appreciation for the drama and detail. Today isn't the day for her antics.

Hester and Angus continue to hide away at Raspberry Farm. They've taken few breaks since the murder. Hester travels to Painter Farm every morning and works in the gardens. Angus often appears for lunch and afterward she returns with him and helps with his work. They keep a low profile. She has mentioned they want, and probably enjoy by now, an arrangement similar to the one she and Nick have nurtured over the past three years— intimate, but business partners and friends as well. She assumes Hester and Angus' inclinations mirror their own. Without additional information, the circumstances of their agreement become more curious by the minute.

The Jeep rumbles into the lot in front of the American Foursquare. Hester, in a long cotton dress and cardigan, clutches her beige drawstring bag, rises from the front step, and trots toward the vehicle. Jewel and her little boy, Kenny, stand in the doorway and wave. The housekeeper, brows furrowed, stares into Stella's eyes for a moment, telegraphing the distinct impression there's a problem.

"Good morning, again. Hurry, Hester. Aiden will meet with you, but you must be quick. Our interview with a potential suspect takes place at ten-thirty. Besides signing a statement, we want another discussion to clarify his alibi. Can you abbreviate your information for us today?"

"Yes, Stella. You and Detective North need my support with every necessary piece of data for your investigation. Angus suggested I avoid further involvement, but I will go against his wishes. I understand my behaviour isn't wise when judged under the guise of potential cohabitation. He may well view me as a contrary partner and change his mind regarding my inclusion in his life."

"Better you discover his real expectations now, Hester, before a deeper commitment. Can you give me any idea what our meeting will cover?"

"No," comes the blunt retort. "I want both of you together and promise not to waste your time. I risk my future with Angus to ensure you and Detective North receive the total amount of intelligence available from me. What happened with Vic Staples' boat after removal?"

"Forensics took the unit to a compound yard for further tests and examinations."

"Do we know when they'll finish?"

"They don't release seized items until after a resolution but ask Aiden when we arrive at the station. Why the interest?"

"You'll understand soon enough. Now, describe recent happenings at the park. Are you satisfied with your new employee? Have I remembered her name—Merrilee Wild?"

"Hester." Stella steals a quick peek at her friend as they turn off the highway and into Shale Harbour. "Your change-the-subject skills need work. I appreciate your reluctance to share your message until we meet with Aiden. I'll respect your wishes—and Merrilee has fast become indispensable. Thanks to Eve, who introduced us and described the position to Merrilee, her addition to the staff means Shale Cliffs purrs."

"I expected you'd miss Alice."

"Oh, I do. Don't misunderstand. I adore Alice, but Merrilee is a sweet woman and a great asset to the business. My goal, after the Staples case, is more time at the park, and more personal involvement." She manoeuvres the Jeep into a spot behind the station.

"Does Detective North expect Detective Matkowski back at work?"

"Not as far as I know, but a topic for another day, Hester. Let's go inside. Maybe Aiden will meet with us right away. Remember, if you can't wait until after the interview for a ride home, ask the front desk to call Jewel or Angus. They can come into town."

While she rummages in her bag, Hester pronounces, "Jewel taught me the basics of knitting. I've brought my project with me." She holds a green sock, half completed, in the air.

"For Angus?"

"Yes. For his birthday. Don't tell him."

Stella smothers a chuckle. "I could never ruin the surprise." *Good grief! The woman manages the craft with four needles.* She can remember how her mother struggled while teaching her how to knit with two. In desperation, she borrowed a book from the library and learned on her own—another one of those life skills which falls by the wayside as competing priorities and new interests shove them into the background.

They trudge into the station. Moyer stands at the front, in his preferred spot. "Detective North said for you to go ahead." He leans across the elevated desk toward Hester. "He told me fifteen minutes, Hester. You have fifteen minutes. Nice seein' ya, by the way."

She squares her shoulders and meets his gaze. "You, too, Sergeant Moyer. I am honoured Detective North released a moment of his precious time to meet with me. Thank you. I will keep a close eye on my watch." As she moves toward the hallway passage and Aiden's office, she turns. "Don't linger, Stella. Detective North is busy."

****

While they gather in his space, Stella places both chairs in front of the desk and extends her hand, offering Hester a seat. She often sits in the second chair closer to Aiden but sees no reason for such an assessment driven position today.

"You are kind, Stella. I wish I could discuss my chosen topics with you alone, but Detective North features as a prominent player in one of my concerns, and I must address him."

Puzzled, Stella nods.

"Clarity will come in due course." She straightens her skirt and unfastens the buttons on her sweater—a garment too heavy for a balmy June day.

They both turn as Aiden whizzes into the room and skids to a stop behind his desk. Still on his feet, he presses both hands on the wooden surface and leans forward. "Hester. Stella. Welcome to you both. I hope you can be quick, Hester. Stella and I are due in a critical interview in thirty minutes."

Hester sits straighter and raises her right hand toward the detective. "I am here to present a pair of important topics for discussion. Neither will take long, although the second may require an explanation from you. The first topic encompasses potential clues. Shall I begin?"

"Fire away." Aiden collapses into his chair with a thud.

"Someone arrived at the farm two days ago and expressed their desire to purchase Vic Staples' boat. They assumed the vessel remained in the barn after the investigation. Can you tell me the current location?"

"In a police compound yard. Did you know the person?" Aiden glances in Stella's direction.

"Let's complete my story. I couldn't hear any actual words while watching from the kitchen window, but will provide the details as told to me by Angus because he won't come into the RCMP station. He's afraid, and rightly so. The last time he cooperated, you arrested him."

"I dropped the charges, Hester." Aiden's monotone illustrates his lack of patience.

"Too bad Angus did not receive a letter of apology. You scarred him for life." She pauses and frowns. "Shall I go on?"

"Yes, Hester. Who wanted to buy Vic's boat?"

"We don't have a name, or rather, Angus didn't ask. The man never identified himself after Angus told him the RCMP took the boat."

"Did Angus describe the guy?"

"His description isn't a problem, Stella. I watched but couldn't hear. He's in his mid-thirties, although I find age harder to assess the older I become, of average size and build, and nondescript. His clothes—let me recall. She closes her eyes. He wore pressed khaki slacks and a zippered jacket. In terms of behaviour—he cupped his ear repeatedly."

Evan Fleguel went to Raspberry Farm to buy Vic's boat? What?

"After he left, Angus said he resembled the man he observed near the barn with Vic on one night earlier in the spring."

Aiden stands. "Thank you, Hester. As usual, you are a tremendous help and I will undertake, once we close the case, a serious push for a formal letter of apology to Angus from the department."

"Please sit, Detective. I told you we must discuss two topics. The second concerns my sister."

Stella checks her watch. "Shall I find us coffee and tea for you, Hester?"

"I'm fine for now. I will wait for you at Cocoa and Café after we're finished here."

As she lifts one brow for Aiden's benefit, Stella leans into the back of her chair and readies for a showdown.

"Discussion of my liaison—previous liaison—is a private matter, as any smart woman understands."

"Don't patronize me, Detective. The act isn't worthy of your status." Hester bends toward his desk. "I will ignore your remark and push forward. Cavelle put her faith and trust in you. She loved you and you said you loved her. To be clear, you used my sister as filler while your wife, in the throes of serious mental health challenges, pulled herself together yet again. Am I correct?"

Although he bowed his shoulders at the assault of her words, he murmurs, "Not exactly."

"Explain, please." Hester crosses her arms.

"Honestly, I didn't expect Rosie to come back this time. Her sisters and I assumed she'd be in the hospital forever. I've never met anyone of Cavelle's calibre—capable, stunningly beautiful, and driven. I hoped in vain for a chance at happiness for once."

"But you found her lacking because she wasn't interested in acting as your housekeeper."

He blushes. "Yes. I'm old-fashioned, I guess."

"Cavelle needs you to approach her and explain the circumstances around the dissolution of your tryst. Tell her the truth—you never imagined your wife's recovery, and you remain burdened with her responsibility inside the long-term bond which is your marriage." Hester squints. "And don't ask me to represent you. Talk with her. She's humiliated and broken. If you care for her, finish the affair with dignity and grace. Do you understand?"

While she swallows her shock at Hester's forthrightness, Stella uses Aiden's moment of silence and gathers her wits. "Does Cavelle realize the purpose of your trip into the station?"

"No. I don't expect either of you will reveal my involvement. I am judged by many because of my socially inappropriate personality. Our exchange this morning illustrates social inappropriateness in a myriad of ways, and Cavelle shall not discover I intervened. Am I clear?" Her head swivels between the two of them.

"I'll call her later today, Hester. I didn't realize, and will keep your name out of any discussion. Sorry."

"Tell her, not me." With her last statement, she stands, buttons her sweater, and turns toward the closed door. "I'm off to the café to wait for you, Stella."

"Let me walk you to the exit."

"They booked our interview in the conference room, Stella. I'll meet you." Aiden gathers a stack of files.

****

"He's the man," Hester hissed. She grabbed Stella's wrist, an unexpected behaviour at the best of times. They were in the detachment hallway. Stella was expressing her surprise at Hester's directness and complimenting her on her courage when Courtney Abraham slid past them. Evan Fleguel and a constable trailed in her wake.

"Who?"

"The one who asked Angus if he could buy Vic Staples' boat. We noticed a car in the yard and no one around two days ago. Angus went for a look. I saw him run out from behind the barn and then talk to Angus."

"You've identified Evan Fleguel, the town engineer."

"What brings him here? He smells sweaty." She wrinkles her nose. The irony of such a remark uttered by a woman once known for the mustard and berry stains on the fronts of her clothes doesn't escape Stella's notice.

"He spent the night here. Listen." She leans closer. "I can't give you the details right now. Wait for me at the café. Our interview should be over in an hour."

"Stella, I will remain at Cocoa and Café. Please telephone the farm and tell Jewel. She'll worry. No need to alert Angus. He's out on the land and expects Jewel to drive me back to his place later in the afternoon."

"Consider the job done." She pats her friend on the arm. Hester, in a second but still unusual show of comradery, doesn't pull away.

"Moyer, do you have a moment to call Painter Farm? Tell Jewel Winslow that Hester will eat lunch with me at Cocoa and Café."

"Sure, Stella. Is she coolin' her jets at the café until you and North finish your interview?"

"Correct, Sergeant."

"Right. Well, I'll contact the farm before my break. I think I'll wander over for coffee and keep her company."

"A kind gesture, Sergeant. You call me Stella, but I don't know your given name."

"Few folks do. Not sure the detective even knows." He shrugs. "Human resources, I guess. My mother thought the idea was cute to saddle me with her maiden name."

"Which was?"

"Briggs. My mother's maiden name was Briggs."

Swallowing a gasp, she asks, "I should call you Moyer?" She widens her eyes and emphasizes her tease.

"Much preferred, Stella—unless I address you as ma'am."

"Unnecessary. Telephone Jewel as soon as you can. She acted none too happy when I fetched Hester earlier."

"Detective North said find him in his office before you go into the interview. He's waitin' for you."

She turns toward the hall. Evan murdered Vic Staples, but the fact might be difficult to prove. Even with the hearing aid battery and the drugs in the crawl space under the barn, Angus' potential identification of him as the man whom he watched with Vic on at least one occasion, the Wigglesworth couple's description of him the morning of the murder, and Hester's identification of him as the person she saw emerge from the far side of the barn and ask after the boat, there still isn't enough hard evidence. If they could find his bloody clothes or shoes and identify the blood as Vic's, the case stands a better chance of being wrapped in short order.

"You were gone a long time," she hears him grumble, when she reaches his door.

"Hester identified Evan when we passed him in the hall on his way with his lawyer to the interview."

"What? Identified him how?"

"She claims he's the guy who tried to buy Vic's boat from Angus. She said he darted out from behind the barn as Angus approached an unfamiliar car sitting in his yard."

196

"Not formal, but enough for leverage, if necessary. We can't hold him on her ID, though."

"Except the fellow is also the man Angus might have seen with Vic at the farm one night."

"Thin, at best. Not clear cut. Before we go, what's gotten into Hester? I was afraid she would shred me into bits earlier."

Stella keeps her voice monotone and uncommitted. "She could. She went easy on you."

"Somehow Hester Painter thinks, because of her assistance in the past, she can march in here and give me instructions on managing a romantic split with 'dignity and grace'." He mimics Hester's pointed tone for effect.

"She does." Her smug expression pre-empts her next remark. "And she's correct."

"I'll call Cavelle later today and explain what's happened."

"You missed the mark, Aiden. In my humble opinion, you've made an incredible mistake in dropping Cavelle." She winces. "My opinion."

"Rosie's hold on me defies explanation. I may never understand why I can't leave her for good." He pauses and inhales a deep breath. "In sickness and in health, I guess." He jumps from his chair. "Come on. Let's begin our interview right away."

CHAPTER 21

Her Opinion Must Count

"You can't hold him one minute past noon, and I'll see him released as soon as possible. Mr. Fleguel shall sign his statement and leave, Detective North." Courtney huffs her annoyance. Her client sits beside her, hunched, hands clasped, with his jacket zipped, although Stella finds the air heavy.

"Staff typed the document." Aiden opens his file folder. "Mr. Fleguel, we discovered inconsistencies while we conducted our investigation, and we will clarify the discrepancies before you sign." He swivels forty-five degrees and nods to Stella. "Shall we begin?"

"You travelled to Raspberry Farm and your purpose was to buy Vic Staples' boat." Stella remains expressionless while she notes the confusion which clouds Courtney's perfect, unblemished countenance.

Evan cups his ear and leans forward. His chest rests against the conference table. "What?"

His lawyer whispers to him before he answers the question.

"Not true. The craft isn't his property. He told me authorities took any evidence away. I assumed I'd discover the vessel at a police compound auction in due course."

"Are you in need of a motorboat, Evan?"

After a quick check with Courtney, who shrugs, he replies, "I fish when I find the time."

"Your statement says you never fished with Vic."

"Correct. We didn't chum around."

"Why not seek a skiff of one sort or another elsewhere? Why Vic's boat now?" His answers make no sense.

Courtney Abraham holds a manicured finger in the air and whispers again.

"I figured I'd land a deal. A Shale Harbour engineer doesn't earn much money in case you weren't aware."

"No hearing aid today." Stella makes a statement intended to change the subject.

"What?"

Stella taps her ear. "No device." She elevates her voice to accommodate the discussion and move them forward at a quicker pace.

"Like I said before—hate the stupid contraption. Beeps in my ear and people sound hollow."

She pauses and Aiden takes over. "Mr. Fleguel, Angus Raspberry identified you as the man he saw on his property with Vic Staples at least once before the murder on May 7. You stated you were never at Raspberry Farm, but now you say you arrived and inquired after the victim's boat."

"He isn't right in the head," Evan accuses.

"You were not at Raspberry Farm before Sunday, June 13, 1982? You're satisfied with what you've told us?"

"Asked and answered, Detective."

"We're not in a courtroom, Ms. Abraham." Aiden's tone holds an edge. "I can ask the same question twelve times if I choose."

"Now, Mr. Fleguel, witness statements suggest you appeared at the residence of Hermione and Jesse Wigglesworth on the morning of May 8. They saw blood on your shoes and jacket. You told them you walked from town but wanted to borrow their vehicle and drive home."

Aiden and Stella wait in silence as his lawyer once again whispers into his ear while she cups her hand and covers her lips.

"My aunt and uncle are old. I've hiked to their house many times." His shoulders heave. "Jocelyn and me, we fight. Often, I leave the house and walk through the night. I don't remember exact times, but I visit their place on the odd evening. Now they're confused and think I walked there the day after Vic Staples' murder."

Stella can't help but notice his satisfied expression. The muscles in his face relax and the flush in his cheeks recedes.

"Your statement stands? You never travelled to the Wigglesworth property on the morning after Mr. Staples' death?"

"No way. I was with my wife. She was sick, so I stayed with her."

"Please explain your wife's medical issue, Evan." She expects their prime suspect will walk out of the police station and not come back. She needs an angle.

"As I told you before, the doctors don't know. I often stay nearby. I sat home the night of the murder, even if she can't remember."

"She reported you were with your aunt and uncle."

"She forgets. Can I ask a question?"

"Sure." Aiden frowns.

"Why do you care if I wear my hearing aid?"

"We found a battery in the cubbyhole under Angus Raspberry's barn, below the crime scene."

"Manufacturers use those batteries in watches and calculators—different contraptions."

"Correct, Mr. Fleguel."

"Detective North. Based on nothing but speculation, you believe my client murdered Vic Staples and hid under the barn at Raspberry Farm until the police left?"

"A theory, Ms. Abraham."

"There's no proof of such an allegation because you are using vague suggestions and dialogue with witnesses best described as unreliable. We ask permission that Mr. Fleguel sign his original statement, adding his visit to Raspberry Farm on June 13. Afterward, he can attend to his wife and his job. He has been cooperative throughout this ordeal."

"Indeed." Aiden opens the manila folder and draws out two pages. After he jots and initials a sentence at the bottom of the second sheet, he pushes them toward Evan, along with a pen.

"I will read the document first, if you don't mind, Evan." Courtney scans the sheets before she slides them in front of her client.

Stella and Aiden sit in silence.

Evan squints at his lawyer, whereby she nods. He runs a finger down each page as he reads before he signs. After he checks with her for a second time, he pushes both pen and paper back across the table.

Aiden stands. "Thank you for your cooperation, Mr. Fleguel. We may well be in touch again."

"Before you go, Evan, one quick question."

He cups his ear and leans toward Stella.

"Where do you shop? Your jacket seems brand new. Boots, too."

"A men's store in Port Ephron called The Working Man. They embroider logos on clothes for businesses. Shale Harbour gets merchandise with the town crest."

"Your coat doesn't have a logo."

Blushing, he points his finger at the empty spot. "They'll add the logo in a few minutes, the next time I'm in town."

"If he's our murderer, we'll never find proof," Aiden mutters in disgust, as they reconvene in his office.

Stella glances at her watch. Eleven o'clock. Hester's been at the café long enough. Although she emphasized patience, Stella understands Hester's moods and expects her wrath if she doesn't soon arrive for their promised lunch.

"He's our murderer," she emphasizes. "I can sit for a minute, but I imagine Hester's foot has tapped steadily for the last thirty."

"Understood. First—his word against the Wigglesworth couple. The Crown won't be happy."

"Hermione presents as stable enough, although Jesse has challenges."

"Agreed. Second, Angus and Hester don't know for sure the man was Fleguel who queried Vic's boat."

"Hester identified him in the hallway. Her opinion must count."

He frowns. "She saw him from a distance and through a window. Contradicted by a good defence attorney in no time, and from my research, Courtney Abraham comes described as the best money can buy."

"So, I wonder how he's so solvent, if he wasn't partners with Vic? His employment with the town doesn't pay a big salary. He said so himself. They live in a new and well-appointed home. Leather couches and oriental carpets aren't cheap."

"I'm sure he's into an ill-advised sideline, but are we able to prove he sold drugs and killed his partner in Angus Raspberry's barn? Third—the battery we found under the building, and the fact he wears or wore a hearing aid, are both circumstantial, even coincidental. Forensics lifted no prints other than Angus'—from anywhere." He slams the pen, with which he has fiddled incessantly, for the last ten minutes, across the desk.

Stella catches it before it tumbles to the floor.

"Sorry. Listen. I'm scheduled for a meeting tomorrow afternoon with Rosemary and her sisters in the Port and I planned supper with Rosie at the

Purple Tulip. Haven't been there since she melted down ages ago." He grins. "Will you take Moyer and interview Luther Greene one more time?"

"Sure, but to what end? We've established he's not involved."

"He might remember a connection he hasn't shared."

She stands. "Make the appointment for after lunch. I can spend the morning in the park. Tell Sergeant Moyer I'll meet him here and we'll drive into Port Ephron—in the squad car, I guess. Poor Luther. He doesn't need another police-issue parked at Royalty Funeral Services."

****

Hester, seated in the bay window, frowns over her sock project as Stella climbs the stairs into Cocoa and Café. Once inside, Stella taps her friend on the shoulder.

"Apologies, Stella. I dropped a stitch and have been flustered with myself." She leans over her tea. "I believe my beverage has gone cold."

"Tiffany will serve us more, I'm sure. The wait was long. Sorry."

"Sergeant Moyer kept me company. We exchanged detailed information regarding uniforms and advertising."

"What precipitated such a discussion?"

"You'll see when Tiffany appears." Hester studies her project again.

As if on cue, Tiffany marches toward their table. "More hot water, Hester? And for you, Stella?"

"More hot water, please."

Stella and Tiffany exchange glances. "Thanks, Tiffany. A pot of berry blend tea for me and what's the special today?"

"Caesar salad with chicken, and a biscuit. Rhubarb crisp for dessert."

"Hester, lunch will be on me. Is the special okay?"

"Yes, but I'd rather eat my meal off a plate, Tiffany." The faces of other customers in the restaurant swivel toward them in response to Hester's sudden barkish laugh.

"Funny, my friend. You fixed your mistake?" She waves at the partially completed sock pressed against the table edge. "We'll both order the special, Tiffany."

"Not a mistake, in the strictest sense, Stella. I dropped a stitch, I repaired my work, and therefore feel deep satisfaction. Now, did you notice her attire?"

Great, a quiz by Hester. After the morning she's spent with the person she believes killed Vic Staples, quizzes aren't high on her priority list. "Let me see." *Humour her.* "Uncomfortable flats for someone who works on their feet. Tight trousers, and a gold shirt with Cocoa and Café embroidered on the left side above the breast pocket."

"Good job. Evan Fleguel's jacket didn't sport the Town of Shale Harbour logo. Did you notice?"

"I questioned that particular circumstance, and he said he'll have the embroidery completed at The Working Man the next time he travels to Port Ephron."

"Right. His boots were new as well."

"Yes, Hester. What's your point?"

"Where are the old ones? I assume he owns a jacket with the logo and broken-in boots. I'm curious."

"Clothes wear out or become damaged."

"Or bloody. I liked his new boots, though. If my sock project doesn't work out, I might ask Jewel to drive me into Port Ephron to find a pair for Angus."

While they munch on Caesar salad, Stella explains how she believes Evan Fleguel is the perpetrator, although certain details make little sense. Why did he risk a visit to Raspberry Farm? There's no solid evidence he killed Vic.

"You need his old boots and jacket."

"Thanks for the advice, but how do you propose I find clothes he possibly tossed in a dumpster a month ago?"

"Your problem. I've given you an avenue for investigation. Make use of my idea. Now," she plops both elbows on the table, which rocks under the weight, "Angus is no longer a suspect. Angus and I can plan our future?"

After she dabs her lips with a napkin, Stella leans toward her friend. "Wait until the case has a final resolution. If Vic Staples' murder remains unsolved, I agree with your earlier assessment. You and Angus will start your formal life together under a cloud. Plot and scheme all you like but avoid announcements until we sort the investigation out. I have ideas, Hester, but I need your patience. As in the past, you were a big help today. And you did your sister proud, I must say."

Stella detects the bare glimmer of a twinkle in Hester's eyes.

On her drive home, she can't wait to review the latest information with Nick. She imagines his shock when he hears her report on Hester's confrontation with Aiden. Hester can be astonishing.

****

"Hi, Stella. Here's a phone message from your sister." Merrilee hands her a pink slip of paper. "I transcribed her words the best I could. She sounded funny."

"Tell me."

"She demanded an account of your whereabouts. When I said you were at the police station, she became excited and assumed Detective North had arrested you. I explained you were involved in a murder case, and she didn't understand how such a circumstance related to you."

The state of Trixie's mind remains a concern. Paulina's execution by Trixie's boyfriend, and her subsequent purchase of his Craftsman cottage, might have been too much for her. She may suffer a predisposition to memory issues and the experiences of the last two years hastened the deterioration process.

"I'll call her right away. Where's Nick?"

"They returned to work before you arrived."

Balancing a murder investigation, a business, and the thought of her sister's mental collapse borders on overload. Her shoulders drop, and her throat burns while she controls buried emotions. "I'll call her," she repeats, "right away, before I start supper."

"Hello. May I help you?"

"Hi, Trixie. You looked for me earlier?"

"Not me. I've been home today. I haven't spoken with anyone."

Deep breath. "Merrilee said you telephoned. I worked at the detachment this morning, in an interview, and I took Hester for lunch."

"Am I interested in your activities? The wedding's in a few days and you promised your help."

"I did, indeed. What do you need from me?" *She doesn't remember her talk with Merrilee.*

"Do you own an outfit decent enough for the wedding? Don't embarrass the family and wear a sweatshirt and jeans."

"Trixie. I found a gorgeous dress—a pale blue affair. You'll approve, I'm sure."

"Okay. Well, I rang you earlier because I didn't know if you took a moment out of your busy schedule and purchased proper attire." The sneer in her voice is unmistakable.

Now she remembers she called. Good grief! She attempts pacification.

"Don't you need my help?"

"No."

The phone bangs in her ear before she gathers her response into words.

They planned on burgers tonight, a tossed salad, and vegetables with dip. She peers at the clock. Nick took the patties from the freezer and they're thawing in the refrigerator. She pulls buns out and grabs a bowl for the greens. While she washes the lettuce, she analyzes her sister's mental health. Trixie needs a professional assessment. Dr. Visser might accept her as a client if Trixie cooperates. After the wedding, and after they solve the case, she'll explore the possibility of encouraging Trixie, with Brigitte's help, to see someone professionally. She didn't warm to Bram Visser, but Velvet Carmichael thinks he's an exceptional psychologist.

"Paul and I are ready for home, Stella. Are you set?" Merrilee stands at the kitchen door, purse in hand. "No late-day check-ins expected. Should be a quiet evening."

"Good grief! Five o'clock already?"

"Yes. Eve's washing her hands, but she'll be off soon, too. I saw Nick on his way along the path with Kiki, and Duke trotted off toward Cloris' place."

"Roll call completed. Thanks, Merrilee. See you tomorrow." She must come across as absent-minded. Not a confidence-builder for her staff.

"Back in a minute," Nick hollers, as he bounds up the stairs. Kiki rounds the corner on two legs.

"Hi, little one. Are you ready for supper?"

The dog jumps and wiggles. Stella sets her pottery dog dish on the floor and pats her while she eats. A warm hand touches her shoulder. She unbends to greet him.

"Good day?"

"Yes. Perfect. Lots of jobs crossed off my list. The park shines. Best start to a season yet. I've high expectations for the summer." He frowns at her. "But you are a woman who didn't enjoy a great day." He squints. "I pointed out the obvious, right?"

"Let's cook supper and I'll describe where we are in the investigation."

During their meal, she repeats Evan Fleguel's statement. She explains they can't prove the battery under the barn belonged to him. His potential appearance at the Wigglesworth property becomes a case of what they said and what he said. Evan's wife isn't sure if he stayed home. She assumed he went to his aunt and uncle's place, but he claims she's too sick and not aware of her surroundings. Now, Aiden insists she take Moyer to Royalty Funeral Services and discuss Luther's involvement again. "I think more time spent with Luther will be a waste."

Nick remained attentive throughout the meal. "Luther might share a morsel of gossip. You could ask him."

Her breath catches. "We've focused on Luther Greene and his interaction with Vic. They were friends and Vic helped Luther out when he needed a machinery operator for the funeral home." She frowns. "And then there's poor Trixie."

"She's not good, Stella. I think the stress of Brigitte's wedding might nudge her over the edge."

"Agreed. She called today when I wasn't here. Merrilee thought Trixie didn't understand why I could be at the police station unless I was under arrest."

"Did Merrilee mention Trixie drove out here?"

"What? No!"

"She navigated the path toward the shop in her big new car. Trixie has no business on that rutted track with her vehicle." He squints. "And she demanded I describe your dress for the wedding. I revealed not one detail," he emphasizes, while he pats her hand. "I told her our clothes are under control. Paul walked alongside and guided her while she backed up the lane."

"I returned her call. When she asked, I said I bought an outfit. Even revealed the colour. Trixie understood my current involvement in a police inquiry, though Merrilee insisted Trixie thought I was in jail." She leans into her chair and clasps her hands in her lap. "I admit, I'm worried sick."

"Options?"

"After the dust settles from the wedding, I'll discuss her mental health with Brigitte again. We'll convince Trixie to see her doctor and get a referral to Dr. Visser—or someone else, if she prefers. I hope she'll relax and return to her old self, though."

Nick stacks their plates and places them beside the sink. "She was incoherent and confused today, Stella. I suggested I drive her home, but she snarled at me. I expect a fight when you and Brigitte eventually talk with her."

Chapter 22

Incriminating Information

Before Stella leaves on her journey to Shale Harbour, a police squad car rolls into her parking lot with Sergeant Moyer behind the wheel. She throws open the veranda screen door. "I didn't expect you here. Come in, Sergeant."

"No problem, Stella. With me driving, you won't need your Jeep." He glances toward the blue sky. "Nice day for a trip into the Port."

"Yup. Poor Luther will be thrilled when he sees a cop car in the yard at the funeral home." She sympathizes with Luther and maintains her belief he wasn't involved with Vic Staples in any way which would cause a murder. "Can I pour you coffee?"

He fills the doorway but doesn't cross the threshold. "No thanks. We'll make good time if we go now."

She pops into reception and tells Merrilee she's leaving. Kiki went with Nick.

Police cars often smell of sweat and dirty socks. Sometimes worse. Moyer's vehicle is no exception.

"Enjoyed a visit with Mary Jo Frost at her new place the other day. She made her high-test stove-top brew."

"Mary Jo's a kind person, Sergeant. I imagine you had fun."

"Oh, yeah." He takes his eyes from the road and glances in her direction. "She can square dance."

Stella muffles a snort, which puddles out of her face as a grunt. "Did not realize. Do you square dance?"

"Not since my wife and I divorced. Years ago."

"Cloris and Duke are square dancers." She's at a loss and can't contribute more. Perhaps focusing on their interview might be wise.

"She and I'll shuffle up a storm at the next shindig in Shale Harbour. There's one planned at the fire hall in July."

Although troubled by her own lack of sincerity, she attempts encouragement. "Should be fun, and a great time for you and Mary Jo, Sergeant."

"Mary Jo invited me for dinner. She doesn't cook much but says she can make a fine roast chicken. I'm gonna take her flowers." He hums under his breath.

A change of subject seems necessary. "You've met Luther Greene. Did he become involved with Vic Staples in the drug trade business?"

"Wouldn't imagine, Stella, but he dug illegal graves for his Uncle Hector, so who knows? People come in different shapes and sizes, both in the mental and physical departments."

"You, my friend, are a philosopher."

"Mary Jo said the same. Now, my ex-wife, she called me a big lout and hated cops, but I can pitch an idea or two." His eyes remain focused on the road. One would never consider him a braggart.

As they approach Royalty Funeral Home, Stella suggests he and his ex-wife weren't a good match. Support with a statement of the obvious.

The wide garage doors stand open, with a hearse parked half in and half out of the right-side bay. Luther holds a can of wax and a soft cloth, focused on the areas of the vehicle shaded by the building.

Stella exits the squad car and waves. "Morning, Luther. Sorry our visit's unannounced. I only have one or two questions." The sun warms her. She unbuttons her denim jacket.

Luther strolls away from the Cadillac and along the driveway, now empty-handed. "Expected you woulda caught your murderer already." His face clouds. "God, Stella. You guys aren't considerin' me, are you?" He stops and places square, tanned hands on his hips. His voice softens. "You brought the sergeant with you."

"Don't misunderstand, Luther. We're curious what else you've heard. Gossip? Did other people discuss Vic? Speculate?"

The young father squints into the sun. "Vic could gossip circles around the rest of us."

Moyer, leaning back against the front grill of the RCMP sedan, crosses his arms. "What kind of gossip?"

"Listen. Vic said I should work in Shale Harbour, but my boy's in daycare and I'm happy with my job here. He told me he could land me a place on the crew at the town because he knew Evan Fleguel's big secret."

"What secret?" Stella's heart pounds.

"Honest answer? I wasn't interested in the work and had no interest in Fleguel. He made his position clear, though. He said his incriminating information could convince Evan to hire me if I wanted. Mrs. Fleguel suffers most of the time, but I don't know anythin' else."

"Come on, Luther. Didn't he tell you?"

"Nope. Vic sold drugs, and I figured Evan worked for him. No more jobs for me with anybody who carries on illegal activities. I dodged a bullet once. Never again."

"Thanks. You've been a tremendous help."

"Where's the detective today?"

"Oh, he's in a meeting here in town, and couldn't arrange time. My apologies for the spur-of-the-moment visit."

Luther grabs his cloth and can of wax after he saunters back into the building. He flaps an arm in the air. "No problem. Hope you finish with this mess soon."

After she opens the car door, she leans inside. "Hold on, Sergeant." She raises her voice. "Luther, may I use your phone and a telephone book?"

"Sure. Yeah. There's an extension here in the garage." She holds a finger toward Moyer and halts potential questions.

"Right over here." Luther leads her to a corner with a wall-mounted telephone and a shelf for the directory installed below.

She finds the number, dials, and waits.

"Hello," comes the weak answer.

"Hi, Mrs. Fleguel, Jocelyn. Stella Kirk here. I wonder if I could make a visit."

"Now?"

"If not too inconvenient."

"In a few minutes? I'm not dressed."

"No problem. We're on our way back from Port Ephron. Sergeant Moyer and I will be a half an hour. May I deliver coffee?"

"I'd be grateful, Stella. My lawyer said I shouldn't talk with you, but since you called and you're buying me a coffee, a visit should be okay."

"Evan home?"

"He mentioned last night he'd work in Shale Harbour today, but he left before I woke.

"We'll stop at Cocoa and Café and buy one of whatever Tiffany and Andrew conjured in the way of pastries. See you soon."

"Thanks, Luther." She trots back, climbs inside the car, and faces Moyer. "We're off to Cocoa and Café to grab coffees and treats before we visit Jocelyn Fleguel."

"Oh, Stella. We are gonna be in big trouble."

****

"A casual talk with Jocelyn Fleguel was in order. Official police protocol demands there be two of us and I made an appointment. If she doesn't call her lawyer, that's her problem. There's my argument."

Behind the wheel, Moyer's cheeks turn rosy red and develop a chipmunk puff.

"We'll take her a cup of coffee and decide if she knows more than she's shared so far. We've reached a dead end if Evan really stayed home."

The flush recedes as he inhales. His shoulders sag. "She has no idea where her husband spent the night. From the report I read, Mrs. Fleguel's doped most of the time." He turns his thick neck and meets her eyes. "People over-medicate. Happened in my family."

"Right." Stella does not understand but won't satisfy her curiosity by asking him personal questions now.

"Here we are." Moyer pulls the big sedan into a space near Cocoa and Café.

"Can I treat you today?"

"Okay. Thanks, but I'll come with you. You'll never carry three coffees and manage the door."

Tiffany fills paper cups with fresh hazelnut brew, a small bag with creams and sugars, and a larger one with carrot muffins. Stella pays the bill before she and the sergeant take their loot to the vehicle.

"I'd love a house," he swoons. "Theirs is great." Moyer parks in the paved double driveway.

"Where do you live now?"

"In my sister's basement. After my divorce, I couldn't afford a place of my own. I help her out and she gives me a break on the rent."

"Ownership takes time, especially with interest rates nowadays. I've never bought property. I moved into my parents' house. Still use my mother's dishes."

He turns off the engine and answers with a toothy tease. "I guess neither of us has been a success in the real estate market." He hauls his unwieldy frame out of the sedan, opens the back door, and retrieves their stash.

One can measure success in a myriad of ways. Stella scurries around and helps while she ponders recent improvements at Shale Cliffs RV Park.

Balancing her coffee and the two paper bags, she makes her way along the concrete path. Jocelyn waves her hand from side to side while she stands in the open doorway.

"Good morning, Jocelyn. Sergeant Moyer and I bear gifts—hot brews and muffins."

The woman nods and remains silent while she swings the door wider. Stella notices Jocelyn's pasty skin and red-rimmed eyes. Yellow flowers pepper her cotton skirt. She's buttoned her white cardigan to her throat. She obviously made an effort to pull herself together.

"Come inside. We can sit in the living room instead of in my messy kitchen. What do we need?" She squints at the bags.

"Spoons for the coffee and napkins for the muffins."

"Okay. I'll find plates, too."

Once Jocelyn's out of earshot, Moyer leans closer. "Mrs. Fleguel's in a bad way. Seen the signs many times."

"Here she comes."

Jocelyn staggers when she places the items on the table. The utensils in her left-hand rattle while she regains her balance and then drops them beside the coffee cups. "Okay," she exhales. Before Stella offers, she reaches for a cup, removes the lid, and sips the hot liquid. "I drink mine black." She wiggles her fingers in the general direction of the offerings. "What kind of muffins?"

"Carrot. Made fresh today by Andrew at the café."

She peeks inside, chooses, and places the warm goody on the tea plate nearest her hand. "Thank you. I feel hungry now."

"Good." Stella glances at Moyer. "We can visit while we eat." Once Moyer picks, she takes the last one.

"I'm glad you called, Stella. I've dithered the past few days and decided my statement needs clarification." She lifts a piece of muffin to her mouth.

"Tasty. I made a statement, didn't I?"

"Not a formal one, Jocelyn, but we talked, and you suggested you weren't sure if Evan stayed at home the night of the murder. You also reported he owns a hearing aid but goes without most of the time."

"I called his Aunt Hermione," she replies, not responding to Stella's assessment.

Stella's heart thumps. "Any reason?"

"Yes. I asked her if Evan spent that night at her place and she told me he did not. She described his arrival before six in the morning. When she questioned him, Evan said he'd walked around overnight and needed her car to come back into town."

"Jesse gave us the same information, which Hermione corroborated."

"He'll say I was asleep, but he wasn't with me. I'm on a variety of medications, but I know when I'm alone." She pauses for a sip of her coffee and Stella holds her breath. "Evan brought me marijuana but wouldn't tell me from where. He brought pills home, too. They give me jitters and I've lost my appetite. I may be sick, but that doesn't make me stupid. Did he buy from Vic Staples? He complained about the cost."

"We've wondered, Jocelyn. How are you managing now?"

"Each day is worse." She closes her eyes. "I need rehab, but Evan says no." She stares out the picture window while she talks, with the paper cup resting against her lower lip. "If he killed Vic Staples, you'll catch him." Her sad acceptance shocks Stella. "The way you dig around—Evan can't stand you."

In a move which surprises them both, Moyer stands and rummages into the pocket of his uniform for his wallet. He pulls out a card. "Here, Mrs. Fleguel. You might wanna call these folks." He passes her the business card.

"Thank you, Sergeant. May I ask why you keep cards from," she drops her eyes and reads the name, "'The Halifax and Area Addiction Recovery Centre' at the ready?"

"My sister's boy is an addict and he ended up sick. They helped him. The place costs money, but the treatment is worth the expense. If you decide and need a drive, call the number on the back. I'll take you into the city."

She stares at the card. "Generous of you, Sergeant Moyer, but a friend will happily deliver me." She stands. "Now, as much as I hate the idea my husband might be a murderer, we can all guess Evan's future. Excuse me." She pauses, then disappears along the hall.

They hear a closet door open. "What the…?" Moyer frowns.

Tears well in her eyes as she offers an olive green zippered jacket, hung on a wire hanger, and covered in a dry cleaner's plastic bag, to Moyer. Stella notices the Shale Harbour logo on the fabric.

"Evan's Shale Harbour work jacket." Stella's statement goes unanswered for seconds. She waits.

"He took this into the cleaners on the day after the murder. He bought a new beige one and new work boots. I can't tell you what happened to his old boots."

"You've never mentioned the jacket before."

Moyer remains upright with the hook of the hanger over his index finger.

"Honestly, Stella, I rarely pay attention. But I saw this," she indicates the plastic wrapped garment, "in the bedroom closet and noticed the paper receipt the business staples on the corner was gone. Hermione said she told you she thought he had blood on his shoes and clothes. When she asked, he suggested mud from the walk, but there was no rain." She inhales. "Afterward, I called the cleaners, and they confirmed the date he dropped his jacket off."

"Why help us, Jocelyn?"

"I need to manage on my own. The sergeant understands and, with his aid," she bends and touches the card on the table, "I will improve. If you want a formal statement, I'll make one."

No support from Jocelyn in the future, despite what Evan may have done in the name of helping her. "Did your husband do business with Vic Staples?"

"He told me Vic needed him from time to time. I assumed town work, but a partnership?" She shrugs. "I didn't pay attention," she says again, with a limp-wrist wave of her hand.

Once in the car, Moyer tells Stella he'll take the jacket straight to the forensics department right after he logs the garment in as evidence. "The plastic bag is helpful." He purses his lips. "Detective North won't be happy."

"Even though dry cleaned, forensics staff might find a trace of blood." She isn't optimistic. "You were a big help, Moyer. She gave us the jacket because you gave her a way out."

****

Evan Fleguel killed Vic Staples. Her gut says yes, but the question remains. Why? A motive proves elusive right now. If the two men were in business, and she's sure they were, what precipitated an altercation? Evan became desperate and murder seemed his one choice? Fear of Vic? Why? Was he afraid Vic would implicate him? How would Vic avoid reciprocal accusations in such a case?

The afternoon scurries past her, filled with reservation requests, kitchen clean-up, returned calls, and organization with Eve so she can take a day off and help her grandmother. By the time supper rolls around and the staff is gone, she's pleased Nick planned their barbecue. She tosses a salad and throws potatoes in the oven. The phone jangles as her love and Kiki wander in the door.

"Shale Cliffs...."

"What the hell, Stella? Moyer reported he logged Evan Fleguel's jacket into evidence and assigned the forensics department to analyze for residual blood stains. You visited Fleguel's house?"

Stella concentrates on measured words and a calm tone. "I called Jocelyn Fleguel after we spoke with Luther. I took her coffee and a muffin from Cocoa and Café. She didn't mind an informal interview because I contacted her first and gave her notice." As an afterthought, she inserts, "There was ample opportunity for Jocelyn to contact her lawyer, and Moyer was a huge help."

In an unsteady voice, he admonishes her. "You can't go rogue in the investigation, Stella. Remember the Owen Ellis-Thomas case?"

"You were unavailable. I had an idea and decided we could test my theory. We gained knowledge and potential proof." She hopes fresh clues might focus him away from her "rogue" behaviour.

"I want you in my office tomorrow morning at nine o'clock. We'll hash out your mess together. I told Moyer to meet us."

With a forced and upbeat tone, although sarcastic, she replies, "Sure. No problem. Shale Cliffs doesn't need my oversight. See you tomorrow. Enjoy your supper with Rosemary." She uses a tactic learned from her sister and replaces the receiver before he has any opportunity for a retort. Aiden North will not bully her.

"Who called, as if I didn't know?" Nick winks while he retrieves the salmon from the fridge. The fillet has been soaking in the soy and maple marinade since noon.

"When we settle for supper, I'll tell you the story. I'm famished. I called a cup of coffee and a carrot muffin lunch, at ten-thirty."

They serve their food and relax on the rattan veranda furniture before Stella launches into the saga of her morning with Moyer. As she progresses from Luther Greene and Port Ephron back to Shale Harbour, a coffee run, and Jocelyn Fleguel, she can't help but notice the indulgence on Nick's face.

"Was I wrong when I contacted and met with Jocelyn?"

"If his jacket has Vic Staple's blood anywhere, you, my dear, become the rock star. I can imagine Aiden's annoyance, though."

"Tomorrow will be a challenge, but I'll take the fall. Moyer shouldn't suffer any consequences. Is that the phone?" She tosses her napkin on the table and slides Kiki away from her feet. "Merrilee was busy today. I expect yet another reservation."

She trots through the living room and into her office. "Shale Cliffs…."

"Stella, where are you?"

"Home, Trixie. I answered, didn't I?"

"With the wedding this Saturday, you said we'd make the cake together. Where are you?"

"Easy, Trixie. First, the wedding isn't this Saturday. She's being married next Saturday, the twenty-sixth. Brigitte organized the caterer, even the cake. Just appear on time."

"No. No. Your dates are wrong, Stella."

"I can't convince her." Val Reguly has picked up the extension.

"Hi, Val. I'm right. Trixie. Relax. Do your best. Try to be calm."

"She's ordered enough food for three hundred people, and Brigitte's guest list shows fifty."

"Cancel the catering, Val. Trixie, give Brigitte a call and hash the arrangements over with her. If you don't believe Val and me, you'll believe her, right?"

"No one wants me at the wedding, and you've confused me, so I won't go."

"What? No! Trixie. You are the mother of the bride. Brigitte's day will be perfect. You'll see."

Trixie hangs up her extension. Val tells Stella he'll cancel the food and says goodbye. Stella calls Brigitte.

"Sorry for the hour, but your mother requires your help. You might need a trip out to the cottage. I'm not sure a call is the answer tonight."

Brigitte's anxiety, coupled with concern, rattles along the line. "Did she order food again? I told Pepper to ignore her."

"You'd better tell Val, because fretting has him overwhelmed."

"I'll go out, Stella. Sorry." The sound of sobs clouds her voice.

"Never apologize, Brigitte. I expect we'll be a team on this one for some time."

CHAPTER 23

My Inescapable Vow

As warm and humid sunshine tumbles through the kitchen windows, she enjoys one last slurp of her coffee before she faces a pissed-off Aiden North. Her visit to Jocelyn Fleguel's home wasn't on the investigative agenda but proved fruitful. She squares her shoulders. If he doesn't want her help in the future, fine. A few degrees of separation from the man and his wife might be better for everyone.

She stops at the reception doorway. "Later, Merrilee. Lots of muffins in the freezer for lunch. Not sure when I'll be home."

"Okay, Stella. We're organized, aren't we, Kiki?" The little dog sits with quiet devotion in her lap.

No time for a stop at the workshop. Nick understands her job, although he shows mild disapproval on occasion. He said that he expects a wave of relief when they resolve this case, no matter how much he respects her friendship with Hester.

While she parks her Jeep in a space at the end of the lot, Moyer stands on the top step, feet spread, hands clasped in front.

She approaches and waves. His solemn nod greets her.

"Good morning. I thought you'd be inside with Aiden already."

"He's mad, Stella. I needed reinforcements. Told him I'd wait for you. Come on. Let's find out what he has to say."

Stella trudges behind the heavy-set sergeant while they make their way along the corridor toward Aiden's office. She grits her teeth in anticipation and vows Aiden won't intimidate her. They uncovered evidence likely lost if not for their visit yesterday. Moyer steps aside and allows her entry. Aiden's focus remains on the folder in front of him.

"Here on time and as promised," she states with false confidence.

"Sit, both of you."

Moyer and Stella exchange glances. He waits until she chooses before he takes the chair beside her. Silence ensues. She doesn't appreciate the detective's principal's-office attitude or his delay. Her paltry contract remuneration won't compensate for his foolishness.

"You two risked our case."

At last. "We treated the evidence with every respect, Aiden." Her calm voice remains firm. She has little to lose.

"I logged the windbreaker, and the lab started their tests right away, sir. We never opened the plastic bag, did we, Stella?"

"We did not. Explain your problem, Aiden."

"Evan Fleguel's lawyer called yesterday and said you absconded with the personal property of her client."

"His wife offered the jacket. We didn't ask and were both surprised. Jocelyn decided, based on her own research, that her husband killed Vic Staples."

"Both of you—tell me what happened, every detail." His voice has settled.

"You received my report, sir. The information's in the file." Moyer remains stoic and formal.

Aiden clutches his chin in his hand while he sifts through the paperwork. "You stated she suggested there was blood on Evan's clothes when he arrived home from the Wigglesworth property the morning after the murder. I told Ms. Abraham I wanted another interview with Mr. Fleguel. They should be here by now." He checks his watch.

With a measure of indignant bravado, Stella launches into a blow-by-blow description of yesterday. She explains Luther Greene's position and his assumption Vic held incriminating information regarding Evan. They contacted Jocelyn in case she remembered, or decided to share more details not mentioned earlier, and she accepted a meeting. They conducted informal interviews with both, handled the evidence with respect, and Courtney Abraham can't complain. Evan's wife had lots of time to contact her. "Jocelyn Fleguel needs rehab. Evan refused his permission, but Moyer gave her the name of a potential resource. She told us she suspects Evan of the murder and therefore wants independence through treatment. I suspect Evan prefers her 'sick'. He has more control." She doesn't miss the cloud which drifts across

Aiden's face. "Jocelyn called Hermione and she told Jocelyn what the couple reported to us. Both women have stated he wasn't with them during the night."

When a knock sounds on the office door, Moyer heaves his frame out of his chair and answers. A familiar technician, dressed in white, hands him a sheet of paper. "Preliminary forensics report for Detective Aiden."

"Thanks, Conrad." Moyer places the document on Aiden's desk.

Stella notices the sergeant doesn't glance at the information. She holds her breath while Aiden reads. His expression darkens. She assumes the lab didn't find any blood, or can't determine if any residue belonged to Vic. Her heart bangs.

"Forensics discovered blood on the jacket," Aiden concedes. "In the zipper teeth."

"Vic's?"

"Too soon. They need more tests, but the sample is large enough, at least. The zipper escaped the dry cleaning. With Luther, Hermione, and Jocelyn's formal statements plus a potential blood match, we'll have sufficient evidence for charges."

"As long as Courtney Abraham doesn't argue that the jacket is inadmissible down the road," Stella mumbles her disgust.

He frowns. "Not much chance. You and Moyer did a good job. My apologies. Now, our task is another interview with Evan. Staff will meet with each player in due course." His frown returns. "Still can't figure out his motive. I understand he did errands and worked with Vic because Vic supplied him with drugs for Jocelyn, but why kill the guy?"

"Jocelyn said he complained the cost of her drugs was increasing. If Vic took on harder products and raised his prices, Evan feared he'd lose access. He blamed Vic, who told Luther he'd insist Evan hire him for work at the town if Luther wanted the job. Vic manipulated him and he couldn't imagine a way out because Vic kept raising the stakes."

"Theories. More theories."

****

Stella assesses Courtney Abraham's annoyance from her flushed cheeks and drumming fingers, observed through the hall window on the way to the interview room.

"Good morning. Thanks for your quick response, Ms. Abraham, Mr.

Fleguel. You've met my community consultant, Stella Kirk. Let's begin."

"Detective North, my client and I have no patience with Ms. Kirk's tactics and will register a formal complaint. Earlier in the investigation, I stated the necessity of my involvement in any interviews at the Fleguel home, and your *consultant* visited without my knowledge."

"Mrs. Fleguel took responsibility. If memory serves," he turns toward Stella and nods, "Stella called and requested permission, which Mrs. Fleguel granted. The department didn't coerce her. Mrs. Fleguel had thirty minutes to contact you before my team arrived. Shall we begin?"

Evan Fleguel remains without his hearing aid. Stella first becomes aware when he looks at his legal counsel with a blank expression. He doesn't understand. Aiden spoke with the fluid assertiveness he often employs in interviews. The result could well be muddled to Evan.

Courtney leans closer to her client and whispers in his ear until he nods and settles back in his chair. "Go on, Detective. Please tell us your methods. You've presented no hard evidence."

"Let's start from the top."

No longer expecting to be home soon, Stella smothers a groan.

"Your client was well-acquainted with the victim. A witness identified him to be at Raspberry Farm on at least one occasion. Police discovered a hearing aid battery in a hidden enclosure under the barn. Mr. Fleguel wears a hearing aid sporadically. He appeared at his aunt and uncle's home, a property on the same road, at the break of dawn the next morning. They described blood on his clothes and boots, although he told Hermione Wigglesworth the stains were mud and claimed he walked to her place from town."

"Not hard evidence, Detective North," Courtney repeats. "You presented us with a tale of witness statements, most not admissible in court."

Without the skip of a beat, Aiden continues. "We contend your client partnered with Vic Staples in the trade of drugs off the cove. In exchange for procurement of supplies of marijuana and harder drugs for his sick wife, he did errands for Vic—dope deliveries to Mildred Fox, for one. We believe Vic threatened him with exposure if he abandoned his assigned tasks, even though Vic raised prices and expected more from Mr. Fleguel in the drug business. Additional financial compensation wasn't part of the deal."

Throughout the time Aiden spoke, Evan squinted at him as if Aiden were in a fog. He focused on Aiden's lips and didn't acknowledge when Stella asked him if he understood.

"What? Sorry. I can't follow what the detective said. You think I hid under the barn and walked along the cliffs? A shore walk at high tide could kill a person. I may be deaf, but I'm not stupid." He puffs his chest and glances at his lawyer. "I was never Vic Staples' employee, either."

"Tell us your location and activities the night Vic Staples died and the morning afterward, Evan." She forms her words with care and makes eye contact with him while she enunciates each syllable. *Give him enough rope....*

"I couldn't sleep. Took a walk. Ended up around the point at Aunt Hermione's and waited until I saw a light in the kitchen. She let me in when I knocked. My shoes and jacket were muddy because I slipped and fell in the dark. I needed a ride to town. She gave me her car and came to fetch it later."

"Jocelyn says you were not at home for any part of the evening, Evan." Stella makes this statement, which suggests he cannot count on Jocelyn anymore.

"She's high most of the time, and never aware if I'm around or not."

Does she sense a bitterness in his voice? "She needs rehab." *Slow and steady.*

"Won't do her any good. I help her."

Aiden takes over and follows Stella's lead. He gazes directly at their suspect. "Please clarify for us, Mr. Fleguel. Were you in business with Vic Staples? Yes or no."

Courtney taps him on the arm and whispers, before she informs them, "My client isn't required to answer such a question, Detective."

"Where are your old shoes, Evan?" Stella focuses on his face.

He squints, leans forward, and cups his ear.

"No." Courtney intervenes with a hand on his arm.

Evan turns toward her, his face blank.

Too many voices at the same time. She realizes he can't follow along. "You took your Town of Shale Harbour jacket to the cleaners and bought a new one." Stella soldiers on. Mindful of his confusion, she manipulates his hearing disability, aware her conscience will nag her later.

"I'll take this windbreaker," he touches his sleeve, "to Port Ephron for embroidery."

"And the old one?"

Their suspect swivels toward his lawyer.

"Forensics found fluid on the zipper. The cleaners missed thick blood trapped between the teeth." Stella's face remains blank.

Courtney Abraham places a firm hand on Evan's arm, but stares at Aiden. "Don't say another word, Evan." She focuses her attention on the detective while she ignores Stella. "Where's my copy of the forensics report?"

"Not yet. He's not arrested. You're out of luck."

"Vic's blood on my jacket doesn't mean I killed him," Evan sputters.

"My client and I require a conference in private."

****

"He thought you said 'Vic's' blood, and you said 'thick' blood." Back in his office, coffee in hand, Aiden studies Stella. "Did you use the word on purpose?"

"Yes. He has profoundly impaired hearing, and I took a chance he'd misunderstand."

"Clever, Stella."

"Val Reguly often misinterprets. He misses a word and assumes another one, which fills in the space in his mind. The confusion can be funny, but dangerous, too." She scowls. "I used Evan's weakness against him."

"Wallow in your guilt later. Grab your coffee. We'll go back in and maybe he'll tell us the truth now."

Once settled in the interview room, Aiden begins. "Let's review the evidence one more time, Mr. Fleguel."

"Listen. I never admitted before, but I was at the farm when Angus killed Vic. I was a witness." His face flushes. "He came home, and I ran behind the barn. Angus killed Vic," he repeats. "When he called the police, I went inside again and checked on Vic. The blood on my shoes and jacket likely happened then. I crawled under the building, into our stash hole until after dark. That's when I lost my hearing aid battery. The damned door on the contraption falls open. Once the tide receded far enough, I walked around to my aunt's place and asked to borrow her car. Told her I slipped in the mud. They're old. They can't tell the difference. I watch her like a hawk, you guys. She's a danger. She worries me sick with her guns." His eyes dart from one to the other. "Okay. Are we good?"

"Why did you run away when Angus got home?"

"What?"

Sergeant Moyer opens the door after a quick tap and says he needs a moment with Stella or Aiden. Stella steps outside the interview room.

"Jocelyn Fleguel called me and said she and her friend are off into Halifax and she won't be back for a while. She reported she found Evan's old work shoes stuffed in a box in the basement."

"Thanks, Moyer. I imagine Aiden will request a warrant. Jocelyn just handed us our final straw."

"She claimed she didn't touch them. I wrote their location and the details."

"Okay. Stand by."

"We discovered no forensic evidence on Angus Raspberry. Even his boots were clean. He isn't our perpetrator, Mr. Fleguel."

Evan stares at Stella as she closes the door. "Sorry for the disruption. Sergeant Moyer said your wife departed for Halifax today; accepted into a drug rehab. facility. The message says she found your bloody footwear in the basement."

"Enough. Are you arresting my client?"

"I'll give Mr. Fleguel every opportunity to confess, Ms. Abraham. The process will be much easier if he decides the truth is the best course of action."

Courtney, once again, whispers in his ear.

"I moved mountains and risked my life for Jocelyn and now she's left," he mutters, with his eyes focused on the tabletop. "My career, my job, my income—on the line. Never enough. In sickness and in health—my inescapable vow."

Stella turns toward Aiden and sees the reflection of their previous discussion, related to his marriage, in his eyes.

"May my team search your home, Mr. Fleguel?"

With silent reluctance, he places a set of house keys on the table. After Aiden contacts Moyer, who arrives and fetches the keys, he begins. "You are under arrest. Mr. Fleguel." Aiden reads him his rights and states the obvious. "You killed Vic Staples. Can you explain what happened?"

Over the next hour, Stella and Aiden listen while Evan pours his heart out despite repeated protests from his lawyer. Jocelyn developed symptoms early in their marriage. Appointments with one doctor, followed by another, absorbed their lives. Her condition baffled medical personnel who blamed her emotions and temperament. Tyna Derhay suggested Jocelyn should smoke pot, which would ease her aches and pains. Once he purchased from Vic, thanks to a reference from Tyna, he latched on to a money-making opportunity where he got Jocelyn's weed for free if he helped Vic with various tasks. He visited Mildred Fox and rolled joints for her or retrieved Vic's stash from under Angus Raspberry's barn when necessary. He mentioned an incident when he thought weird Angus had noticed him. Most often, the guy stayed in the house. Once his girlfriend arrived, exposure became riskier.

"And what caused the altercation?" Stella still can't fathom an obvious motive.

"His supply of marijuana dwindled, and so Jocelyn tried amphetamine instead. He said his sellers expected distribution of harder drugs because they'd make more money. After a few months, he told me I'd have to pay more for the pills because the product cost increased." He runs his hand over his scalp, which makes his hair stand straight in the air. "He threatened to report me to my boss—Phil Lewis—if I refused to work for him and pay more for the amphetamine."

"Vic Staples blackmailed you."

"He did more. He appeared in the office one day and asked for Phil. I hustled him outside. He demanded I handle his 'errands' or my days as the town engineer were over."

"You killed him the next time you were at Raspberry Farm."

Evan holds his head in his hands. "I don't understand what came over me. He insisted I deliver amphetamine to a location in Port Ephron and collect money. I'm aware of the place. The people there are scary, and I refused. Vic teased me and called me names. I grabbed the first tool within reach."

After Evan realized he killed Vic, and he observed lights approach, he ran out the back and around the side, where he hid in the underground spot where Vic kept his extra stash. He stayed put until the commotion quieted and the tide drifted out. They have a clear picture of the rest.

Stella glances at Aiden. "One more question, Evan." She leans closer, in the hope he'll understand her. "Did you go back to the farm to find the drugs?"

"Yes. I didn't want the boat, but pretended to be interested after I ran around to the back side of the barn before Angus heard me arrive."

"Your visit to Raspberry Farm put you in a position where a witness later identified you."

The phone in the interview room bleats. "Thank you, Sergeant. We're almost done here." He turns toward Courtney Abraham. "The forensics report has matched the blood found on your client's jacket zipper with the victim. My people located his work shoes in the basement of his home." He stands. "You two can come with me to Booking. We'll complete the paperwork. Please wait for me in my office, Stella."

Her stomach rumbles. He's taken his own sweet time, but she hears him approach. "Sorry for the delay."

"No problem. I'm sympathetic toward Evan."

"Why? He beat a man to death with a crowbar and blamed the act on a poor sod who didn't even understand the operation."

"Remember when he spoke about his inescapable vow? He broke the law because of his wife, who turned him in and left town. He sacrificed his life for no purpose in the end."

"A valid description of me."

She doesn't reply.

🐝

CHAPTER 24

I Value Your Opinion

Three occurrences happened in quick succession after her return home from the detachment in Shale Harbour. Nick asked for her company at the hotel for a celebratory dinner, a rare offer made despite commencement of the tourist season. Eve overheard her reluctance, because they keep the office open until eight, and offered coverage. Hester called for an update, and they'll meet after supper at Raspberry Farm.

Shale Harbour Hotel vibrates with the murmurs of guests. Nick secured their favourite spot in the back room, where three antique dining table arrangements occupy the space. Pepper, ponytail swinging, describes the lobster and mango salad special and states she'll return with their drinks in a minute or two.

"I, for one, am happy the Staples case has concluded. You were right, as usual, when you thought Evan Fleguel killed Vic. What did Aiden say?"

"Not much." Stella fiddles with her napkin. "He's pleased Evan confessed. We still need meetings with the peripheral witnesses and players, but I won't attend each interview. I'll accompany him tomorrow morning." Her shoulders sag. "I'm tired." Her forced smile withers.

"Last time, Pepper. No more deliveries. Tiffany suspects, and we can't see each other anymore."

She observes, through the doorway, a tray with two glasses of white wine in Pepper's hand, although neither Pepper nor her companion are within her line of vision. Stella whispers, "Could the man outside in the hall be Andrew? He delivers pastries and sounds like Andrew Blair. I've seen Andrew here before."

Nick swivels in his chair. "No idea."

Pepper trots inside with their drinks.

Stella adopts her best supportive tone. "Someone we know?"

"Andrew brought me muffins for tomorrow. We run out often. I guess they're busy and I'll send staff to fetch them from now on." She blushes.

She lied.

After she's gone, Nick's eyes roam the room. "We should buy Shale Harbour Hotel."

"What?" She sputters and wine dribbles below her bottom lip.

"I caught wind of a rumour at Bacon Hardware. A guy from Fisher's Contracting said Eugenie Charlebois wants to sell."

Her heart pounds and her palms sweat. "Any reason?" Nick has money and invested a portion into the park with funds inherited from his father's sister. She expects there's much more but doesn't pry. He's indicated, on more than one occasion, that cash isn't an issue, but buy a hotel? Can he be serious?

"This operation could provide income for twelve months of the year if we employ more staff, modernize the building, and tidy the grounds. Tourist seasons are busier. People explore their own neck of the woods now. I should talk with Eugenie."

Despite her reluctance, the inheritance belongs to Nick. She silently balks at the idea of more responsibility but keeps her concerns to herself for tonight.

A young woman unfamiliar to Stella delivers their entrées. "Thank you. And you are...?"

"Hi. My name's Vanessa. Have you met River and Saffron?"

"Yes."

"Well, I'm Saffron's sister, here for the summer."

"Welcome to Shale Harbour, Vanessa."

The salad doesn't disappoint. After supper, they drive to Raspberry Farm. Hester seemed impatient on the phone, although Stella explained they closed the case and obtained a clear confession. Despite her expressed relief, she said she wants a discussion about another issue. Stella hopes Cavelle isn't her concern.

Hester stands, stoic and controlled, on the back steps which lead into the kitchen. "I've waited, Stella. You promised to be here at seven and my clock says fifteen past."

Stella glances at Nick. "We took our time on the drive, Hester. Such a glorious evening. Sorry."

"You shouldn't promise someone and not appear," she huffs her annoyance.

"We've discussed this particular weakness before."

"Hi, Hester. We solved the case. Now you and Angus can resume your life together. No gratitude?"

"My apologies. We are grateful—both of us. We will proceed with our lives, which is the reason I asked for your company at the farm tonight. Shall we take a walk?"

"A walk?" She frowns.

"Yes. Angus stayed inside. He wants to speak with Nick. He wishes to repair the old barn where the murder occurred. I suggested the structure sits too near the water's edge and Mother Nature will swallow his work in due course, but he insists on a complete restoration. Nick can advise him." She nods in Nick's general direction and points at the house. "Are those decent shoes, Stella?"

"Loafers."

"Good. I thought we could trek over toward the look-off. We'll use the trail at the edge of one section of River and Saffron's property. They don't mind.

"Okay. Enjoy your visit with Angus, Nick." She feels herded by a pushy Border Collie but follows Hester.

They trudge along a narrow and well-worn path. She sees the public site in the distance and wedges her body between Hester and the tall shore grasses which sputter in the light wind. Her eye catches Hester's left hand, where a sizable peridot replaces her small silver friendship ring. "New?"

She pauses. "Angus' gift. We planned a ceremony." She stares at her finger. "He inherited what we now refer to as my partnership symbol from his grandmother."

"Ceremony? I thought you didn't believe marriage to be necessary."

"We don't. Our commitment will be in front of family and friends—you and Nick, Cavelle, Jacob and Maeve, Donamae Kutska, and Ken and Jewel— and little Kenny, too. Did I tell you Jewel expects another baby?"

"No!"

"Before Christmas. We are excited." Her expression clouds. "I want to spend time with her and assist when I'm able."

Stella pats Hester's arm. Her friend doesn't withdraw. "You and Angus could move to the farm for December through February. You both would help make life easier for everyone."

"Sometimes, Stella, you display exceptional wisdom. After our commitment ceremony, I think a thorough discussion of the possibility, with both Angus and my siblings, is in order." She brushes a wisp of hair off her cheek. "Here we are. We plan to recite our mutual truths in the presence of the nine people we care for most. Will this place suffice?" The glimmer of a smile crosses her serious face.

The view from the point fills Stella's eyes with the reason she considered her move back home came with advantages. Clouds roll and the lavender light of a June sunset fades. She holds her breath for a second. "You couldn't find a more stunning vista for the backdrop," she whispers.

"Are you not familiar with this place?"

"We found River and Saffron here once, but not near dusk. Hester, what's the date for your event?"

"July tenth. No need for any intrusion on Brigitte's wedding. At sunset. What do you think? As strange as this life-changing circumstance might be, I value your opinion."

As Stella opens her mouth in response, the crack of a rifle shot slices through the calm of the evening. She ducks. "What the hell, Hester?"

Her friend, unperturbed by the noise, sits on the bench and pats the space beside her. "I understand Hermione Wigglesworth performs target practice with her long guns in the backyard of her home. The idea frightened me at first, but I'm told she possesses adequate skills and won't shoot someone by accident while they enjoy the sunset. Evan Fleguel, her nephew and Vic Staples' murderer, discouraged her gun activities as much as possible. Since he's incarcerated, we hope River talks with her. Accidents happen. Bullets go array, no matter your talent."

"I might mention rifle shots when I see Aiden. Okay?"

Another crack rips through the silence. Stella winces.

"Okay."

****

Her staff hasn't arrived. She yawns and sips Irish cream coffee while she waits for Aiden. They plan to debrief the owner of the boarding home, and her residents, at seven-thirty, while the men eat breakfast and before they head off to work. With Kiki still upstairs and Nick in the shower, she wanders out on the veranda and settles in a rattan chair. A moment of solace eludes her as Aiden's car appears.

"We'll meet with Etta Graney and her three boarders first. Can't hinder their jobs."

Stella observes his face when they drive past Grey Cottage Realty and round the corner toward the boarding house. She expected a remark or a wistful murmur, but silence and no change in his expression.

Etta Graney flutters at the front door. "The men are inside. Can I pour you coffee or tea?"

"Not today, Mrs. Graney. We won't be long."

She shows them into the dining room, decorated with tired and faded wallpaper, dated from the wars. Wall sconces illuminate the space in a dirty yellow ambience. The chandelier hangs with missing bulbs, covered in dust, and unused. Cam Keller, Brad Masterson, and Wally Lavender slurp hot drinks and gobble scrambled eggs, bacon, and toast with jam. The odour of a diner permeates the air.

"Good morning, gentlemen. Stella and I wanted you to receive the results of our inquiry from us and not through the rumour mill. Evan Fleguel has confessed to the murder of Vic Staples. He engaged in business with Vic."

The men listen while they eat. Etta sits wide-eyed and sips her tea. Aiden provides the basic details. "The Crown may ask for formal statements based on our previous interviews. One of my staff will call and request your appearance at the detachment if such an event becomes necessary."

Brad opens his full mouth, but Aiden continues. "You may sign paperwork in the evening. We don't want anyone to lose time at their place of work. Questions?"

"Luther Greene wasn't involved, Detective North?"

"No, Mrs. Graney. Luther became a valuable resource, but he did not do business with Vic Staples."

They stop at the town office next. Tyna Derhay jumps from her desk and greets them at the counter. "The three of us are here. Gavin went into Philip's space already. Myrtle," she shouts over her shoulder. "Cover for me. The police have arrived." They follow her.

"Hi, Stella. Guess who got offered a full-time job in Shale Harbour?" Gavin stands beside Philip's file cabinet, arms outstretched.

"I gather the town has adapted to Evan's loss." She hates the idea of unverified information circulating around the community and experiences a moment of sympathy for Evan. The same gossip and innuendo happened after Paulina's murder. She swallows her urge to clarify assumptions and judgments.

"We're here to give you the results of the investigation, as you were each interviewed at one point or another." Aiden continues with his spiel. "If statements require more detail, the detachment will contact you." He turns toward Tyna. "The Crown won't lay charges, but your involvement with a drug dealer has not gone unnoticed, Ms. Derhay. Consider yourself cautioned."

Tyna opens her mouth, but Stella catches her eye and raises one finger. Tyna remains quiet.

Once in the car, Aiden suggests they grab coffee before driving over to the Wigglesworths'. He itemizes on his fingers. "You've spoken with Angus and Hester. And Donamae Kutska? Shall we stop in and speak with her as well?"

"Good idea. You call Luther and I'll see Mildred in the park. Oh, can I tell Mildred someone from your office could be out for a formal statement? No need for her to find a lift to town."

"Perfect." Once seated at a table in the back of Cocoa and Café, French Vanilla brews in hand, Stella addresses Brigitte's wedding. "They invited you and Cavelle."

"I won't attend, as you might expect, although I imagine Cavelle will go. She can't disappoint her best friend. Has she not mentioned the wedding?"

"Not a word, and Hester isn't aware of her plans. One other issue. When Hester and I took a walk to the look-off last evening, we concluded Hermione was target practising. We heard rifle shots."

"You didn't file a report?"

In a tempered tone, she replies, "Consider the report filed. I know the road curves. I was afraid, as the crow flies, she might have reached us."

"I'll speak with her." He winces his policeman's disapproval.

Stella's pleasantly surprised when she sees Hermione, Jesse, Saffron, and River seated on the front deck, but finds Donamae's presence curious. Donamae—a friend of the family? She wasn't aware.

After they're up the steps, greeted, and offered refreshments, which they refuse, Aiden launches into his prepared recitation of the case and explains how their statements may or may not be required. Collateral information depends on the demands of the Crown. "My notes and Stella's reports are available already. If they want signed statements, the office will be in touch. A pleasure to see you here, Ms. Kutska. You've saved us a trip."

"We visit now and again, Detective. We're neighbours." She pats Hermione's arm.

"Your nephew's crime has created challenges for you, Mrs. Wigglesworth, Mr. Wigglesworth." The old man's shoulders bob. "But we appreciate your forthrightness—although somewhat slow at first—while you assisted us in the case. Mrs. Wigglesworth, may I discuss an issue with you in private for a moment?"

Hermione surveys her guests with round eyes. Stella hears Jesse mumble, "Guns."

While Aiden and Hermione are in the kitchen, River and Saffron tell Stella how they've committed more time to Hermione and Jesse. In Evan's absence, River will help on the property. Both Donamae and Saffron can assist Hermione with Jesse's care. Their arrangements are coordinated so Hermione and Jesse can remain in their home for as long as possible.

Aiden returns without Hermione. "Mrs. Wigglesworth will join you in a few minutes. I cautioned her from further target practice and suggested she contact the gun club in Port Ephron. Thanks for your patience today, everyone."

Back in the car, Stella breaks the silence. "I gather your talk didn't go well."

"She never said a word, but if any human can conjure thunder, the candidate is Hermione Wigglesworth. The park?"

"Yes. One more visit. I'll see Mildred after lunch. We're finished for now. Big day tomorrow."

****

"Hey, Mildred. How's my favourite camper?"

"Fine as the weather." She raises her flabby arm toward the blue sky. She's settled in her basket chair on her deck. "No complaints from me. Still on the right side of the grass. What can I do for you?"

"The investigation has wrapped. You were a tremendous help. Someone from the detachment may pop by for a formal statement. I guess a visit with you depends on what the Crown attorney might want."

"Evan Fleguel confessed?"

"Correct, but sometimes a confession isn't enough. He hired a top-notch lawyer."

"Fleguel delivered my weed?"

"Right. Your description made a difference."

"Happy comin' to the aid of law enforcement." She cackles. "Good-lookin' law enforcement."

"See you later, old girl. The family has a wedding. I'm a busy lady."

The shrill sound of the phone greets her when she walks in the door. She hears Merrilee on the other line and runs toward her office. "Shale Cliffs RV...."

"I have no drive tomorrow. Can you and Nick fetch me?"

"By all means, Trixie, but where's your new car?"

"Val can't deliver Brigitte and Mia in his old wreck. They don't need my vehicle after the ceremony because they'll use Carter's."

"Okay, Sis. Understood. We'll collect you. Be ready by one. With the wedding at two, that gives us lots of time to arrive and settle. Will Mia still give her mother away?"

"Yes. Sweet and stupid. Wish the job was mine."

Stella sputters a response after her sister's harsh evaluation. "Why stupid?"

"What if the kid takes off or has a tantrum? She could ruin Brigitte's big day. I can't run after her in my dress."

"Relax, Trixie. When Mia sees Carter by the altar, she'll be the perfect little angel." "Okay. One o'clock, right?"

The slam of the phone receiver clunks in Stella's ear.

****

Churches are not her forté. Seated in the front pew, Nick by her side, she closes her eyes. The smell of religion washes over her—musty wood, lemon oil, candle wax, and layers of devoutness. Her family never attended church. With purpose, she's avoided the rituals. Brigitte started accompanying Carter. She used the excuse that Mia needed the experience—empowerment to make an intelligent decision one day. Nick pats her knee.

They're ready, despite the hectic morning. Trixie called three times and double—triple-checked when she was to be collected. Stella drove out to the manor to ask her father, one last time, if he'd come to the wedding. He didn't know her. He didn't understand. Despite his advancing issues, she needed to be able to say she tried. When she returned, a guest, unhappy with their reservation—not a magnificent view—arrived at the office. Their haughty entrance rattled Merrilee. Stella intervened. In the end, Merrilee assigned the couple a site they found more suitable, and the unsettled waters of reception smoothed once more.

Nick must have waited at the foot of the stairs for ten minutes. Her teal blue wrap dress accents her waist and doesn't advertise her weaknesses, considered by her as many. While she made her way along the worn treads, he stood at the bottom with a scarf in his hand.

"Did Trixie send me an accessory?" She reached for the fabric.

"No," he replied. "I bought you a shawl, not to be confused with a scarf, which I know you hate. A gift—say," he hesitated, "a birthday present."

She wrapped the soft woven material, splashed with every blue shade she could imagine, around her shoulders. "My birthday's long past and proved perfection, as I recall. Splendid, Nick." She twirled in front of him. "Perfect with my dress." She placed a hand on each shoulder and kissed him. "Thank you."

When they arrived at Trixie's, she wasn't ready. Stella felt the pinch of flesh from her bitten lip when she finally saw her sister dressed in a mermaid gown the colour of oysters. The sweetheart neckline plunged, and the waist cinched her into a sausage state. She hobbled toward the car on stiletto heels and insisted she sit in the front because she couldn't fold into the back without damaging her dress.

Reality bursts through her reverie. An usher escorts Trixie down the aisle. Stella imagines her sister yearns for the role of bride. She snuggles in beside Stella and whispers, "How did I do? Where's Cavelle?"

"Fine. You did fine. I haven't seen Cavelle. Did she say she'd come alone? Aiden won't be here." Stella closes her eyes again, absorbed by the scent of reverence once more.

"I saw her car a block away. I thought she was here. The last time we talked, I suggested she sit in front with us. Nice shawl. A gift from Nick? You'd never buy one on your own." Her lip curls.

Val scurries along the outer aisle and slips into the space beside Nick. He isn't interested in a spot nearer Trixie.

Stella leans across Nick's lap so Val will hear her request. "Can you let me into the office to call Cavelle?"

"Sure. Come with me. We'll hurry. They'll start in a minute. Brigitte and Mia are already in the vestibule."

Jewel answers and reports that Cavelle dressed and left for the wedding.

Stella, while she trots ahead of Val back to her seat, turns and notices Rosemary North tucked into a corner at the edge of the entrance. She peers straight at Stella and wiggles her fingers. Glee, Stella thinks, adequately describes the expression that plasters Rosemary's face.

Before she sits, Aiden's Citation skids to a halt in front of the door. Brigitte and Mia stand poised for their trip down the aisle but turn toward the interruption. Aiden rushes at Rosemary and grabs her arm. She bellows and resists. The congregation reacts with a collective gasp.

With no awareness of the action which has transpired at the entrance, Carter and his cousin Brent enter from a side room at the front and take their places. The organist chords the introduction of the wedding march, perhaps with unnecessary vigour, but the music covers the disruption. Everyone stands. Stella presses her lips near her sister's contrived messy hairdo and murmurs, "Jewel says Cavelle left for the church."

Brigitte, preceded by one of her friends as the bridesmaid, and Mia's tiny hand clenched in hers, begins the walk. The little girl turns from side to side and smiles as Carter coached her. For now, the bride and her daughter become the focus—the commotion outside forgotten by the assembled congregation. Stella scans the group of fifty guests, fingers twisting her shawl. Cavelle is nowhere to be seen.

About the Author

L. P. Suzanne Atkinson was born in New Brunswick, Canada and lived in Alberta, Quebec, and Nova Scotia before settling on Prince Edward Island in 2022. She has degrees from Mount Allison, Acadia, and McGill universities. Suzanne spent her professional career in the fields of mental health and home care. She also owned and operated, with her husband, both an antique business and a construction business for more than twenty-five years.

Suzanne writes about the unavoidable consequences of relationships. She uses her life and work experiences to weave stories that cross many boundaries.

She, her husband, David Weintraub, and their dog, Spencer, make the fabulous Summerside, Prince Edward Island, Canada their home.

Email – lpsa.books@eastlink.ca
Website – http://lpsabooks.wix.com/lpsabooks#
Face Book – L. P. Suzanne Atkinson – Author
Face Book – lpsabooks Private Stash

Titles:
Emily's Will Be Done (2012)
Ties That Bind (2014)

Station Secrets: Regarding Hayworth Book I (2015)
Hexagon Dilemma: Regarding Hayworth Book II (2016)
Segue House Connection: Regarding Hayworth Book III (2017)
Diner Revelations: Regarding Hayworth Book IV (2018)

No Visible Means: A Stella Kirk Mystery #1 (2019)
Didn't Stand a Chance: A Stella Kirk Mystery #2 (2020)
Sand In My Suitcase: A Stella Kirk Mystery #3 (2021)
Fictional Truth: A Stella Kirk Mystery #4 (2022)
Mallory Gorman Won't Be Buried Today: A Stella Kirk Mystery # 5 (2023)
Fate Deals The Cards: A Stella Kirk Mystery # 6 (2024)
My Inescapable Vow: A Stella Kirk Mystery # 7 (2025)

Watch for:
No More Deliveries: A Stella Kirk Mystery #8
The eighth and final installment in this cozy mystery series
set in Shale Cliffs RV Park
Coming in the spring / summer of 2026